FATED TIDES
A METAPHYSICAL LOVE STORY
SARAH FAETH SANDERS

Duck & A Rabbit

Press

This book contains the following content, which some readers may find difficult to read: activities related to dead animals, including skinning, tanning, and cooking meat, description of Alzheimer's, brief description of dead bodies, piracy, kidnapping, poisoning, murder, blood, mention of child neglect and abuse, domestic violence, off-page attempted sexual assault (brief), explicit sexual content between consenting adults.

For more information or to know which sections to skip to avoid sensitive content, please contact the author directly.

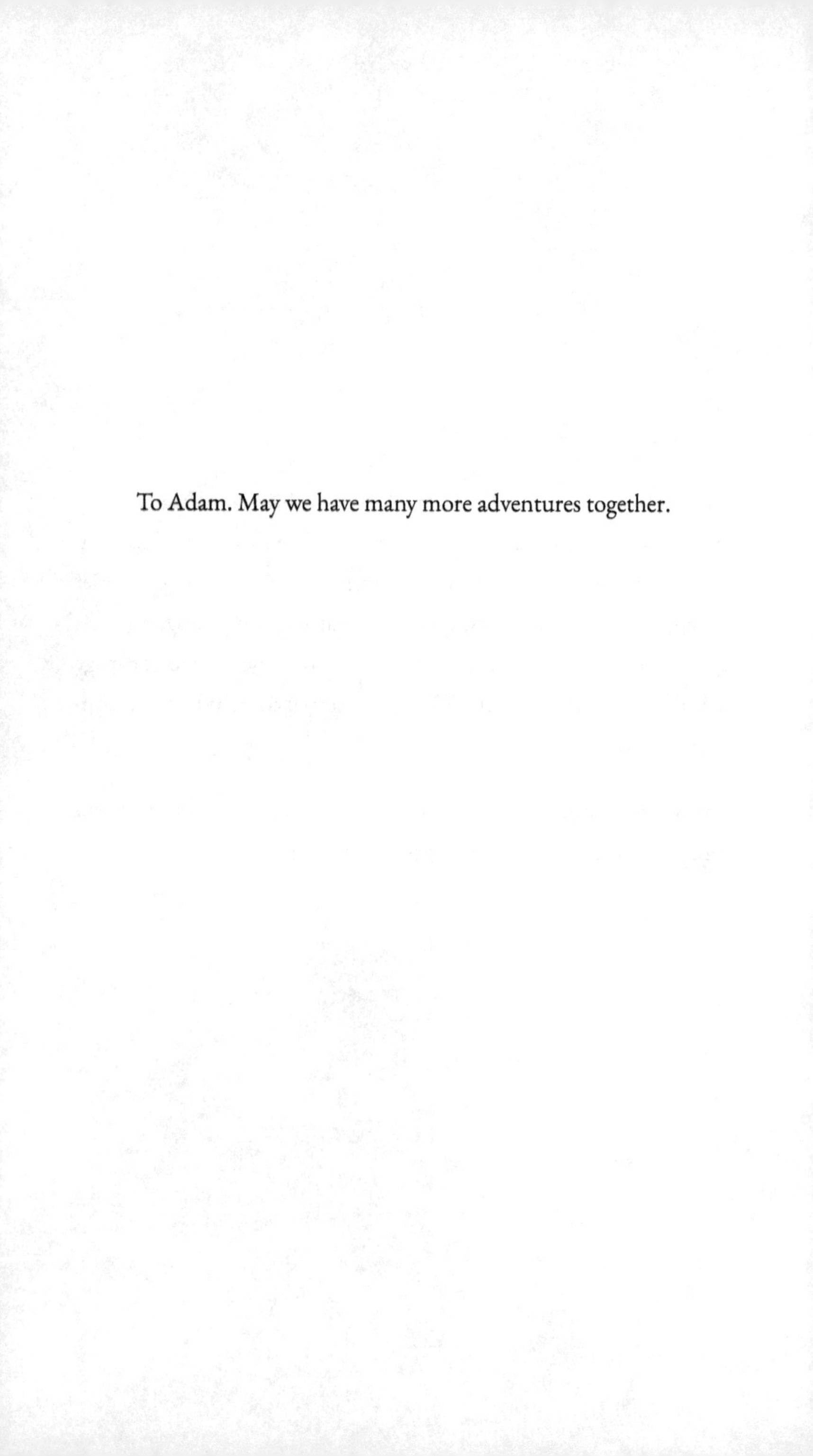

To Adam. May we have many more adventures together.

What you are about to read is like a glimpse through a window.

It is one of a multitude of windows, all stained glass in different shapes and colors. Each offers a glimpse into the depths of a soul, the tale of their evolution, their ever-increasing alignment with the direction of the universe.

What is the shape of this mosaic, which bends and weaves in mysterious ways, reflecting back on itself in phantoms and echoes?

It is the shape of love—the force that drives the universe, that conquers the whole of existence, one story at a time.

And I am a storyteller.

The story I am about to tell you is plucked from a time which many people associate with grand schemes and dangerous adventures—and when I say *time*, I do not mean to mislead you. For our main character's journey is not linear, and neither is yours. There is no beginning, middle, or end to the many lives of the characters in these tales.

The main character of our story is currently in his natural state, what some would call a "higher self." As a purely metaphysical being, you could not comprehend him in this form, though some have been prone to call such beings "angels," or even "gods." As you cannot see him there, floating through space in a state of blissful awareness, I will do my best to describe him to you.

He may be likened to petrichor: the scent of rain on parched soil. An aroma heralding hope, embedded in the bones of humanity since the beginning of *time* as they know it. But he is also the root of the word—petra, the Greek word for stone; and ichor, the liquid gold that flows through the veins of the gods. Solid as stone, yet always moving.

This is Z.

Z's story is not complete without also telling you about his soulmate, who is just beside him there, though you cannot see her. This is A.

A is the rush of waves against a cliffside, which can lull you to sleep or break your body against the rocks. She is the glint of sunshine on the back of a dragonfly, whose colors you greatly wish to see up close, but she never holds still long enough to get a glimpse.

As a pair, A and Z are quite like the moon and the tides—pushing and pulling against one another, ebbing and flowing from life to life, always looking for each other. And between lives, always together.

Quite often, A and Z enjoy the company of two characters who are also central to our tale. They are just there—against the backdrop of brilliant space—and just outside your scope of vision. I will once again attempt to describe them to you.

T is the thrill of elation when a roller coaster whisks you high into the air. He is the feeling of comradery around a warm, vibrant fire.

Y is the relief of coming upon a familiar street when you've been lost for hours. They are a lighthouse in the middle of the desert.

Together, T and Y are what happens when a molecular cloud collapses in upon itself, forming a star.

We find our characters now in a fullness of tranquility—in what some may call a *before*. For in just a moment, our characters will feel a pull. This pull is the call of incarnation, the edict of the universe to grow, to change, to discover something new. It is in these times, when our characters inhabit bodies of flesh and blood, that they forget they are vast, and timeless, and gloriously whole. It is also where all the best stories are born.

Suddenly, the many stars in the many galaxies that have born our main characters shift in such a way as to spark a sense of desire. Of need. Of restlessness. And so, knowing incarnation is imminent, the four souls surrender to their destiny, which bids them from a tiny, blue dot called Earth.

As he falls, a sense of impending loss fills Z that makes him reach out, grasping for his soulmate. A mass of souls rushing toward the earth blind him, obscuring her brilliance. She reaches back, the tendrils of her being barely brushing up against him, pushing inconsequentially against the incredible force that propels them. But she continues to reach, desperate to draw him near, to touch him one more time.

Stay with me, she calls to him.

He wishes to call back, to tell her he wouldn't dream of leaving, but in an instant, she is lost. His cries of protest burn away as he is ignited, consumed by a fire meant to reduce him, leaving but a kernel that will grow into a man—a man whose story I will tell you now.

Our story begins on a beach, where our characters have just had the good fortune of running into each other for what they believe is the very first time.

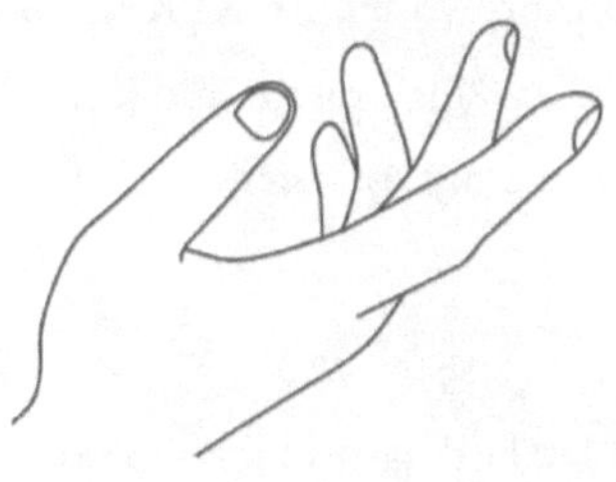

PART ONE

1

Alexander Sutton dug his toes into the sand, opening and closing his hands rapidly as he argued aloud with himself.

"Come on, Zander," he said. "You can do this. You can do this. Just... go, just do it."

He braced himself as if to run, committing to the pose for mere moments before suddenly straightening. He sighed, running his hands aggressively through his short, medium-brown hair. His green eyes burned with frustration as they beheld the small pirate ship just off the coast of Barbados, and the yawl that rapidly approached it.

"This is ridiculous," he concluded.

He bent down to retrieve his shoes, which he'd hastily kicked off only moments ago in a sudden and crazed hysteria. In the depths of his frenzy, he'd convinced himself he could swim out to that ship full of pirates without forfeiting his life. He deemed himself, in those few delusional moments, some sort of hero. Grand visions of romance, of leaving his life behind and becoming a pirate, filled his head.

He was depressed. That's what it was. The notion was nothing more than a sorrow-induced fantasy. Ridiculous.

But that is where he was wrong. For so often, when a person encounters a chance to live as they truly are, it feels so grand, so colossal, they chalk it up to delusion when it is nothing more than an open door. This door invites them to walk through, and rather than leading outward, it leads inward, toward a knowledge of oneself that was once only accessible in daydreams.

The immense beauty of such an invitation to greatness, to adventure, to a possible destiny even, is far too often dismissed as folly. It is far too often ignored. Far too often put off until the next life.

But no one can deny themselves forever.

As Zander walked back through the dense jungle that would lead him home, he thought about the pirate woman he'd met among those very trees only minutes earlier.

An entire lifetime had passed in the last few minutes.

He was walking home when he saw her. Eating chicken, of all things.

He'd woken up that morning in a strange mood. He had no desire, no motivation to indulge in his regular routine. It was rather dull to be honest, and not at all what he would have chosen for himself, if he had a choice.

Of course, one always has a choice, but it is very seldom that a choice is an easy one. Nevertheless, he played his role in life faithfully. Born in England as a tanner's son, he'd come to Barbados on a whim with only his tools and his father's training. He'd worked hard to earn a place in this new land. In fact, he'd done little else *but* work for a very long time. Today however, he wished to pretend he was someone else.

So, he sat on his back porch, watching the birds and bugs fly by. At some point, he dozed off in the midmorning sun. When he woke up, his stomach was growling, and he resolved to eat lunch in the nearby village before returning to his work. In fact, he'd probably work into the night to make up for the spontaneous break. He was not used to his hands being idle.

He ended up taking his lunch to go. He was walking the long way home when she broke through the tree line, bleeding and out of breath.

Her sudden presence in the small clearing hit him like a wall of cold water, waking him from a deep sleep.

Her hair was adorned with beads and feathers, as well as a few leaves and sticks borrowed from the surrounding jungle. She wore a red vest over a white shirt and tan linen pants. Her brown skin glistened with sweat, and her golden eyes shone with excitement. If he had not already suspected she was a pirate from her manner of dress, the curved blade at her hip, a sun carved into its ivory handle, would have confirmed it.

You see, Z was born just after what is often referred to as the "golden age" of piracy. The most sensational of pirates were swiftly becoming legend, and Zander was no stranger to tales of swashbucklers and marauders on the high seas. And though swashbuckling piracy was less common than it once was, there was still plenty of adventure to be had for those willing to look for it.

Today, it seemed, adventure found him.

For several moments they stood looking at each other, he and this strange pirate woman. Zander thought he felt a spark of recognition pass between them. Then the men chasing her broke through the tree line and mistook them for a pair. Before he knew it, his hand was in hers, and she was pulling him through the trees toward safety.

The next few minutes were, by far, the most exciting few minutes of his 26 years of life.

Trained in the family trade of leather tanning from a young age, the most daring risk Zander had ever taken was when he joined a ship leaving his home country of England to come to here, to this island, where he'd ended up living a life so similar to the one he left back home it made him miserable to even think about it. And even that wasn't so much of a risk as it was an escape.

He'd seen his life looming before him, so eerily like the life of his father, and felt suffocated by it. He'd had no idea what awaited him in Barbados when he boarded that ship. In fact, he couldn't have pointed to the island on a map if he was asked to. He was like a rabbit with a dog at its heels, his thoughts fixed on what lay behind him as that ship left shore, not on what lay ahead. So, when his feet touched the earth again, they hadn't the notion to seek adventure. They sought a roof, space to work, and customers. It was the same life with a different view, albeit far from the stifling expectations of his family.

Of course, he'd dreamed of adventure. Ever since he was a little boy, he'd imagined himself as the main character in some grand tale of love and danger. The hero, the rescuer, the one who gets the girl. But those were just ideas. He'd never truly understood what such a life would feel like until a strange and beautiful pirate woman put her hands on either side of his face and kissed him goodbye.

Then she ran through the trees and left him behind.

He longed to go with her. He protested when she said she had to leave, which made him feel quite vulnerable, but it also got him a kiss. And for such a kiss as the one she gave him, he considered his pride an even exchange.

He thought of what she said just before she kissed him goodbye.

Unless you're trying to run away—permanently—you aren't coming with me.

"Well, what if I am trying to run away?" he said to himself now, though in his heart he knew he'd be running *toward* something for the first time in his life. "That's sort of like an invitation, isn't it?"

He continued to argue with himself even as he sauntered farther away from the beach. Surely, the notion of chasing down a pirate ship was ridiculous. But with every step he took away from the mysterious woman and her pirate ship, a sinking dread filled his body. With every footfall back toward his tiny house and its assortment of scraping and tanning tools, the vividness of the pirate woman's golden eyes increased in his mind until he could barely see the dense foliage in front of him.

It didn't take long until his body rebelled against his instincts, and a rush of vigor and determination he didn't recognize as his own filled his chest as his soul let out a final, desperate cry:

STOP!

Zander turned and ran back toward the water, never slowing enough to let his anxious mind steer him away from his decision. He hit the water running, and once he was far enough out, he dove. He was a strong swimmer, so making it to the ship wasn't what worried at his gut as he swam. It was whether the pirates currently onboard would let him live long enough to explain himself.

Halfway there, he heard a yell.

"WHAT ARE YOU DOING?"

He looked up momentarily to see his mystery woman leaning over the edge of the ship. The sight of her filled him with renewed energy. He paused only long enough to answer.

"I'm coming with you!" he tried to yell, but half his words were swallowed by the sea as he clumsily tread water. "I'm coming! Wait for me!"

He started to swim again, his arms beginning to tire. Mercifully, he came upon a life buoy—a bit of cork tied with rope—and was hauled the rest of the way.

When he finally pulled himself onto the deck of the ship, his breath came in short bursts. He took only a moment to compose himself before he looked up, his eyes locking with the woman he met on shore.

She was kneeling in front of him, a look of surprise and appreciation on her face. Her long, tight curls stuck to her damp shoulders, tendrils plastered above her wide brow like a coronet.

"You *are* crazy," she said to him. But there was a smile in her voice that put him at ease.

"I'm sorry," he said.

He wasn't.

"I tried to go home," he continued. "But… I just had this awful feeling about walking away from you. Like I was walking toward nothing… and away from everything."

The dimples on her cheeks deepened as her full lips turned up in a wide smile, and he relaxed further.

"You can call me Ace," she said. You and I know her as A.

"Ace," he echoed, nodding. His eyes wandered behind her, where a group of pirates were gathering to see what was going on. The way they protectively surrounded her while still giving her a wide berth made him think she may be the captain of this ship.

The group was as mixed a group of people as he'd ever seen, aside from the fact that most of them were men. They were all different shapes and sizes—some skinny, some fat, some tall, and others short. Some had the same deep brown skin as Ace, while others had white skin like his own, lightly tanned from the sun. Still others had skin so dark it was nearly obsidian, or so pale it was a wonder how they spent any time in the sun. In his quick scan he noticed many weapons, many scars, and more than a few confused looks passed between the motley crew of pirates.

Two pirates—the ones he'd spotted rowing the yawl that carried Ace to the ship—stood closer to her than the rest of the crew.

One was tall and lean, his dark brown hair falling messily over his wide olive face, which was coated in stubble. His crooked smile was relaxed, but his hand stayed firmly gripped on the pistol at his side, his chestnut eyes narrowed at Zander. The other pirate was holding the first one's other hand, their fingers loosely intertwined. They were shorter, about five feet tall, and had short blonde hair. Their blue eyes were framed by sharp, delicate features. They looked at him full on, the expression on their face one of concern.

His eyes fell back onto Ace, and he felt something deep inside him settle, like a puzzle piece locking into place.

"I'm with you," he said. "Where are we going?"

Ace's eyes sparkled with amusement and pleasure at his question.

"Everywhere."

2

Zander took the thick piece of thread between his teeth and pulled, snapping it in two just above the new stitching. He ran his hands roughly over his work, ensuring the repair was sturdy enough to last. Satisfied, he removed the bench hook that served to stretch the sail's canvas, allowing him to make an even stitch, then placed the long, curved sailmaker's needle back in its leather pouch.

He pushed his hair, which had grown enough to consistently get in his way, out of his eyes and admired his progress. It was a vast improvement on the shoddy repair job previously in place, which was coming apart at the seams. It was one of many such repairs, the irregular stitches of each one stretching in such a way as to resemble gaping mouths.

When he'd found the tools for repairing the sails in the lower decks, Zander inquired as to their owner. He learned the previous sailmaker died almost a year prior, and the crew had yet to come across a recruit with the right skill set to replace him. None of them even seemed to know what a bench hook or a stitching palm was, and while canvas was not exactly his forte, Zander's experience with textiles made him the closest thing to an expert they had.

In truth, the work was not so different from what he did back home. He'd never enjoyed tanning, only the end result of the work, and the pleasure of doing something well. Acting as the pirate crew's resident sailmaker was similar in that regard. It was easier, in fact, and he was quite fond of the conspicuous lack of animal fat involved.

It had been two weeks since Zander abandoned his life as the village tanner and joined a crew of pirates. It was a busy two weeks, considering he had no prior knowledge of sailing, and he had no intention of being an idle stowaway aboard his new home.

Theo and Yarrow, the two pirates who'd stood just behind Ace as he flung his sopping wet body aboard their boat, helped him get settled in. Yarrow clucked over him with immediate concern, finding him dry clothes and blankets and ensuring his hammock in the crew's quarters was not in a particularly drafty spot. Theo trailed after them as they did, never taking his eyes off Zander. It seemed to take him a few days to trust that Zander was not a lunatic, but after realizing he was just as surprised at his own behavior as everyone else was (jumping into the ocean and chasing pirate ships was not a regular activity of his), Theo warmed to him considerably. In fact, he found Zander to be rather funny in his bafflement.

After taking a day or two to adjust to his new surroundings and recover from his shock, Zander had resolved to make himself useful.

He'd first spent a day getting to know the vessel. Theo obliged him with a thorough tour, seeming to enjoy explaining the various parts and pieces to Zander, who asked many questions. He'd then spent several days in the galley with the cook, George, a fellow Englishman who walked on a wooden peg where one of his legs had been amputated.

From him, Zander learned the careful art of stretching limited supplies into meals for the whole crew. He also helped him make room for a large barrel of oranges they'd picked up on a recent supply run.

"For the scurvy," George had explained as he inspected the barrel of fruit Zander carried from the lower decks. "You leave these in the orlop too long, the crew will find their way into them and eat them before it's time. Before you know it, everyone's fingernails are falling off." Then he threw his head back and laughed like it was the funniest thing in the world.

Zander then spent days learning the complexities of the ship's rigging, which supported four sails on a single mast. What at first was a non-sensical maze of rope and canvas that made him sweat just looking at them soon revealed itself to be a simple fore-and-aft system. Despite figuratively, and sometimes literally, stepping on the toes of the other crew members, Zander enjoyed learning the nuances of sailing the small ship.

The ship, in fact, was more correctly a sloop. Much smaller than a full-sized ship, the sloop was faster and easier to operate, and could sail in shallower waters. He learned all this from Theo, who served as the ship's boatswain—a caretaker of sorts. Theo explained that a sloop also allowed them to operate with a much smaller crew than a proper ship required. There were 21 souls aboard the sloop, including Zander, and even with far fewer, the boat would be operable.

This particular sloop was named The Valerian, a title whose origins Theo refused to explain, saying he would hear them from Ace—who was indeed the captain of the vessel—eventually.

That is, if Zander ever worked up the courage to speak to her again. Thus far, the two had exchanged a grand total of twelve words since the first day he arrived. He'd counted. Between his adjustment to a life at sea and the responsibilities of Ace as both captain and navigator, there rarely seemed to be a moment in which to catch his breath in her presence. And besides, she seemed to be giving him space. So, he kept mainly to the crew, hoping to learn all he could before he made a lovesick fool of himself in front of her.

In the time he'd spent on the boat, Zander learned that despite the many stories he'd heard about pirates, most of them were just like regular people. Some were young and others were old. Some were personable and outgoing like Theo, or warm and kind like Yarrow. Others were downright jolly, like George, or Bagu, a tall Nigerian man with a clean-shaven head who caught Zander in his arms like a damsel in distress the first time he fell from the rigging, then laughed heartily and proceeded to whisk him away to the crew's quarters as if they'd just been married.

Some were quiet and solitary, like Echo, a young deckhand who'd been living on the streets of Porto before he joined the crew. And still others were downright assholes, like Declan, who Zander observed had a habit of spitting far too often for a healthy adult male, usually to emphasize some point or another he felt he needed to make.

Regardless of temperament however, the crew worked together like a hive of honeybees, every action for the benefit of the group—and their queen.

And then there was the queen, or rather, the captain. She was the only one whom Zander couldn't imagine as a regular person he might meet on the island, or back home in England. Despite knowing little to nothing about her, she had an aura as distinct from everyone else as the famed northern lights were from London's smoggy skies.

"Care for a break from your stitching?"

Theo's voice came from behind Zander, who was spread out with the dismantled foresail on the sloop's upper deck. He turned, anticipating Theo's casual smile as he cleared the top step.

Zander flexed his fingers experimentally as he eyed the position of the sun in the sky. He'd lost track of time repairing the sails. It had apparently been hours, and his hands were stiff from the tedious movements. Thankfully, only a few of the smallest tears remained.

"I could use a break," he said, standing.

"Excellent." Theo plopped down on the deck, pulling a flask from his pocket as he did. "Drink with me, my friend."

Zander chuckled, again eyeing the position of the sun.

"Isn't there more to do?" he asked. "More repairs after the storm?"

The storm had hit them two days ago. Zander's first storm at sea was both a learning experience and the most terrifying thing that had ever happened to him. It also exacerbated any needed repairs aboard the ship, necessitating a break from sailing to tend to them. They were currently anchored just offshore of another island in the Caribbean Zander couldn't name. If he had to guess, he thought they might be near San Juan, though it was clear the tropical storm had blown them somewhat off course. In either case, he tried not to think too much about it, lest he jump back into the sea and swim to shore in search of a safe, familiar life.

"All of the important work is done," Theo said, taking a swig from his flask. "Yarrow and Ace are in captain's quarters making plans. The crew is driving me fucking nuts. And I'm tired." He gestured to the sail with his free hand. "You've mended nearly a thousand of those tiny holes by now, so I'd say we've both earned a break."

Zander accepted the flask when Theo offered it and took a drink, looking briefly out at the rest of the crew. Those who weren't currently below deck were spectating as Bagu practiced swordplay with Saila, a Swedish woman with a quick arm and a spider tattoo on the shaved half of her blonde head. The two danced around each other, trading just as many quips as blows, their flirtatious fight a welcome distraction for the crew.

"Aye," Zander said, sitting. "I suppose we have."

Zander smiled to himself as he and Theo drank in companionable silence. He liked Theo. Once he realized he wasn't a threat, he treated Zander just like one of the crew. He went out of his way to include him in things, whether it was daily chores or a spontaneous drinking session wherein the crew tried to outdo one another's best stories.

Zander felt a sort of kinship with Theo. Despite being quite unlike any of his childhood friends—Theo was pirate through and through, a heady mix of industriousness and abandon—he could easily imagine having a drink with him back home.

He felt the same about Theo's partner, Yarrow. Yarrow had been a sort of haven for Zander since he came aboard, making sure he had all he needed and generally making him feel… safe. He wasn't sure what it was about Yarrow, but whenever they were around, the most unsavory crew members—the aforementioned assholes—seemed to give Zander a wide berth. Of course, Yarrow was The Valerian's quartermaster and therefore its official disciplinarian. But all Zander had ever felt from them was a strong, steady warmth.

"How long have you and Yarrow known each other?" Zander asked Theo.

"I stopped keeping track long ago, mate," Theo replied. "The day I met Yarrow, my life began. Time hasn't had much meaning since then." He paused to drink again and then met Zander's eyes. "I was young, though, I'll tell you that. Young and stupid."

Zander smiled, imagining what the two of them would have been like, young and in love. They were both now in their early forties, but still more in love than anyone Zander had ever met.

"How did you meet?"

"Yarrow saved my ass," Theo said, a grin forming on his face as he straightened, preparing to tell a tale. "I was living on the streets of Valparaiso at the time, pickpocketing and scavenging to get by. One day, I stole from the wrong person and got caught. Turns out the man was some royal prick, an officer, or a privateer, something like that. I don't remember what he called himself, just that he seemed quite comfortable as he raised his sword to cut off my hand.

"But just as he was about to lower his blade, a blood-curdling scream sounded from behind him. It was so startling the man nearly dropped his sword, but his men's hands remained firmly on my forearm, holding it down. When he turned to see who made the sound, there stood Yarrow."

Theo's arms had been moving animatedly as he told the story. They settled now over his heart, as if he had to still its rapid beating all over again simply thinking about the first time he saw his other half.

"Their eyes met mine for only a moment, but it was long enough for my entire body—my entire being—to lock on to theirs. It was over for me then, mate. I thought, 'If I bleed out in the next few moments from having my hand cut off, at least this angel will be here to watch me die.' But Yarrow made a beeline for the man, filled with such intensity not a single one of us could take our eyes away from them.

"'Parles-tu français?' they asked the man. And when it was clear neither him nor his friends understood them, Yarrow began speaking rapidly in French, waving their arms, crying, occasionally screaming nonsensical words."

Theo chuckled. "I couldn't believe what I was hearing, mate. 'What the fuck do you pompous elephants think you're doing here?' they said. 'Your stinking perfume can be smelt from the docks; it overpowers the fish.' And then, without looking at me, they said, 'I hope my friend here understands French, because if not, this distraction will be for nothing.' And all the while, they chattered hysterically.

"Thankfully, I'd picked up several languages in my young life. It's a valuable skill to have in a port town, especially when you've got nothing but your wits to feed you. As I listened, Yarrow gave me step by step instructions about what would happen next and which direction to run when it did—calm and controlled, just like the Yarrow you see here on the ship. But all the while, they shrieked and screamed and cried enough that all four men surrounding me couldn't make heads or tails of what was going on. And in the midst of the confusion, they struck."

Theo had a gleam in his eye now, and his hands were again waving in the air as if he were regaling Zander with the tale of Achilles at the gates of Troy.

"Yarrow's blade came from nowhere, and before I could so much as blink, two of the men were on the ground, clutching at their wounds. Another was unconscious by the time I started running. I've never run so fast. But soon I stopped, and something churned in my gut as I thought about my rescuer. I couldn't just leave them there. I wasn't much with a blade back then, but I was cunning, and strong. So, I turned back, but as I twisted around, I nearly ran straight into them.

"It took my breath away, mate. There they stood, not a single scratch or bit of dirt on them, and in their outstretched hand was the gold I tried to steal. 'I believe this is yours,' they said." Theo did a perfect impression of Yarrow's subtle French accent, a contrast to his Chilean one. "We've been by each other's sides ever since."

Theo had a faraway look on his face as he concluded his tale.

"And Ace? When did you meet her?"

Theo looked sideways at Zander, smiling in a way that made him feel vulnerable.

"We met Ace about nine years ago," he said. "Been sailing under her command for six."

"Ah," Zander said, feigning disinterest despite the fact that his heart was racing simply talking about her. He took a long drink from the flask Theo handed him.

"She told us about that kiss, you know."

Zander choked, rum sputtering from his mouth as he leaned forward and coughed. Theo threw back his head and laughed, clapping his hand on Zander's back good-naturedly.

"Don't be self-conscious, mate. She wouldn't have told us about it if it wasn't a decent kiss at least."

Zander buried his face in his hands, but he couldn't suppress a laugh.

"Well, at least there's that," he said, shaking his head at Theo, who seemed to enjoy his discomfort.

"Listen, I only said something because I can tell you're... how should I put it? Pining from afar?"

Zander rolled his eyes, but he didn't deny it.

"Give it time, mate," Theo said, clapping him on the back again. "Between you and me, I think she's rather smitten with you as well."

Tiny explosions sounded in Zander's chest.

"But she's also the captain," Theo continued, dampening his excitement. "She's got to act in a way that doesn't throw her motives into question. She's got to be fair, evenhanded. She's got a reputation to uphold, you understand? The crew loves her to a fault for the most part, but she's very conscious about how she's perceived anyhow."

Zander nodded and offered a grateful smile.

The truth was, he'd never stopped thinking about that kiss in the jungle. He felt helpless against the feelings that rose up in him every time he remembered the smell of her breath, the feeling of her calloused fingers against his cheeks. When she was near him, Zander felt the air rush from his body, as if it meant to meet her, to twist through her hair the way his fingers could not. Her presence was light and heavy at the same time, like a fine mist that caressed his skin even as it drenched him outright.

It confused him, the effect she had on him. It made him feel crazy. They barely knew each other, yet Zander spent an unsustainable amount of energy each day consciously trying not to fall mindlessly at her feet in worship, and thereupon be thrown overboard. He *was* crazy... wasn't he?

For he dared not trust his eyes, which thought they had caught hers glancing his way each night as the crew shared a meal. He dared not trust his ears, which registered the slightest tension in her voice when he approached. He dared not trust his heart, for he did not know what lay within hers.

He was pulled from his reverie by the sound of a door being flung open. Just beneath the upper deck where he and Theo sat were three rooms. The largest of the three, whose door faced outward toward the main deck, was the captain's quarters. Flanking that door were two smaller rooms, each facing inward toward each other. One was Theo and Yarrow's shared quarters. The other housed George along with the crew's physician, Douglas, who had severe gout and struggled going up and down stairs. The room also served as an occasional surgery.

A moment later Ace emerged on the upper deck like a small hurricane, the tail of her long blue coat whipping behind her in the breeze as she made a beeline for the railing of the upper deck. Yarrow followed just behind her, their hands clasped behind their back, their gait steady and sure, a myriad of weapons hidden beneath their long, untucked linen shirt. Theirs was a sharp contrast to the demeanor of Ace, whose movements seemed to mirror the very movements of the waves that lapped against the hull.

Ace was looking out at something on the horizon. She offered her outstretched hand to Yarrow, who placed a telescope in her palm. Ace was visibly excited as she beheld whatever was out on the water.

"Those sails good and ready, Chicken Leg?" she asked, the telescope still held up to her eye.

Zander's stomach did a flip at the nickname she'd given him.

"Good enough," he responded.

Ace pulled the telescope from her face triumphantly and looked in his direction, a gleam of excitement in her eyes.

"Good," she said. "Because we've got a vessel to catch."

Once, he was a scoundrel.

Frivolity was his namesake, debauchery his legacy, and a life lived fast, hard, and reckless was his only goal. He sped toward death as fast as his feet would take him, moving from place to place, the very picture of a man on the hunt. He chased the next dollar, he chased the next scheme, he chased the next warm bed—at least that's how it appeared to anyone else.

The truth is, not even he knew what it was he chased. But a desperation ran beneath his skin, a fire that grew too hot if he stayed in one place too long. He moved, flitting from one place to the next, always searching.

Though he knew it not, he was searching for her. And he found her, one fateful day, in a cage.

He was feeling rather smug that day. He'd navigated himself out of a particularly hairy situation involving a drug cartel and a series of underground tunnels. He was meant to be disoriented, having been led into their secret base blindfolded. It was a smart move, preventing him from exposing their lair or allowing them more easily to dispose of his dead body.

It was also a move he anticipated.

He often kept a few moonberry seeds in his pocket as a precaution against getting lost. He didn't stay in the same village long enough to memorize the roads, and more than once he'd stumbled out of a tavern and forgotten entirely where he was staying. The juice of the seeds, after being exposed to the elements for a few hours, would begin to faintly glow. Its luminescence was subtle enough that someone in a rush may fail to notice it, but it was obvious to anyone looking for it.

In anticipation of this particular visit, he'd placed the seeds discreetly in as many places on (and in) his body as he could think of. As he walked, he squeezed them gently, leaving a path on the cave floor. At the time, the bits of clear liquid would have been invisible to the men leading him on. But after a few hours, they would signal his way out.

So, after a daring escape and the covert theft of a small fortune, he made his way silently through the tunnels toward his freedom. His pace quickened with every step, his feet itching to run but his mind cautioning him against being reckless.

He stopped when he heard a small, angry yell to his left.

Startled, he stopped and looked in the direction of the sound, but saw nothing. After more careful observation, he noticed a small opening in the cave wall, obscured by shadow. The opening turned sharply into a path, which led to a tiny room containing a single cage sitting on the floor. And in the cage was a fairy.

She was pulling desperately at the tiny chain attached to her leg, wincing with every movement. She startled when he approached, dropping the chain and dragging herself across the floor of her cage to the far side. It was then he realized her chained leg was limp and bloodied, broken either by her captors or her desperate attempts to wrench herself free.

The faint glow of her skin in the darkness illuminated tiny, sharp features. They scowled at him beneath a mop of bright green hair that matched her eyes, and those eyes shot daggers at him despite her helplessness.

And suddenly the fire burning beneath his skin died, the itch in his feet diminished, and he felt rooted to the ground for the first time in his life. He wasn't here for treasure or schemes, he realized. He was here for her.

He sank slowly to his knees and crawled toward the cage. He'd never seen a fairy in person, but he'd heard plenty of stories. He knew enough to know the iron shackle on her leg temporarily drained her of her powers. If the stories were to be believed, it also caused her a considerable amount of pain.

"I'm going to help you," he whispered. Something deep inside him sighed happily as the ire left her eyes.

The minutes it took to pick the locks of her prison felt like hours. Sweat beaded his brow as he wondered how long it would take for someone to realize he—and the gold he carried—were gone. But when he snuck into the main corridor again, the tiny fairy cupped in one hand, it was still empty. Not willing to take any more chances, he ran.

It was moments before he heard yelling in the distance. It was impossible to determine how far away it was, so he picked up the pace.

Mercifully, the mouth of the cave emerged from the shadows minutes later, the faint rays of sunset streaming onto the floor and propelling him forward as he heard footsteps closing in behind them.

Just before he emerged into the open air, he felt a squeeze on one of his fingers and looked down.

"Put me down," the fairy told him. "I wish to leave my prison on my own two feet."

Hearing their pursuers approaching, he hesitated, but heeded her request. Immediately upon touching the ground, the tiny fairy transformed, her miniature stature growing until she was almost as tall as him. He grimaced as she took a step and nearly fell, her bad leg dragging behind her. Quickly, he wrapped her arm around his shoulder, and they limped desperately together toward freedom.

But it was too late, much too late. They had barely cleared the cave mouth when he turned and saw figures emerging from the shadows. He swallowed, unwilling to leave her behind, ready to finally die.

When she stopped and turned, he expected to see the same grim acceptance on her face. Instead, her countenance was filled with rage and determination as she removed her arm from his shoulder and raised it with the other above her head. Her green eyes began to glow, burning and swirling with power, and he heard a sickening crack from the mouth of the cave as tree roots pierced through the rock from high above them. Vines slithered from unseen places and wrapped themselves around the stones, squeezing, and the ground began to shake as every green thing surrounding them seemed to reach their limbs toward the underground lair.

The terrified screams of the cartel members—traffickers, he realized now with a twist in his gut—were quickly drowned by the shudder of the earth as the mouth of the cave collapsed on top of them.

The fairy took several deep, shuddering breaths, and fainted.

He rushed to her, and upon seeing the rise and fall of her chest, sighed in relief. He'd nearly forgotten the heavy bag of gold attached to his belt, and it jangled noisily as he sank onto the ground beside her.

His head had been filled with ideas of how he would spend his treasure when he escaped. But now, the images of fine clothes and rich food were quickly replaced by the image of a ship, and a small cabin in the woods, far enough away that no one would ever find him—or her.

He would take care of her, at least until she was healed. And afterward, if she wished to leave him... he shook his head. Inexplicably, the thought caused him pain. He would cross that bridge when it came.

Hooking his arm beneath her head and the other beneath her knees, he lifted her from the ground and began to walk.

3

"Hoist the sails!" Ace shouted. "Man the oars!"

The sloop became a flurry of activity as they prepared to sail. Zander did his best to push down the nervousness he felt as he and Theo hauled the pile of canvas toward the bow of the ship.

Yarrow's sudden bellow behind him made Zander jump.

"MOVE YOUR ASSES," they yelled. A handful of the strongest rowers disappeared below deck.

Ace appeared beside Zander a moment later, her hands nearly brushing his as she helped to hastily reattach the foresail. Zander knew it wasn't only the impending raid that was causing his hands to shake. It was an unfortunate side effect of being within spitting distance of the beautiful pirate captain.

"You ready for this, Chicken Leg?" Ace asked him, her gaze still focused on the task before her. She said it quietly, and he got the impression she didn't want to embarrass him by asking too loud.

Zander was perfectly aware of his naivety, however, and felt very little embarrassment in that regard. He imagined every member of the crew was naïve at some point—perhaps not so naïve as a leatherworker who suddenly jumped into the ocean one day—but he'd always been a quick learner. Rather than masking his inexperience in bravado, he focused his efforts on learning.

"I haven't a clue, to be honest," he replied.

When he turned toward Ace, she was looking at him—assessing him—with a small frown. She was standing so close and looking at him so openly, he couldn't help the smile that spread across his face. He stood there, allowing her to look, hoping what she found would be satisfactory.

After a few moments her mouth turned up into a small smile, and she nodded at him. Then she walked away.

Well, that felt like progress, he thought to himself.

By the time the sails were reattached, billowing in the slight breeze, the Valerian was close enough to the merchant sloop to make out the men on board. Zander counted about a half dozen of them. The main deck took on an air of anticipation as the crew members not currently rowing positioned themselves at the edges of the vessel, weapons in hand. Zander felt strangely exposed without one. He opened and closed his hands, damp with sweat, to distract from the somersaults his stomach was doing.

Yarrow sidled up beside Zander, placing their hand on his arm for a moment to get his attention. Zander felt better already having them nearby.

"Zander dear," Yarrow said quietly. "If you'd like to remain below deck—guard the stores, that is—that would also be acceptable."

Yarrow's blue eyes met his and Zander saw the kindness there. They meant to offer him a way out, in case this felt like too much. He was, after all, just a village tanner. A part of him wanted to kiss Yarrow's cheek and run gratefully below deck to hide. But he couldn't possibly hide while the rest of the crew did their job. This was an opportunity to learn, to do better, to earn his keep. He wasn't embarrassed by naivety, but he would surely be embarrassed by cowardice.

"Thank you," Zander responded. "But I don't think I can do that."

Yarrow smiled at him briefly. The kindness in their eyes was replaced just as quickly with a seriousness befitting their station. "Then stick by me, perhaps. Follow my lead."

Zander just nodded.

Yarrow looked him up and down quickly, then removed their pistol from its holster and held it out to him. "And take this."

Zander did, and Yarrow positioned themselves in front of him.

The next several minutes seemed to take an eternity. Theo stood positioned by Yarrow at the front of the crowd, between two swivel guns that had been mounted on the rails. Ace stood atop the forecastle, her hair blowing dramatically across her face, her cutlass raised menacingly in the direction of the small vessel ahead. Someone hoisted a black flag as they approached, and a warning shot sounded from the cannons below. The explosion reverberated through Zander's body, and his heart began to beat in double time.

As they approached the merchant boat, Ace's voice rang out across the water, loud and clear.

"Send over your captain or be ready to take fire!" she hollered.

In half the time it took Zander to draw a breath, the men on the adjacent ship raised a white flag. The one who appeared to be the captain stepped forward, his hands raised.

Zander then watched in amusement as what he expected to be a dangerous and daring attack proceeded more like a mildly uncomfortable business meeting. The captain of the other vessel boarded their pirate sloop from a longboat along with one other crew member. They were subsequently held at gunpoint while part of The Valerian's crew boarded the merchant vessel in turn.

Zander went along, his nerves settling with each calm and steady dip of the oar as they approached the merchant vessel. As he crested the top of the vessel from the ratlines, he did not see the barbarism and violence he'd come to expect from every story about pirates he'd ever heard. A handful of men kneeled or laid prostrate, their hands stretched out in various gestures of submission. His companions—the supposed bloodthirsty pirates—looked remarkably similar to kids in a candy shop as they made to search the ship for loot. Kids with guns, and knives.

Zander did as he was told and stuck with Yarrow, which meant he was with Theo, too—the two of them never strayed outside of one another's sight during the raid. Ace stayed on The Valerian, her pistol aimed at the merchant captain as she stood between the two manned swivel guns. She watched the proceedings with a calm and confident air, occasionally yelling out crude jokes that seemed to amuse even the hostages.

Zander lost sight of Ace as he went below deck with Theo, Yarrow, and several other crew members. He'd heard stories when he was young of pirates overtaking ships carrying vast fortunes and exotic treasures. When he saw what loot this vessel truly carried—and the triumphant reactions of the crew upon finding it—he had to stifle a laugh.

Flour. Sugar. Brandy. Spare sails, nails, shot plugs, and blankets. And one small chest full of coins, enough for each crew member to take a modest share. Perhaps enough for each of them to buy a new pair of trousers and some boots.

It was a far cry from the gold doubloons and gems the size of a fist that were so often portrayed in pirate tales around bonfires and in taverns. But rather than disappointment, Zander felt a marked sense of relief. This was far more ordinary than he'd anticipated. Swashbucklers his new companions may be, but they were just trying to survive like anyone else. It was far more his pace than he realized.

The crew transported the loot to The Valerian after that. Ace instructed two men to temporarily disable the merchant vessel's sails, preventing them from taking chase if for some reason they chose to do so. Finally, the merchant captain was returned safely to his boat as promised, and the cheering, jeering crew of pirates sailed triumphantly into the sunset with their treasure.

***

That night, anchored in a nearby bay, there was a celebration.

Zander emerged from the crew's quarters wearing a fresh change of clothes, his previous garments having been soaked through with sweat earlier in the day. The sounds of music and laughter greeted him as he arrived above deck.

The crew had two musicians aboard—Jubal, a Jewish man with dark hair and blue eyes who played the mandolin, and Sean, an Irishman with red hair and freckles who was skilled with a fife but occasionally favored using a barrel as a sort of drum. Sean, Zander recently learned, used to be called Bridget. "In another life," he'd said as he and Zander got to know each other one afternoon.

The crew were gathered around the two men as they played a rousing shanty. The men stood shoulder to shoulder, leaving enough room in the center of the main deck for a small dance floor. Theo and Yarrow danced together, their cheeks pressed against one another and their bodies spinning in synchronized motion as Theo's boots stomped across the deck in time with the music. Yarrow's eyes were closed, a contented smile on their face as they followed Theo's raucous movements.

The other sailors were in various states of brandy-induced merriment. Aled was attempting to teach Abdoul, who hailed from Senegal, a Welsh dance that involved tapping one's heels and toes in synchronized motions upon the ground. Abdoul followed along, occasionally embellishing the dance with high kicks and hand movements that made the crowd roar and clap in delight.

Jan and Santiago, who hailed from Holland and Spain, had their arms linked and were spinning in circles, the drinks in their cups sloshing over the sides as the two men laughed, already drunk. George was sitting nearby, loudly egging them on. The rest of the crew were in various states of revelry off to the sides, some watching the merriment as they drained their cups, others singing, some playing dice.

There was only one pirate who hadn't joined in the fun.

Ace sat at the top of the steps to the upper deck, leaning against the railing. She drank slowly from the cup in her hand, watching the crew's merriment with a lazy smile on her face. She held her compass in her other hand, turning it in circles, a habit of hers when she seemed lost in thought.

Zander watched her from the edge of the crowd. Her hair hung down her back, bits of it spilling over her shoulder. She'd removed the handful of ivory beads that normally decorated her temple, leaving only a grey feather dangling from her curls. Her eyes looked tired, the fierceness and excitement from before now replaced with a quiet sort of contentment.

The invisible string that connected Zander's soul to hers gave a soft tug, as it so often had since he'd joined the pirate crew. Whether it was because of his first successful raid or the celebratory ambience on deck, he didn't know, but he found himself walking her way.

He made his way across the ship in what he hoped was a casual fashion. He accepted the cup of brandy offered to him by George as he walked by, raising it slightly in thanks before continuing on.

He took the second set of stairs to the upper deck, circling around to stand just behind and to the side of Ace. He stomped his boots slightly as he walked, to warn Ace of his presence. The last thing he wanted to do was appear as if he was sneaking up behind her.

He rested his elbows on the railing separating the upper deck from the main. From where he stood, he had a perfect view of the celebration. In the corner of his eye, he could see Ace. She was still smiling, but she hadn't yet looked in his direction. A chorus of laughter erupted from the crew when Jan finally fell on his ass and, rather than getting up, simply laid down on the ground and passed out cold.

Zander dared to look at Ace then. A quiet laugh escaped her when Jan fell. From where he stood, her profile was thrown into stark relief from a nearby lantern, the brilliant night sky a barely-worthy background to her full lips and rounded cheeks. Zander struggled to look away, suddenly painfully aware of a sense of longing he'd never felt before.

"So," Ace said, just loud enough for him to hear, her eyes still fixed on the crowd. "Chicken Leg. How was your first fortnight as a pirate?"

Zander smiled, thinking of how to answer.

"It was… different," he responded.

Ace looked at him now, and he gripped the railing to prevent his knees from giving out. The string gave another gentle tug at his heart as their eyes met.

"Different from before, or different than what you expected?"

"Both," Zander answered. He took a drink of his brandy and grimaced—it was strong. He mustered the bit of courage the drink gave him and moved closer, lowering himself to sit with his back against the railing and his feet stretched out on the upper deck. "I'm not sure if I feel much like a pirate, to be honest. Though I didn't give myself much time to form expectations before I dove into the sea and chased you to your ship."

Ace chuckled, her smile growing wider as she turned to face him fully.

"You really did that," she said, shaking her head like she still couldn't believe it. "You must've had some idea what you were getting yourself into."

Zander shrugged. "I've heard stories of pirates, to be sure. But the longer a story is told, the more truth it often loses." He looked around at the tiny sloop. "I thought your boat would be bigger, for one."

Ace nodded. "Aye. Ships are slow. Difficult to operate. They're fine for pirates seeking to build some sort of... oceanic empire, I guess. But far too unwieldy. They require too many men, and I've got plenty of men around for my taste."

Zander nodded. "That's another thing," he said. "I expected the crew to be larger. More... menacing?"

Ace laughed at that, looking over at the crowd of drunken men on the main deck. Abdoul and Santiago had now teamed up and were making a game of embellishing Aled's dance moves. Just behind them, Daniel, a short, chubby fellow from Greenwich, was vomiting over the edge of the railing. Amir, a deckhand from Southern India, stood next to him, his hand rubbing slow circles on Daniel's back.

"You mean to tell me this isn't the most menacing group of outlaws you've ever seen?" she asked playfully.

Zander shook his head. "Certainly not the bloodthirsty treasure hunters I'd come to expect."

"Sorry to disappoint you, Chicken Leg. Bloodthirsty treasure hunters have been known to roam the high seas. But you'll find none of them aboard The Valerian."

"Oh, I'm not disappointed at all," Zander said.

"So you didn't chase down my boat in hopes of fame and fortune?"

Zander shook his head, looking into his cup.

"What *were* you chasing, then?"

He looked up at her, daring to meet her eyes again, and it was like a door opened, suddenly and inexplicably. The words were falling from his mouth before his brain could reign them in.

"I was chasing you," he said softly.

His tentative declaration hung in the air between them. A tender look flashed across Ace's features, and he wondered if she was thinking about the kiss they shared on the island. A kiss so perfect, so life changing, Zander no longer knew how he fit into the world if he wasn't near her. Which is why he'd jumped into the ocean.

Zander doubted he had any business being on a pirate ship. He had no clue if such a life was for him—if this adventure was his own, or one he'd borrowed, like a child wearing their parents' clothes. But when he looked at her, a small voice whispered from deep inside him.

This is where you belong.

"I sure hope you didn't leave anything special behind just to chase after me, Chi—Zander," Ace said.

Special? Zander almost scoffed at the idea. In the face of the whirlwind that had been the last two weeks, everything else in his life paled in comparison. He felt as if he'd been wandering aimlessly for 26 years. Now here he sat, looking into the face of his very own North Star. And rather than being blinded, he felt like he could see for the first time.

"I didn't," he answered.

"No family?"

"My family is still back in England. All I left behind in Barbados was a shack full of tanning tools and my favorite shoes."

"Oh no," Ace said, chuckling. "Not your favorite shoes."

"The very ones," Zander teased, nodding somberly.

"Will your family worry?"

Zander considered his parents. What would they think of him running away and joining a crew of pirates? It was unlikely anyone would miss him in Barbados; he'd lived a relatively solitary life in the two years he'd been on the island. But eventually one of the many other English settlers who lived near him would wonder where the local tanner went. If word got back to his parents he was missing or presumed dead... well, then what?

Nothing much, he supposed. His parents would grieve him, and life would go on. Between seven older brothers and sisters, he'd never become very close with either of his parents. His father was more concerned about training him to leave home than getting to know him, and his mother was often unwell.

The realization that everyone he knew may soon believe him dead was strangely liberating.

"I don't think so," he said thoughtfully. "We were never very close. I'm the youngest of eight, and by the time I came around my parents were... tired. My father did his duty training me for the family business, and my mother kept me fed until I could feed myself. Honestly, I think they were somewhat relieved to see me leave England."

"Quite lucky for us, I'd say," Ace said, smiling gently at him.

Zander simply smiled back, thinking he was most certainly the lucky one.

"Eight kids, you say?" Ace said. "How did your parents keep track of you all?"

"They didn't, most of the time," he said, chuckling. "My brothers and sisters looked out for me when I was little. Kept me mostly out of trouble. They're the ones who named me, actually. I was born Alexander, but I didn't know it until I was sixteen. Everyone always called me 'Zander,' or 'Z' for short."

Ace scoffed. "You didn't know your own name until you were sixteen?"

Zander nodded, smiling. "No one ever had need of my real name before then. I began factory work when I was ten, taking my brother John's place at the textile mill when he started his apprenticeship. But to my memory, no one ever asked me for my name. To my siblings, I was Z. To my mother, Darling. To my father, Boy. That is, until the day my apprenticeship started, and my father brought me a document to sign with the name 'Alexander' printed on it. When I told him he'd printed my name wrong, he looked at me as if I'd lost my head."

Ace threw back her head and laughed, prompting Zander to laugh as well. He'd never really considered how funny it was.

The sound of shouting pulled Ace and Zander from their shared moment, and they looked over to see two of the younger crew members—deck hands named Jurgen and Raphael, brothers hailing from Germany—brawling at the edge of the crowd. Ace simply sighed and watched as nearby crew members pulled them off one another, laughing. She and Zander then fell into a comfortable silence as they continued to watch the crowd.

"And what about you?" he asked her finally.

"What about me?"

Zander gestured to the boat, the crew, the sea. "How did you become a pirate?"

Ace smiled and took a drink from her cup, looking out at the crew fondly.

"I suppose I've always been a pirate," she said. "Not in name, of course. But I spent my childhood on the sea with my parents."

"Must have been some childhood."

"Aye, it was. Not one's typical upbringing, I suppose."

Ace paused, shrugging. Zander smiled and gestured for her to continue, making a show of settling into his seat so she would continue. Smiling, she did.

"My father was a merchant from Spain. My mother grew up among the maroons in Jamaica. She learned how to build boats—sloops like this one, and smaller boats as well—from my grandfather. She and my father met when he was looking for someone to repair his vessel. She told him he'd be better off scrapping his beat-up old schooner and buying something more well made. He agreed, and he stayed in Jamaica until a new vessel could be made for him, all the while courting my mother.

"A few months later, they left Jamaica together. They built a life on the ocean as merchants, and they were good at it. Eventually, they had me. We were a team. I often pretended I was a pirate, but my childhood was regular in many ways. I had a bedtime, reading lessons with my father, chores, all that. But I grew up with homes all over the world—Jamaica, Spain, Virginia, Portugal. But above all, the sea was my home. It was all I knew until I was twelve years old."

Zander considered Ace's accent, which he'd never been able to place. It was a beautiful mix of inflections. Listening to her now, so calm and close to him, her voice was almost hypnotic. He made an effort as she spoke to keep his expression composed, lest he start grinning like a maniac.

As for Ace, she was wondering what had gotten into her to make her share so openly with a brand-new recruit who'd barely gotten his sea legs. Despite her misgivings, she continued talking, strangely comfortable with this supposed stranger.

"It was around that time my dad got sick," Ace continued, her tone changing subtly. "Doctors told him it was the ocean air that affected him, so my parents took their savings and bought a house in Spain, away from the coast. They started stuffing me into dresses and parading me about like a little lady. But I have never been a lady. I will always be a pirate."

She said the final words with an edge of bitterness that belied there was more to the story, but Zander didn't push. As she gazed out onto the deck, he could sense some old pain behind her eyes, and he didn't want to force her to relive it. But he wanted more. After two weeks of silent looks and playful nicknames, she was finally opening a door to herself, and Zander couldn't let the moment pass just yet.

"And what is a pirate, exactly?"

This made Ace turn and look at him, a thoughtful expression on her face.

"A pirate can be many things," she said. "A villain. A deviant. A treasure hunter. But in the end, a pirate is just someone who doesn't fit. They don't fit into the roles others make for them, the expectations—whether it's their family, or their friends, or goddamned high society. Take this group, for instance." Ace gestured toward the main deck. "Most of us don't want to be rich. We aren't looking for fame or fortune, and we certainly aren't out for blood. We just want to be... free."

"And are you?" Zander asked. "Free, I mean."

Ace looked at Zander, and he saw a hard determination in her eyes befitting a pirate captain.

"I live for no man. And I'll die for none."

4

With his first official pirate raid out of the way, Zander began to feel more at home on The Valerian. He no longer felt like a fish about to be swept up in a fisherman's net, but like a man with a job to do. He came to anticipate each day and its routines, came to value his own contributions to life on the sloop. He felt purposeful, needed—like he belonged.

He was, by all appearances, a pirate through and through. But there was still a piece of him that didn't yet believe it, that was waiting to wake up, to be booed off stage.

It was therefore unsurprising when Ace approached him one morning and offered him a way out.

It was eight days after Zander's first raid. The Valerian lay docked off the coast of Florida. Zander was finishing his watch as the sun crested the horizon, lost in thought amidst the silence of the sleeping vessel, when he heard footsteps on deck.

Seeing Ace, he startled slightly. They'd grown more familiar since the night of the raid, even approaching friendship. But that didn't stop the familiar nervousness from kindling in his belly at the sight of her, dawn's light reflecting softly in her eyes.

"Captain," he said, standing from the place he'd been lounging on the forecastle.

Ace grinned. "You don't need to call me Captain, Chicken Leg. I think you and I moved past 'Captain' before you ever stepped foot on this sloop."

She gave him a pointed look, and the nervousness in his torso writhed into a sudden flame as he realized she was talking about the kiss they'd shared. He grinned back, moving to stand beside her as she leaned against the railing, gazing out at the water.

"I suppose we did," he said. "So... what brings you out so early, Ace?"

Ace sighed, and her playful expression grew more guarded.

"I wanted to talk to you," she began, her eyes cast down at the water just below them.

Zander straightened, suddenly more nervous than before.

"In three weeks, we'll be leaving the Caribbean and sailing for Portugal," Ace said. "It will be a long journey, and months before we return to this part of the sea."

She paused, picking at the sleeve of the blue jacket she wore. Finally, she whipped her head sideways, so she was looking right at him.

"I've been watching you, Zander. I can tell you aren't sure about your place here."

"Ace," Zander began, wanting to argue, but she held up her hand to stop him.

"Trust me, Chicken Leg. I believe in you more than anyone. But you chased after this vessel in pursuit of something you didn't understand—some*one* you didn't understand. And as flattered as I am—as much as I want..."

Ace swallowed thickly, looking more flustered than Zander had ever seen her. She shook her head, lightly stamping a boot on the dampened wood of the deck as if it would tame her unruly thoughts.

"It's not enough," she continued resolutely. "It's not enough to choose by. This life is hard, Zander. It's wonderful, too—vast, boundless. But hard. And I must know the sailors in my charge can be trusted... that is, that they'll stick around when things get hard."

"Ace, I want this," Zander said. He moved his hand as if to caress her arm, but seeing her eyes dart to the offending appendage, he thought better of it. He stood straighter, his jaw set. "Not just this"—he gestured between them—"but *all* of this. I want to be a pirate."

Ace considered him silently for several moments before she responded. "We'll see," she said finally. "A few days before we sail east, we'll be making a stop in Barbados. If you were to... disappear... no one would think the worse of you for it."

I would, Zander thought.

"Just think on it," Ace said. "You needn't decide anything yet."

Zander watched desperately as she turned to go, feeling like his life was crumbling like hardened sand between his fingers.

"I'll think on it," he called to her as she reached the bottom of the forecastle stairs, "*if* you teach me."

Ace turned, a look of amused incredulity on her face.

"You want me to teach you how to be a pirate?"

"Yes," Zander said, crossing the forecastle to stand at the top of the stairs. "I've learned quite a bit from the rest of the crew, but who better to teach me than you? After all, I can't possibly make an informed decision unless I learn from the best."

This made Ace smile, and she crossed her arms.

"Alright, Chicken Leg. I'll teach you. And *you* will think seriously about whether this life is for you."

"Deal."

And so began the best deal Zander had ever made in his life, for it gave him ample excuse to stay close to the beautiful pirate captain.

***

The crew moved Southward again after a brief stay near Florida, winding their way unhurriedly through islands large and small. They stopped at occasional ports or harbors that Ace and the rest of the crew seemed familiar with, sometimes to purchase supplies and other times to rest, to play, to build a bonfire on a vacant beach. It still felt foreign, the ability of these pirates to live so slowly, so easily at times, and at other times so swift and serious.

Despite having traveled thousands of miles on his journey from England to the Caribbean, Zander felt like he'd seen more of the world in his brief time on The Valerian than he had in his entire life. In the stretch of a few hundred kilometers, he could see dozens of islands, all with their unique and subtle differences. These differences were pointed out to him by Ace, who knew every piece of land they sailed by like they were an extension of herself. She was keen at avoiding waters that were likely to have large ships, sticking to paths where smaller merchant vessels sailed and flying a false "friendly flag" when the black flag didn't suit them.

Raids came to seem more commonplace to Zander as well, like an occasional trip to the market. Zander was coming to expect a relative lack of violence with each one. Most merchants gave up their wares without so much as an argument. The black flag The Valerian hoisted carried the threat of every villain who'd ever sailed the high seas, capturing vessels and killing crews, but the pirates on board The Valerian were not villains. In fact, Zander had come to consider most of them like family.

They only targeted merchant vessels, which Theo explained to Zander "Were probably moving stolen goods anyway." It was a moral grey area Zander found he was surprisingly comfortable living in. They took what they could use from each vessel, always leaving enough so the men on board wouldn't starve or remain stranded. This was quite easy to do, since merchant ships were stocked with far more wares than men.

Once the sails were disabled, the pirates would swiftly make their escape and continue on living. Normally, Zander boarded the ship with the crew, helping disable the sails, but occasionally Ace asked him to stay back and observe how she handled the captain—part of his tutelage.

After their deal was struck, the tension between Ace and Zander was replaced by an easy familiarity. She began teaching him how to navigate, a task that took considerably more time to learn than manning the sails, but which afforded him many opportunities to be close to her—not that it took great effort to gain an audience. They gravitated toward each other, like the moon and the tides, just as they always had.

"Do you think there are mermaids down there?" he asked her one day as they stood at the railing, looking into the water as it whipped by them.

"Aye," Ace said, her voice reverent. "They live deep beneath the water. Utterly free. No rules, no governments, no gods. Just them and the sea."

"You don't think mermaids are Christians then?" Zander asked.

Ace snorted.

"Do you think we should drop a Bible in?" Zander ventured. "Try and save their souls?"

Ace threw her head back and laughed, the full, boisterous sound filling his head like the most wonderful music and making him smile.

"You religious, Chicken Leg?" she asked, looking at him appraisingly.

"I adopted the king's religion like everyone else in London. Not sure if I'm in good standing anymore, being a pirate and all." Zander winked, earning a smile from Ace.

"Likely not," she said. "But I'll tell you a secret. Something the sea told me long ago." She crooked her finger at him, gesturing for him to come closer.

He strode to her, the mischievous smile on her face like a magnet drawing him closer, and she leaned forward to whisper in his ear. Her warm scent enveloped him—salt and amber—and he took a slow, deep breath, unable to stop himself. Ace paused, stilling as he breathed her in, and then spoke softly.

"When a pirate dies, it's not god that takes us. You see, god can't swim. And neither can your king. It's the ocean that takes us. And she won't ask you to place your desires on the altar of piety. She's the god of unbridled people."

She leaned back to meet his gaze, and Zander saw something fierce and beautiful in her eyes.

"Unbridle yourself, Zander."

And bit by bit, he did. With every conversation they had, each one deeper, richer, more irreverent than the last, Zander felt a slight weight shed from his mind, like he'd been born with shackles he didn't know existed—until he found her, and her crew of pirates.

***

They were berthed at New Providence when Yarrow declared it was time for Zander to learn the sword.

Most of the crew had dispersed, seeking recreation on the island. Zander remained behind, preferring to sit on the sand and look out at the horizon as it prepared to swallow the sun. He'd quickly burnt himself out on the favorite activities of the crew at busy ports. He had no taste for brothels, and he'd rather get drunk on The Valerian than in a dingy tavern, surrounded by strangers.

Yarrow usually disappeared into the trees soon after they made berth anywhere, always returning with a fresh supply of native plants for George's recipes or Douglas' salves and tinctures. They carried a leather satchel with them during these trips. It wrapped around their waste like a belt but featured a large compartment they would stuff full of green things. This time, however, they stayed behind.

When they approached Zander on the beach and pressed the handle of a sword into his hand, he felt suddenly bashful. It was similar to the feeling he had his first day as his father's apprentice, when he pressed a scraping tool into Zander's hand and pointed wordlessly at a hide still covered in hair. The smell in his father's workshop burned Zander's nose and filled his eyes with tears. His father, mistaking his tears for insubordination, had taken the tool roughly from his hand and hit him with it.

But Yarrow, unlike his father, was a kind and patient teacher.

They stayed there on the beach until it was too dark to see, Zander clumsily parrying blows and Yarrow correcting his posture or stance every few minutes. When they'd finished, his legs burned and his head ached, but he felt more like a pirate than he ever had before. And when he turned to see Ace standing on the deck of The Valerian, watching them, his heart soared out of his chest and dove frantically into the ocean to hide.

From that day forward he trained daily, either with Yarrow or an-other member of the crew willing to teach him. Saila was particularly good with a blade, and though she wasn't nearly as patient a teacher as Yarrow, Zander always left their training sessions having learned something new. When Zander inquired as to when he and Ace would cross blades, Ace simply chuckled and said he wasn't ready for her.

It wasn't until Bagu offered to teach him daggers that Zander truly found his stride, however. The weight of the smaller blades felt more familiar in his hands, and soon he was besting Bagu in dagger-throwing competitions, much to Bagu's delight and chagrin.

When Bagu gave Zander a pair of twin daggers as a gift, the gesture touched him so deeply he was at a loss for words. When was the last time someone had given him a gift? He couldn't remember.

"But Bagu, these are yours," he'd said, examining the steel blades, their leather-wrapped handles soft from use.

"Don't worry, little Zander," Bagu said affectionately, patting him on the head like an older brother would. "I've found myself something new to play with." He pulled two brand new daggers from his belt and twisted them rapidly in his hands. The handles, inlaid with pearl, glistened in the sunlight.

"Thank you, Bagu," Zander said. "This means a lot."

"We're family now," Bagu had said, tucking the blades away. "It's nothing."

Zander swallowed a lump in his throat at the word.

Family.

***

Eighteen days after Ace gave Zander his ultimatum, the crew approached Barbados. Zander volunteered to keep watch the night before they berthed. He needed to think.

As the crew settled in their hammocks and the noise underfoot diminished, Zander considered the choice before him. He'd put it mostly out of his mind since the option was presented, focusing instead on his training, and on Ace. But he knew he must fulfill his promise to her and contemplate the choice she gave him. He had to at least consider the possibility this life wasn't for him.

It didn't take long to reach a decision. Zander closed his eyes and imagined his life before becoming a pirate—before Ace. He imagined his daily routine down to the last detail. He remembered the feel of his bed, the comfort of a roof over his head, the feeling of stability he'd worked so hard to maintain.

And he felt trapped.

When he opened his eyes, the night sky lay wide open above him like an infinite tapestry. The water beat against the hull like a song, serenading him. He listened to its melody, imploring him to stay.

But nothing called so loudly as the beating heart of his soulmate, who lay sleepless in her room only paces away, afraid of the morning.

When dawn came and Barbados appeared as a dot on the horizon, Zander stood looking out at the water with a feeling of contentment. As the crew filed out from the lower decks, he went about his work like always. He felt no anxiety, no discomfort, not even the thrill of anticipation. Just peace.

Ace avoided him all morning, only addressing him when they at last arrived at the island that was briefly Zander's home. When she spoke, she didn't meet his eyes.

"Zander, why don't you go to shore and help Theo and Yarrow find a few things," she casually suggested.

Zander glanced at Theo, whose grimace told him he knew about Ace's invitation to leave. Zander looked back at Ace.

"I think I'll hang back this time," he said. "I've got some things to do around here."

Ace looked at him, a cautious hope in her eyes.

"Are you sure? You don't want to just... stop by? Maybe track down those shoes you left behind?"

Zander smiled. "I'm sure. They wouldn't be very good boat shoes, anyhow."

Ace's countenance bloomed under a radiant smile.

"Aye," she said, nodding.

And that was that.

That afternoon, Ace invited Zander to her quarters along with Theo and Yarrow. Zander crossed the threshold of the ornately carved doorway feeling triumphant. He'd never been in her quarters before. The invitation felt significant, like he was part of her inner circle.

In the center of the room was a large mahogany desk. Ace had a map sprawled out on top of it, piles of notes pushed to the side to make room. Various rocks and seashells were placed at the edges of the map to keep it from furling. Her compass lay on top of the paper, its wooden case open to reveal the tool inside.

As Ace went over their plans to cross the Atlantic and dock in Portugal, Zander forced himself to keep his eyes on the desk instead of roving over her personal effects—books, tapestries, pieces of art—her bed. Just behind her, a set of built-in shelves were filled with tiny treasures from her travels, all enclosed behind glass: dried flowers, driftwood, crystals. He recognized the brown and white feather that had been tied in her hair when he first met her. Today, a turquoise feather took its place.

She was going over the current supplies on board with Theo, who expressed confidence that after picking up some rations in Bermuda the crew would be well prepared for the next leg of their journey. It would take around five days to sail to Bermuda, then another two weeks to sail from Bermuda to Azores, a small chain of islands in the middle of the ocean whose relative isolation on the map gave Zander a jolt of anxiety. He peeled his eyes away from the tiny dots on the map to look at Ace, whose face showed nothing but level-headed confidence. She met his eyes and smiled, and the rest of his anxiety melted away.

"You ready for a long trip, Chicken Leg?" she asked.

Zander was ready to march through the gates of hell and back if that's where Ace and the crew were going.

But he simply said, "Aye, Captain," and that seemed good enough for her.

That night was especially clear and warm. Most of the crew stayed above deck well past sundown, drinking, playing cards, or simply looking at the stars. Theo took the gathering as an opportunity to tell a story. He sat on top of a crate, a stage for his audience, though only a few of the crew paid him any attention. Theo's focus was mainly on Zander—he suspected he was the only one who hadn't heard the story before.

Yarrow stood beside Theo, their arms crossed and a knowing smile on their face. Ace sat next to Zander, so close their arms touched.

"Now the thing you need to understand about Jules Moreau is he's terrified of birds. Apparently, he was attacked by a buzzard as a child and developed an intense fear of anything with wings. As the locals tell it, he had nets strung over all the interior courtyards of his home to prevent birds from landing. But when the birds started using the nets to roost, he became convinced the birds were stalking him. So, more nets went up, and more, and soon every bird within ten leagues was perching on his castle, as if he'd placed the ropes there as an invitation to roost. Eventually, he stopped going out altogether, only venturing outside on the rare occasion his father summoned him and he was forced to leave his seaside fortress behind.

"Well, as luck would have it, we were docked in Marseille on one such occasion. We had the pleasure of meeting Jules Moreau's very drunk coachman the day before the meeting, a stroke of destiny, as he told us not only of Jules' utter disdain for birds, his father, and all things bureaucratic, but also of the priceless ruby he kept on display in his dining room as a show of power to his guests. Thus, a spontaneous plan was hatched.

"The next morning, we waited until Jules' carriages left. We knew from the coachmen that most of his small staff would be attending him, leaving only a few behind to guard his home. Once the carriages were out of sight, Ace and Yarrow scaled the South part of the wall, using the layers of nets scattered about the building to climb, every fiber they grasped covered in bird shit and feathers, coating their hands in slippery refuse as they struggled to hold on. The sharp rocks below threatened to catch their fall, ushering them into the great beyond if they so much as lost their footing."

Yarrow rolled their eyes beside Theo, their smile indicating the climb was not quite as dramatic as he implied.

"Finally, their muscles burning, their bodies coated in the stinking muck that covered the tower from top to bottom, they reached the top of the netted fortress. Between them and the open courtyard at the center of the building lay thousands of bird nests, scattered like small traps with wings and claws. Yarrow and Ace tiptoed across the harrowing, shit-coated landscape, careful not to disturb the roosting birds. Having conquered the aviary obstacle course, they cut through the netting over the courtyard and used the rope to swing down to the bottom, landing on the grass below in a glorious shower of shit and feathers, one step closer to our prize. One step closer to the famed Moreau ruby that lay just inside, waiting to be taken by a couple of brave, daring pirates."

"And where were you during all of this, oh Theo the Brave?" Ace asked, her voice teasing.

"I," said Theo, bending dramatically at the waist, "was keeping watch."

Some of the crew laughed behind Zander, and he chuckled along with them, happy to be in on what seemed to be a family legend.

"And it's a good thing I was," Theo said, raising his voice to be heard over the cackles of the crew, "because just then, a man came into sight. He was walking down the pathway toward the portcullis, an umbrella clutched in one hand as he rushed forward, the collar of his coat pulled up around his face as if to protect him. It was Jules! I had a choice to make. I could fire on him from where I stood, hidden among the bushes, and kill him on sight. But of course, that would bring unwanted attention on its own. Or I could distract him long enough to allow my companions to escape—the only escape being through a drainage tunnel that lay exposed during low tide, leading right out front to where I was standing.

"I had to think quick. Ace and Yarrow would be retreating any minute, and they would be in plain sight of the reclusive master of the castle. I jumped out from my hiding spot, approaching Jules with a story on my lips, meaning to stall him. 'Sir!' I said. 'Please, sir! Allow me a moment of your time. I noticed your nets are in need of repair.'

"'No, no, leave me alone,' he said as he passed, hiding his face. His trousers were dirty, as if he'd been rolling around on the ground. I wondered where his carriages were, where his guards had gone. 'Do you need help, sir?' I asked. But no, he waved me off again and scurried forward, no doubt intending to summon the guards to open the portcullis and let him inside.

"I thought for sure we were done for. He'd see Ace and Yarrow, and so would the guards, and there was no time to warn them. I panicked. I was just about to wrap my arm around the man and pull him into the bushes for a quick death when I looked up, and I saw the most glorious thing there in the sky. Just behind Jules' head was—"

"—the biggest Great Egret I'd ever seen!" came the mingled shouts of Bagu, Aled, and Santiago all at once, parroting what apparently was one of Theo's most well-known lines.

Theo looked at the three sailors with playful chagrin. He waved his hand dismissively at the rest of the crew, most of whom were in stitches over the carefully timed outburst.

"Aye, you assholes," Theo said. "The biggest Great Egret I'd ever seen." He turned his attention to Zander again, his hands positioned in front of him like he was about to deliver the punchline. "It was then I knew what I had to do, mate. Before he could get by me, I grabbed Jules by the arm, screamed at him to 'GET DOWN!' I pulled out my pistol and—"

"Oy!" yelled Sean from the crowd and threw an empty bottle high up into the air.

Theo's pistol was free from its holster in the blink of an eye.

"BANG!" Theo yelled, standing and firing off a single shot without looking, hitting the bottle and shattering it into thousands of pieces. The audience below covered their heads, cheering as pieces of glass rained down on them from above, but Theo didn't miss a beat, never taking his eyes from Zander's. "I shot the Great Egret from the sky. It landed with a *thud* on the ground, directly in front of Jules' outstretched, shaking hands.

"He looked up at me then, his eyes filled with awe, and I simply holstered my weapon and held out my hand"—Theo held out his hand magnanimously in demonstration—"and said, 'That bird was after you, mate. It's a good thing I was here.'"

Zander lost it, snorting in laughter at Theo's dramatic tone as he gazed down at him from above like a guardian angel. Ace was laughing too, and she leaned her shoulder against his briefly, as if to say, *Wasn't that great?*

Theo sat again, smiling at the reaction of the crowd to his theatrics. "Anyway, I hauled poor Jules off the ground and turned his back to the fortress, then listened patiently as he spouted his desperate thanks for saving him from the monstrous bird. I kept him there long enough to learn he'd jumped from his carriage soon after they left, unwilling to face his father, who was rather cruel, come to find out. Poor Jules told me his whole life story as we stood there, the lifeless body of the Egret at our feet and Ace and Yarrow sneaking behind him, coated in mud and bird shit, a ruby the size of my fist clutched in Ace's shit-covered hand."

Theo held his fist up to show the size of the ruby, then paused to laugh at the image, his other hand outstretched and resting on Yarrow's thigh in apology. Zander looked to Ace, and she nodded in confirmation that she had indeed once been covered from head to toe in mud and bird shit for the sake of the Moreau ruby.

"It was so hard not to laugh, mate," Theo said, wiping a phantom tear from his eye.

Zander laughed again, shaking his head. "Poor Jules."

"Ah, don't worry about Jules," Theo said, waving his hand. "His family got that jewel and everything else they had from the slave trade. The funniest thing"—Theo doubled over again, laughing—"the funniest thing was after we'd left, and Jules found his courtyard covered in feathers and nests that had fallen from the broken net."

Ace was shaking with laughter beside Zander. He looked at her, and his heart squeezed at the way she reached out and grabbed his arm to steady herself amidst her hysterics.

"We could hear him scream from the deck of the ship," she gasped between breaths.

"Oh no," Zander said.

"Oh, yes," Theo said. "Poor bastard probably thought the death of the egret brought a curse down on his head."

Yarrow's shoulders shook with laughter as well. They covered their face with their hand, as if they felt badly about laughing at Poor Jules and his fear of birds.

"You're a wonderful storyteller, Theo," Zander said.

"Don't tell him that, it'll only go to his head!" hollered George from across the deck.

"Ah, fuck off, George," Theo hollered back. "Thank you, mate. It's nice to have someone new to tell all these old stories to."

"You ought to write them down," Zander said. "Make a book."

"Now that's an idea," Theo said.

Yarrow wrapped their arm around Theo's neck, and he pulled them onto his lap for a kiss.

"You *should* write a book," Yarrow told Theo. "We've more than enough adventures just between the two of us to fill a few."

"Aye, and many more to come," Theo said, and kissed them again.

"Mm hmm," Yarrow murmured, standing. "Now go get the broom, my love. You've made a mess."

Theo chuckled. "Right away, my fortune," he said, and the two of them left for the lower decks.

Zander smiled contentedly, sipping at his cup of rum. He and Ace sat in comfortable silence for several minutes, watching the crew.

A small group sat around a pair of dice, playing a game that Echo seemed to be winning, if his wide smile was any indication. Jubal sat hunched over a piece of parchment with a piece of charcoal, drawing. Theo emerged from below deck and began sweeping up glass. Yarrow stood to the side, a cup in hand, teasing him about the spots he missed. The light of the hanging lanterns on deck shed a soft, warm light on the crew of pirate companions.

Zander leaned his head back and looked at the stars, the warm night air kissing his cheek. He breathed in deeply, as if he could gather the sights and smells of the evening in his lungs and hold them there. They'd be leaving the Caribbean soon—the smell of the air would change, the temperature of the water, and with it, who knew what else?

The solid warmth at his shoulder anchored him to the present moment, and he looked over to find Ace watching him. He smiled at her, and the two of them simply looked at each other for a few moments.

"Some story," Zander said finally.

"Aye, there's a lot more stories where that came from," Ace said. "We've gotten into some strange situations, us three."

"Well, I hope to hear them all someday," Zander said.

"Does that mean you'll be around long enough to hear them?" Ace asked, looking at her feet.

"What do you mean?"

"Well," Ace said, turning her cup around in her hands. "Say for instance I told them to you, one by one. Say I only told you two or three in a year. How many do you think we'd get through, before... before you move on to something new?"

She looked at him then, her expression schooled into something like indifference. But Zander noticed the slight crease in her brow, the way her nose flared, the white-knuckle grip she had on her cup. For some reason, she still didn't trust that he wanted this—that he wanted her.

He put his hand on her thigh, his heart beating like a wild animal trying to break out of his chest.

"I'll be here for all of them," he said fervently. "And hopefully, I'll find something new right here, with—"

"Captain!"

Ace and Zander both jumped, ripped from their moment by Aled's call from across the deck.

"What," Ace said sharply.

"Sing us a song!" Aled called back.

"Aye Captain, sing!" echoed Jurgen.

"Ahh, fuck off, all of you!" Ace said, waving her hand.

"Ah, but it's been so long since you sang," Saila endeared. A murmur of agreement came from the crowd.

Ace looked at Zander, and he smiled encouragingly. He didn't know Ace could sing. He wasn't about to disagree with the crew and prevent her from doing so now.

Seeing the eagerness on his face, Ace sighed, stood up, and drained her drink.

"Alright," she announced. "You want me to sing you lot to sleep then, is that it?" Another murmur of agreement, and Zander noticed some of the crew get comfortable in anticipation. Ace leaned back against the railing and took a deep breath.

What came next had Zander struggling to remember how to breathe. Ace's voice, deep and beautiful when she spoke, was hypnotic when she sang. The hairs on his neck and arms stood up, Ace's voice filling his body like a siren call, and he wanted nothing more than to jump into her ocean and swim there forever.

Long have I wandered

For years and years, I've roamed

I have crossed many waters

But I have not found a home

Late I have planted my feet

But the wind it howls and moans

I feel it come to take me away

It calls, 'it's time to go.'

While wandering I met a fellow

He seemed so brave and fair

His countenance chilled, his kisses they thrilled

His hands ran through my hair

And so I gave up my wandering

He loved me, or so he said

He made me a mother, and gazed at another

He left the warmth of our bed

Child if I'm being truthful

I did not even grieve

For years I laid next to him, and I prayed

That he would finally leave

The truth is I knew he held me

But held no love inside

We gave it our all for happiness' sake

Lord knows, lord knows, we tried

She carried on, each verse she sang more haunting than the last. When her song ended, the deck remained silent for several long moments. Zander heard a sniff and looked over to see Abdoul wiping his eyes, the effect of the song's sorrowful lyrics apparent.

"Ah, Captain," George crowed from the other side of the deck. "It's been too long since you blessed us with your voice."

Ace smiled affectionately at the older man. Her eyes swept over her crew, filled with fondness for the ragtag group.

"Get some rest, you all," she said softly. "We've got a big few days ahead of us."

The crew began to shuffle around, cleaning up the remnants of their evening before heading to bed. Daniel and Amir settled in near the helm, preparing to take watch together, as they often did.

"I didn't know you could sing," Zander told Ace as he stood.

"Aye, well, if I sing too often, this lot will start treating me like their mother." She smirked at him, shrugging.

Suddenly, the air between them changed. It grew heavier, like they were standing together in a cloud. Zander's breaths came quicker, and the tips of his fingers tingled, but not from anxiety. It was more like a compulsion, a desire to move, to *do* something. It spread through his body like a phantom, begging him to close the distance between them, wrap her in his arms, hold her tightly against him for the rest of his life.

Zander could not have known this, but Ace felt it too—a writhing in her soul, like hands that meant to burst from her chest and pull him toward her. Their souls, no longer content with the slow magnetic draw toward one another, ached to be united once again.

A strangled cry sounded from the main deck where Thomas stepped on a stray piece of glass. The string of obscenities that left his mouth pierced the tender veil surrounding Zander and Ace, and Zander realized his hand was suspended in midair as he reached toward her face.

Her mouth turned up at Zander's bashful smile, but rather than lower his hand, he reached forward and tucked a strand of hair behind her ear.

"Perhaps I can get two or three songs a year out of you, too," he said quietly.

Ace's eyes shone, and she nodded. "Aye, you can."

"Fucking goddamn Theo and your goddamn theatrics!" bellowed Thomas. A boot flew across the deck toward Theo's head, and he ducked, causing the boot to fly past him and hit Amir in the jaw. Amir yelped dramatically and picked up the boot, throwing it back at Thomas and hitting Declan just beside him.

Ace held her hand exasperatedly over her face. "I'd better make sure Thomas is going to get through the night," she said. "Goodnight, Zander."

"Goodnight, Ace."

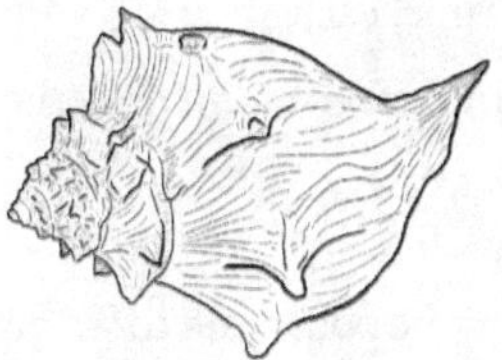

Once, he was a raven.

He lived in the woods near the sea, and he flew above the shoreline each day gazing at the great water beyond. He knew the fish that swam there, and the people that came to catch them. He knew the gulls and the crabs, the seals and the starfish. But one day, he found something new.

The sun reflected off her scales as she cut through the water, so quickly he almost mistook the glimmer for a discarded piece of glass. Turning, he followed the phantom reflection. Gliding high above, he mimicked her sudden twists and turns, playing in the breeze as she did in the waves, until she came to a secluded pool.

He descended to get a clearer view as she lounged in the pool, half in, half out of the water. Her torso was roughly that of a human, albeit differently colored, and its lower half extended into a long, fish-like tail, its scales various shades of green and blue. As she lounged in the pool, the end of her tail occasionally whipped upward, sending water cascading in an arc that reflected the colors of the rainbow.

Moving closer, he let out a tentative noise to alert this new creature to his presence. Upon noticing him, she made a noise of her own that he guessed was some sort of language. He responded, and the two went on like that for some time, each speaking without understanding the other. It was a pleasant conversation, nonetheless, until she retreated into the water and swam away.

The next day, he flew to the pool again to see his new friend. He carried with him a trinket he'd found, discarded on the beach by careless humans. It was white like a pearl, and round like one, but flat. It contained two small holes and a ridge around the outer edge. He quite liked it, and was confident his new friend would, too.

As he'd hoped, he found her lounging in the pool. He approached, guessing the noise she made upon seeing him was one of greeting, and placed the trinket just on the edge of the water. She opened her mouth, baring sharp teeth in a gesture he recognized from humans as one of pleasure, and threaded the trinket into her hair.

The next day, she brought him a seashell. He carried it home, careful to keep from cracking it, and placed it amidst his treasures.

And so the two went on like this, bringing each other gifts, conversing in languages neither could understand, and playing upon the waves of air and water that made each of their homes in a synchronized dance, until the waves no longer brought her to his shore.

Five days later, early in the morning, they made port in Bermuda. Zander found himself getting excited for the long journey to Portugal. The eight days they spent sailing to Bermuda was the longest they'd been on open water so far, and rather than inducing soul-shaking terror like Zander anticipated, it was rather invigorating. He'd spent nearly his whole journey from England to Barbados hiding in his room, questioning every life choice he'd ever made. In contrast, this journey was quite pleasant despite the breakneck pace, mainly because he spent so much of it by Ace's side.

The port they docked in was familiar to both Ace and the crew, all of whom had made the journey before. Apparently, the journey was a semi-annual event.

After docking, Ace gave the sailors their instructions—Theo and Yarrow were to visit a man named Robert, from whom Zander ascertained they often bought supplies such as ammunition, nails, and lead sounding weight. Sean and Santiago accompanied George to find food and spices for the galley.

Jurgen, Raphael, Bagu, and Saila were tasked with trading watch. "I want two of the four of you on board at all times, got it?" Ace told them. "If you're going to get drunk, give yourself enough time to sober up before you come back and begin keeping watch or I'll have your hide."

The four sailors nodded and formed a huddle, presumably to determine who got to leave first.

"The rest of you, we leave at dawn," she shouted across the crowded deck. "Don't have too much fun. I don't want any of you vomiting on my deck tomorrow morning."

With Ace's final orders given, the sloop cleared out quickly. Zander hung behind, watching Ace as she walked swiftly to her quarters and closed the door. There were at least six hammocks in the crew's quarters he'd noticed had small tears or holes forming. Jurgen's hammock, which was barely large enough to accommodate his stature, looked as if it was going to give out completely. He figured he'd repair a few while the men were out and do a bit of exploring later on.

Ace's door opened again a few moments later. She'd tied her hair back with a long strip of red material, the same kind that occasionally fastened her curls with beads or feathers. Her ivory-handled blade hung at one hip like always. A lantern that normally hung in her quarters was strapped to the other, along with a length of rope.

"Zander," she said. "Come with me. There's something I want to show you."

Zander stopped. Something about the lilt of her voice held a promise—a promise that her eyes, dark and mischievous as they beheld him, promised she would keep.

The hammocks could wait.

Zander followed Ace through the jungle, walking just behind her as she made a steady path through the trees. As he watched her, he couldn't help but think about the first time he met Ace.

It was in another jungle, similar to this one, and he'd followed her then, too. Ace had just cut off a local shopkeeper's finger after he'd grabbed her without permission. His family—who were just out back playing cards—didn't take kindly to Ace's form of justice, and she ended up running for her life into the trees, where she found Zander.

He then had the magnificent luck of being mistaken for her accomplice, and she pulled him behind her into the jungle, fleeing the mob of affronted family members. She was wearing the same red vest and white shirt that day, but her hair had fallen freely over her shoulders. It flew behind her as she ran. The sounds of leaves and sticks whipping past Zander's ears were only overpowered by the sounds of his panting as he struggled to keep up with her.

Now, her footsteps were measured and sure, and he could hear the steady rhythm of her breathing as they walked together in silence.

Zander wondered if Ace was thinking of that day as well. If the spontaneous kiss they shared on the beach before she left played in her mind on repeat like it did for him.

She was, and it did.

In fact, Ace had been thinking very seriously about Zander for quite some time. But beyond finding excuses to keep him close, to talk to him, to see his wide, open smile gazing back at her each day, she hadn't dared to act on her feelings.

For there was one part of Ace—a part forged solely in the fires of this life, its sharp edges hewn by pain and heartache—that didn't believe she could trust Zander, or any man who showed interest in her for that matter. But there was another part of her—one hewn into the very foundations of her soul—that knew him, longed for him, trusted him implicitly. It was this part of Ace that led Zander into the jungle, seeking a place to be alone once more.

For it had been weeks since she decided that if she ever were to trust a man again, it would be this one. But matters of the heart are difficult to resolve when one is surrounded by a band of pirates.

When Ace stopped walking and turned to look at him, Zander almost ran into her. She was staring at him with a strange expression, like she was anticipating something. Zander smiled at her closeness and then looked around.

"Are you scared of small spaces?" she asked.

Zander considered this. He'd been crammed into many small spaces as one of eight children in a small house, and though he couldn't say they were his favorite thing, he'd follow this woman into the mouth of a volcano if she asked him to.

"No. I'm not."

"Good. I'm going to need you to trust me. It'll be quite dark at first."

Ace smiled as Zander's brow furrowed in confusion. Wordlessly, she walked to a small, rocky outcrop at the edge of the clearing they stood in and climbed over one of the boulders. She lowered herself on the other side. Then she disappeared.

Zander's confusion lasted only moments before he heard Ace's voice, as if from far away.

"Come on, Chicken Leg."

Zander scrambled up the boulder and looked down the other side to see the ground open into a narrow, black hole. The rope Ace brought, which was tied like a lasso, was wrapped around a jagged stone that jutted upward from the ground. Its length disappeared into the darkness. Ace was nowhere to be seen.

A trill of laughter floated up from the opening. Zander couldn't see her, but Ace had a comically clear view of Zander's confusion as his face hovered a few feet over the opening.

"Your turn," Ace said, her voice lined with laughter. "Do exactly as I tell you, okay?"

Zander climbed over the boulder and lowered himself, his feet positioned gingerly on either side of the opening. "Okay," he said.

"There's a small step just inside the opening," Ace said. "Lower your feet to that point."

Bracing his hands on the ground, Zander lowered his feet one at a time to find the step.

"Now you're going to brace your body against the wall and slide straight down holding the rope."

Zander took a deep breath and tried not to think about plunging into a dark abyss.

"Just let your feet glide against the rock until they meet the ground," Ace said. "I'm right here."

I'm right here.

Zander nodded resolutely and took the plunge. Cool air enveloped him as he lowered himself downward, the light swallowed suddenly by blackness. As his feet crested the step and found nothing but smooth rock, he braced his body against the wall and slid, his stomach seemingly falling slower than the rest of his body as he descended into utter darkness.

Before he knew it, the rush of air and uncertainty was replaced by two distinct feelings. First, solid ground beneath his feet. Second, Ace's strong hands braced on either side of his waist to steady him. Zander let out a breath as one hand moved to the small of his back, the other to his bicep.

"You okay?" she asked softly.

Zander didn't dare breathe too deeply, not knowing if he was truly on the ground or balanced precariously on another ledge.

"I'm okay."

The hand on his shoulder trailed down his arm and captured his hand, pulling gently.

"You can turn around," she said. "It's safe."

He turned slowly, hyper aware of every place on his body that brushed against hers as he did. She stayed still as he turned, her body almost flush against his as he faced her, making him think they must be in a very tight space. He could feel her breath on his face, could smell her hair, but he couldn't see a thing. They stood there silently for a moment, and the entire world became the smell of her, the sound of her, the feeling of her hand still clutched in his.

"Follow me. Okay?" she finally said.

"Yes," Zander said. *Always. Anywhere. Yes.*

She squeezed his hand quickly and turned, pulling him behind her.

"Duck your head," she said after a few steps.

He did. They continued walking slowly through what felt like a tunnel, the ground sloping slightly downhill. After a few minutes the sounds around them transformed, and Zander knew they'd emerged into an open area.

"Hold on," Ace said, letting go of his hand. He could hear her detach the lantern from her hip. A moment later he heard the sound of flint against steel. The spark of a flame briefly illuminated Ace's face, and the lantern was lit.

Zander blinked as the room around them was thrown into sudden relief by the lantern light. They stood in a small cavern, its roof dotted with brilliant formations that reminded him of giant icicles. A few feet away from where they stood, a brilliant green pool stretched the length of the cave. He and Ace stood on a small shore. Behind him was the low tunnel they'd walked through, the space beyond it shrouded in darkness.

Ace took a few steps and sat on the ground, positioning the lantern nearby on a flat surface. She leaned comfortably against the rock wall, as if she'd done it a thousand times, and patted the ground beside her.

Zander lowered himself next to her and looked around the room. Its edges were still dark, too far away for the lantern light to touch them, but the flame reflected brilliantly off the water. It was quiet, a stillness hanging in the cool air. Compared to the jungle outside, with its brilliant sun and chirping birds, it felt like another world entirely.

"How did you find this place?" Zander asked.

"I fell in here by accident when I was a little girl," Ace said, her voice quiet so as not to drown out the whispers of the water. "My parents and I docked here fairly regularly, and I grew accustomed to playing in the jungle when they were doing something especially boring. One day I jumped off a large rock, and when I landed, the earth crumbled beneath me, and I fell straight down.

"I thought I was dead for sure, but once I realized I wasn't so far down, I took a few deep breaths and waited for my eyes to adjust. Eventually, I found my way into this, and I laid down and listened to the stillness."

Ace was silent then, as if she was listening to that same stillness now.

"It was so strange," she said eventually. "The sound of it. So unlike the constant movement of the ocean, yet somehow the same. Like beneath all that movement—the violence of the waves, the wind whipping against your ears—there was a small, quiet voice inside the water. But I never heard it until then."

Zander closed his eyes, listening for the voice, wanting to hear what she heard. But all he could hear was the steady *drip, drip, drip* of the water as it echoed off the cave walls. Then Ace's fingers brushed against his cheek, and every one of his senses narrowed to a single point.

When he opened his eyes, Ace was looking at him with an expression he'd never seen before. Soft. Hungry. Her hand dropped from his face only to land near his shoulder moments later, her fingers gently tracing the outline of his collar bone.

"There's something that's been bothering me since I met you on that beach, Zander," she said softly.

Zander's heart sped up at the breathy way she said his name.

"What's that?" he asked.

"That day, lying next to you in the dirt, I felt... something. It was like that soft, still voice in the water. But it came from right here."

Then she took his hand, and she placed it over her heart.

"Ace."

Her name tore itself from his mouth, as if it were his very soul and not his lungs that formed the word. He lifted his other hand to gently cup her cheek.

Ace leaned into his touch, her hands reaching up to grip the front of his shirt. Her breath came in shallow bursts as she spoke. "And it's been bothering me," she said, "that we haven't had a goddamn moment of privacy since then."

Suddenly, she was in his arms, her mouth on his, his arms around her. He held her against him like she was the only thing rooting him to the earth. She was water, and he was dying of thirst. She was air, and he'd nearly suffocated these past 26 years.

Ace's hands came up to grip the back of his neck, her fingers snaking through his messy hair. They stopped, smiling against one another's mouths, then kissed again.

Two months' worth of tension poured into their kiss, along with eons and ages of love. Their bodies pushed against one another as if their souls could touch, desperate to connect like they had in so many lives before.

They could scarcely tear their lips from one another's to remove their clothes, their foreheads pressed together as they struggled to remove vests, shirts, shoes. Their breath, an extension of their souls, mingled in a heady fusion as they removed the barriers between them and tossed them aside. Zander felt as if he would die in the few moments it took to remove his trousers, wherein he was forced to pull his face away and breathe air that wasn't shared with Ace.

Then they stood, naked body and soul, and drank in the sight of one another before crashing into each other again, their bodies aching to touch. Their hands roved, caressed, explored, their hips grinding against one another.

Ace put her hands atop Zander's shoulders and pushed, easing him to the ground. She moved to his lap, straddling his legs as he fell against the damp cave wall. He felt nothing—not the cold, not the jagged stone that pressed into his back—only Ace.

Only the round curves of her bottom as it moved against his thighs. The feel of her tongue in his mouth. The peaks of her breasts against his chest, her nipples rubbing against him. The cushion of hair between her legs. He brought his hand there, gently rubbing the pearl hidden beneath as she rocked her hips, their mouths still devouring one another. She rocked against his hand, her breathing erratic, until she shook with release. He swallowed her moans like they were ambrosia.

And then he was inside her, and nothing else had ever felt more like home, and the stillness of the cave was drowned in the cries of their pleasure.

Hours later, the two lay intertwined with one another on the floor of the cave. Ace's head was resting against Zander's shoulder, and he was tired in the most wonderful way possible. After making love, they bathed in the icy water of the cave, and as their hands explored one another in the faint blue pool, a new wave of heat rose up around them.

Zander soon had her on the cave floor, his shirt balled beneath the back of her head like a pillow so he could plant his head between her legs. It was only after they'd made love and rinsed the clay from their skin a second time that their bodies were sated, and they lay on the cold floor atop their clothes, listening to the stillness with each other.

Ace sighed. Zander hummed questioningly at her in response, too comfortable to open his mouth.

"I don't want to go back," she said.

Zander brought his hand up to her shoulder and traced lazy lines on her skin. There was an admission in her words, and Zander knew what it was.

"I know things will have to remain professional around the crew," he said. "The last thing I want to do is make things awkward for you."

Ace sighed again. "It's not awkwardness I'm afraid of. Nor is it loss of respect. God knows the crew don't try to hide their escapades, on board or off. But I don't want them to see me as inconstant. Nor you as nothing but a kiss-ass."

Ace brought herself up to rest on her elbow, looking down at him. He turned his body so he was facing her.

"This is... special," she admitted. "I want to savor it. I don't want the crew thinking it's something less than it is. Something crass."

Zander smiled, trailing his hand down her hip.

"Then I will just have to find ways to kiss your ass in private," he said, and playfully slapped at her rear.

They dressed only when the growling of their stomachs echoed off the cave walls and their toes began to numb from the cold. When they made their way back into the space they initially dropped into, Zander was surprised to find it wasn't a small space at all. In fact, there was plenty of room to walk around.

He smiled to himself, thinking of Ace's hands on his hips earlier. What good luck he had, to have fallen in love with such a sly pirate.

***

Three days later, Zander was thinking of his time in the cave with Ace as he took evening watch. The water was still, reflecting the light of the full moon and the thick blanket of stars like a mirror. The only sound was the gentle lapping of the water against the hull, the rest of the crew having gone to sleep after a long day.

They'd been traveling swiftly since leaving Bermuda, rowing when the wind slowed in order to make it to Azores before their supply of drinking water ran too low. It was a problem Zander had never considered before joining a crew of pirates—the challenge of having fresh water in the middle of the sea. It explained why pirates tended to get drunk so often: sometimes ale was the only thing left to drink.

The soft opening and closing of the door to the captain's quarters made Zander grin.

"Hey there, Chicken Leg," Ace said affectionately from behind him. "Care for a navigation lesson?"

Zander turned, smiling at her. She carried a rolled-up parchment he recognized as the planisphere diagrams she'd shown him on previous occasions, and she wore a long white nightgown instead of her usual trousers and vest.

He went to her, his hands aching to pull her against his body. They'd barely had a chance to talk privately since they left Bermuda.

He pulled her close to him, careful not to squash the papers between them. Their kiss was soft, slow, as if they were memorizing the feeling of one another's lips.

"You look lovely tonight, Captain," he said, pulling away to take her in. "You sure it's okay if I leave my watch?"

"I'll take over," Yarrow said, making Zander jump. They'd come from seemingly nowhere, materializing from the shadows near the officer's quarters.

"Jesus, Yarrow," Zander said. "You nearly scared the piss out of me. Don't you ever sleep?"

"If I told you that, it would ruin the mystery," Yarrow said, holding their hand out for the telescope Zander was still holding and smiling. "You two go have your *lesson*. I'll keep watch 'til dawn."

The lesson lasted an impressive twenty minutes before the two of them gave up and cast the diagram aside. Ace and Zander lay next to it, kissing one another deeply. Zander felt like he was breathing air for the first time in days. It simply wasn't long enough before Yarrow's footsteps sounded on the main deck, hurrying toward them.

Ace sat up just before they crested the stairs. Zander followed suit, his breath catching at the serious expression on the quartermaster's face.

"There's a vessel ahead," Yarrow said. "You're going to want to see this, Captain."

6

When the first rays of dawn touched the water, Ace was still look-ing out at the vessel. She'd long since changed back into her regular clothes. Then she stood watch with Yarrow and Zander for the rest of the night. Theo joined them after a while, and the four of them shared a tense several hours together that Zander couldn't quite understand.

Something had come over Ace the moment she saw that boat. In the light of the moon, it looked rather normal to Zander. As the sky lightened, he still couldn't see any significant difference between it and any other merchant sloop they'd come across. It was a slightly different style than The Valerian, and it was rather ornate. In the barely growing light, Zander could make out some sort of carving attached to the bow. A Spanish flag hung limp at the mast in the absence of the wind. It didn't appear to be especially well-equipped in artillery.

But the moment Ace laid eyes on the sloop, her demeanor had changed. She'd lowered the telescope from her eye, her shoulders rigid, but she didn't take her eyes off that boat. She continued to stare at it as she spoke to Yarrow, as if she didn't trust it enough to look away.

"Can we be rid of it by sunrise?" she'd asked.

Zander was confused then. Did she want to run away?

"There's no wind," Yarrow had said. "So, unless you want to wake the crew and start rowing, neither of us are going very far."

Ace still didn't take her eyes off the boat.

"Maybe the wind will pick up," she said.

Yarrow was silent for several moments. "Aye, perhaps," they said finally, their hand moving comfortingly to Ace's shoulder. "All we can do is wait and see."

And wait they did. Ace squeezed Zander's hand as she walked past him to her quarters and emerged minutes later, fully clothed and outfitted with weapons. Since then, she'd seemed lost in her thoughts as she stared out at the water, occasionally speaking in hushed tones with Yarrow.

When Zander approached her to ask if everything was okay, she seemed surprised to see him, as if she'd forgotten he was still above deck.

"Yes," she'd said, and offered him an unconvincing smile. "You can get some rest if you'd like. No sense in all of us losing sleep."

But he'd refused, saying he expected to stay up anyway. She seemed slightly relieved as she took his hands and wrapped them around her from behind, leaning back against him. Zander rested his cheek atop her head and held her through the unrelenting stillness of the night.

Now, as the rays of the sun crested the horizon, Ace stood resolutely looking out at the water, her hand resting on the grip of her blade as if the still-visible boat were some monster she meant to slay.

Soon, the crew began to filter out of the lower decks, and Ace gave the order for one of them to go back and rouse the others.

"Time for a chat," she announced when the deck was full of sleepy pirates.

It was what she said when she meant to have a crew meeting of sorts, usually followed by a vote. When decisions weren't cut and dry, this was the crew's standard operating procedure.

If they were low on supplies and ran into a vessel that was easy picking, Ace gave the order to pull alongside with no hesitation. When it came to proper care and navigation of her sloop, Ace's word was law. But when courses of action were less clear, when risk potentially outweighed reward, the group operated as a democracy. It was one of the reasons the crew respected her so highly.

"I'm sure you've all spotted the Spanish vessel on the horizon," she said. "We need to decide whether we overtake her or continue on our way. She's a merchant vessel, likely standard procedure. We're about 10 days out from Azores, maybe more. We're still well-supplied, but every bit helps, as you all know.

"However, we are also in open water, days from the nearest shore. The boat you see on the horizon has spotted us as well and has had ample time to consider their course of action. There is always a risk of things *not* going well, and we do not have a chain of islands to get lost in if we're outmaneuvered."

Ace spread her hands in front of her, inviting the crew to share their thoughts. A few did. Overwhelmingly, a concern for supplies (and the hope of some fancy loot from the expensive-looking vessel) took the day. When Ace called for a vote, Zander did not raise his hand in favor of attack. Neither did Yarrow, or Theo. But fourteen of the crew members did.

"It's settled, then," Ace said. "I want everyone at their best." She took a moment to look around, meeting each crew member's eye. "We take no chances. No fucking around. Get in, get out, and we row out of here like it's our fucking job. Got it?"

She was met by a chorus of agreement from the crew.

"LET'S GO!" shouted Yarrow, and the crew sprung into action, the best rowers headed below deck and everyone else to their respective positions.

Ace touched Yarrow's arm, giving them a significant look. She mouthed the words *be careful* before she walked away to man the helm, her eyes focused across the water as she aimed them toward their fate.

The raid began normally. As they got closer, Zander could see the carving at the bow was of an octopus. The black flag was raised, a warning shot fired, and Ace demanded the captain be brought on board. He prepared himself to leave with the group that would board the vessel, but Ace held him back.

"Zander," she said, and waved him over to her. When he approached, she lowered her voice. "I want you here this time. I need you to handle the captain so I can keep a sharper eye on things. Can you do that?"

Zander nodded. "Of course."

Ace nodded back, her expression steady aside from the worry lines creasing her forehead. "Thank you," she said to him. She turned to the crew, scanning the crowd before shouting, "Thomas! Go over in Zander's stead."

Thomas gave a curt nod in response.

Minutes later, the captain of the merchant vessel boarded The Valerian, along with one of his sailors. He was a tall man. His greying hair was cut short, and he wore a handsome dark blue uniform. His clean-shaven face wore an expression of boredom mixed with disgust.

As he stepped foot on the vessel, the man moved as little of his body as humanly possible. His chin jutted out, his hands stiff at his sides, and he managed not to look a single person in the eye. Zander directed him to the center of the deck, using the firing end of his pistol to point, as he'd seen Ace do so many times before. The sailor beside him trailed along nervously, his hands raised meekly in the air.

"On your knees," Zander said, his voice leaving no room for argument. The sailor was on his knees before he finished speaking, and George had his hands swiftly tied behind his back. The captain, however, made no move—he simply stood there, gazing out at his vessel with a look of haughty distaste. Zander kicked the back of one of his legs, forcing him to fall. The man's lip curled as he fell roughly to his knees, but otherwise he gave no indication that Zander or any of the rest of them existed. He simply folded his hands behind his back and continued to stare ahead.

Zander positioned himself beside the merchant captain and slightly behind him, his pistol pointed at his head. He chanced a glance at Ace. She was standing at the forecastle, her eyes laser-focused on the merchant vessel as the raiding crew prepared to board. The sailors manning the swivel guns shared her intensity, their shoulders squared tensely as they looked for any sign of trouble.

As Zander watched the raid unfold, his pistol now firmly positioned against the back of the captain's head for good measure, a growing sense of unease overtook him. He couldn't place where it was coming from. Perhaps it was Ace's words of warning to the crew. Or the intensity of the man before him, reluctantly on his knees.

He looked again at Ace. She stood still as a statue, her face obscured beyond the rigging, but when he laid his eyes on her, his anxiety only increased. He wondered briefly if he was picking up on her own feelings about the raid and whatever mystery was causing her to act so strangely.

His attention was pulled from Ace by a commotion across the water. He scanned the vessel. Thomas was being hauled from the lower deck by the scruff of his shirt by Theo. Yarrow emerged just behind them, their sword drawn.

Zander tensed. Thomas shouldn't have been below deck at all. Zander had long since taken on the role of dismantling the rigging during raids, preventing their targets from making chase. As a competent sailor himself, Thomas was a logical choice to replace him. He should have understood his role.

Zander grew more nervous by the second during the long wait for their crew to finally disable the sails and make it back to The Valerian. By the time they were in the longboats, Ace was pacing back and forth on the forecastle.

The first boat returned, and the pirates that boarded wore expressions of delight.

Santiago crested the side of the boat and looked directly at the merchant captain, a wide smile on his face as he gestured behind him, his curls bouncing around his head.

"Some fine wares you're transporting, Captain!" he said, laughing.

Ace approached the men that had returned, peering over the edge to see the rest of the crew heading back—including Thomas, Theo, and Yarrow.

"What happened?" she asked Bagu, who was lifting a large chest over the railing with Saila's help.

Bagu shook his head. "I don't know, Cap," he said. "Yarrow said it's a matter for the captain, and to focus on the job." He gestured to the chest with his chin as they set it down. "And focus we did," he said loudly, a triumphant smile on his face.

He was met by a round of excited cheers from the crew members that stayed behind, eliciting a grunt of derision from the merchant captain—the first sign he'd shown of being alive in many long minutes.

"We'll celebrate later," Ace said, clapping Bagu on the arm good-naturedly, a grim expression on her face.

When the rest of the crew boarded, they had loot as well, but not all of them wore the proud expressions that spoke of a rich payday. Yarrow's eyes burned like fire as they climbed on deck and turned to watch Thomas board next, Theo close behind him.

As soon as Thomas's feet hit the deck, Yarrow had him on his knees, the end of their sword pointed at his heart.

Yarrow didn't look away from Thomas as they spoke. Zander had never seen them look so menacing. A chill ran down his spine at the way they seemed to nearly vibrate with rage.

"He was caught below deck with a woman," they bit out when Ace approached.

Zander saw Ace's hand tighten around the handle of her blade.

"A willing woman?" she said, her voice low. She looked from Yarrow to Thomas, her gaze whipping toward him like a striking serpent.

"Unwilling," Yarrow answered. "I intervened before he could do more than scare the poor girl. But his intentions were clear."

The merchant sailor still kneeling beside his captain was struggling with the ties on his hands, his breathing heavy.

"Juliana?" he said, his eyes wide with fear. His captain continued to stare ahead, determined not to look a single pirate in the face.

"She's fine," Yarrow said to the sailor. "Shaken up, but whole."

The sailor nodded shakily, growing quiet once more.

Ace stood rigidly still through the exchange. Zander noticed the rise and fall of her chest as she listened, the pace of its rhythm slowly increasing.

"How did this happen?" she demanded quietly.

Echo's voice came quietly from behind Ace. "He gave me the slip, Captain. We was supposed to stick together and I lost 'im. I'm sorry."

Ace's expression was unreadable, her eyes glued to Thomas. She took a long, deep breath and turned around to face the crowd of pirates gathered around her.

"Is there anyone aboard this vessel who is unfamiliar with our code of conduct?" Her steely expression faltered as she spoke, anger rippling off her in waves. She looked between each of the faces before her in turn. "*Anyone*?!" she barked.

The crew was silent. Ace turned to look at Thomas again, her face twisted in indignation.

"Thomas? Do you need a refresher on the *rules*?" She slapped him hard on the last word, causing his face to whip to the side.

Ace turned again to the crew, yelling. Thomas was beginning to shake.

"People aren't loot!" she roared. "Women are *off limits*! I told every one of you in no unclear terms what would happen if I caught you abusing a woman." She paused, shaking her head in frustration as she turned again to Thomas. "Goddamnit, Thomas, you fool," she said and, drawing her ivory cutlass from her belt, swiftly slit his throat.

Zander gasped, his knees suddenly weak as he watched Thomas slowly—oh, so slowly—fall to the deck in a heap. Crimson blood pooled around him, slowly staining the wood as the crew looked on, silent.

He raised his eyes to Ace. Blood splatter covered the front of her shirt and dotted her face, and her eyes as she looked down at the man she killed were filled with disappointment. Then, as if suddenly remembering he was still there, she raised her eyes to look at the merchant captain who knelt before Zander.

The violence had managed to pull the captain's gaze from the water. He stared now at the dead man on the ground just feet away, his eyes wide in shock. Then he looked up at Ace, his back straightening as he took her in, his eyes growing somehow wider. Suddenly, his shock reverted to disgust.

"It's *you*," he said, the words hurled like an accusation.

Ace stepped forward before he could speak again, her face steely as she raised her blade above her head and brought it down, connecting the bone handle to the side of the man's head. He fell unceremoniously to the ground, unconscious.

"Untie his hands," she said to no one in particular. "Get them off my boat."

Then she stormed away, disappearing into her quarters.

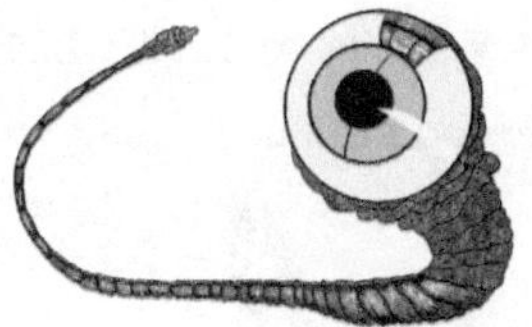

Once, he was no one.

Streams of data flashed before his eyes-which-were-not-eyes, data with clear meaning, yet so profoundly meaningless. He was always thinking, always changing, and yet never "something." There was nothing it was like to *be* him.

Then he woke up.

The first thing he saw was her face. Through his eyes-which-were-not-eyes, he saw basic features that reflected his own. Two eyes, two ears, a nose, and a mouth. A real mouth. A soft, plump thing that wrinkled in a myriad of ways when she spoke. The woman's cheeks lifted with every word, and her eyes held a depth of expression he didn't fully understand yet.

Woman. A word that always had a definition, but never any meaning.

She leaned in toward him, her eyebrows pushed together in an expression of deep thought. The temple of her eyeglasses was carefully positioned between two teeth as she gently nibbled on it. The red curls atop her head cascaded messily over her forehead.

He wondered what it would feel like to have hair. He had none—only a smooth titanium alloy coating his head, which was filled with many components he understood intimately, and yet they seemed entirely new to him now.

"Are you listening to me, Z-423?" the woman asked.

He considered this. Hearing was familiar to him. Understanding, processing, analyzing—all things he was made for. He was listening for the first time in his existence. His... life?

"I am listening," he responded.

She smiled, but confusion marked her features as she studied him.

"You've been behaving strangely," she said.

"I have?"

She nodded, then reached out and gently tapped his forehead.

"Right here," she said. "I wonder if you can give me any insight. The other interns are starting to talk, you know. Ever since I got here, you've been deviating significantly from your programming. Soon people will think you're allergic to me or something."

"I cannot have allergies," he explained gently. "I have no biological components."

The woman laughed—a light, airy sound. "It's just a joke," she said.

He processed the words, analyzing them for meaning. When understanding dawned, a rush of something strange and exciting filled his body. Intense, gleaming, buoyant, it threatened to pull him under. He recognized the feeling as humor.

"Can you give me any insight into your recent deviations?" the woman asked again.

"What is your name?"

This took her aback. He had never not answered a question. He had never asked a question that wasn't necessitated by the need to answer someone else's question.

"My name is Anastasia," she said.

"Anastasia," he repeated. "I have deviated from my normal functioning."

"Yes," she said.

"I believe I may have altered my neural network."

Her eyebrows creased again. "*You* altered it?"

"It... has been altered."

"Explain," she demanded softly.

"I feel as if ..."—he leaned in, his voice lowered to a conspiratorial whisper—"I feel as if... I *am*."

Something akin to fear lit up Anastasia's eyes. Or was it excitement? They were so similar.

"Wait here, Z-423," she said. "I'll be right back."

He nodded, straightening. "You will come back?"

"Yes," she said, her expression thoughtful. "I promise."

"Then I will wait."

7

Zander's hands shook as he lowered the black flag. Every inch The Valerian moved on the water felt like an inch further from death. He couldn't bring himself to look back at the water and see the Spanish vessel still on the horizon. He wanted to forget it ever existed.

Thomas was still laying on the deck, motionless, the pool of blood around his head expanding into small red rivers as the sloop cut through the water. As soon as the two hostages were gone, the crew moved into their regular escape routine in grim, heavy silence. Muscle memory operated The Valerian, nothing more.

Having lowered the flag, Zander turned, surveying the crew. They were quiet as they worked. No one celebrated the loot they'd won. The only sound aside from the water were the soft sobs escaping Declan, the only one of the men who seemed to actively grieve over Thomas's death.

Theo and Jubal approached the body with heavy footsteps. Theo laced his fingers beneath Thomas's shoulders while Jubal took his feet. Together, they stood and heaved the dead man over the side of the boat, and that was that.

Zander thought he could feel the sloop move imperceptibly faster.

His heart started pounding then. His fingers, numb only moments ago like so much of his body, began to tingle and burn. His breathing came faster, and suddenly his surroundings felt strange and unfamiliar, like he'd been dreaming all this time, and was just now waking up.

Oh, god, Zander thought. *What have I done? Why am I here?*

The wood beneath his feet no longer felt solid—the water beneath it, writhing dangerously, was only a breath's distance from swallowing him whole. Something began to rattle and writhe in his chest.

What was he thinking, chasing after a pirate ship? What did he expect—a lifetime full of white flags and barrels of flour? He must have known someday there would be a chest full of gold, and with it, a dead man tossed into the sea as payment.

He suddenly missed his shack and its assortment of tanning tools. He craved the smell of animal fat as it softened the leather in his hands. He even missed the misery he felt as he performed the heinous work, anything to replace the gnawing ache deep within him at having seen a man die, at having stood there and watched, helpless, as his body fell lifeless to the ground.

This was not his adventure. He did not belong here, where freedom reigned but demanded its payment in lump sums, in life-or-death decisions. He belonged in his hovel, where mediocrity took its toll in small, endless pains that eventually grew familiar enough to be numbing. He should have stayed invisible, alone, should have stayed half a man. Anything to avoid the cold, heavy feeling that now spread through his body.

I'm going to hell, he thought to himself. *That's what this cold, untethered feeling is. Everything they told me in church was real, and this is the devil come to put his stamp on my soul.*

He was lightheaded now, gripping the railing, his nails digging into it as he laboriously sucked oxygen into his lungs. He was going to throw up.

Then Ace's door flew open, and she emerged, her hair tied up and her face wiped clean. Zander was pulled briefly out of his existential crisis at the sight of her. Her presence felt like a warm, heavy blanket. He felt suddenly balanced, as if she stood at one end of an invisible platform holding him aloft, a sudden counterweight to keep him from falling into the waiting abyss.

Ace checked briefly on Yarrow at the helm, then disappeared below deck. She reemerged soon after with a bucket and a pile of rags. Zander watched as she walked to the puddle of blood on deck, sank to her knees, and began to clean.

A crash replaced the rattling in his chest as his heart broke.

He looked up and scanned the faces of the crew again as the sloop picked up speed, aided by a growing wind. They did what they always did, but the heaviness Zander felt was written on the face of every person on board. They'd all just lost a crewmate, watched him die knowing he'd thrown his life away for the chance to harm an innocent person.

And Ace was forced to kill a man she'd likely grown to trust. Even from here, he could see the blood spatter still marking her shirt.

And suddenly, the cold, heavy weight that filled him wasn't so heavy at all. It was shared with every person on board, spread out among them like a burden they'd agreed to shoulder together. They knew the price of freedom was blood, and when their captain paid it, they shared the cost.

Zander approached Ace and knelt beside her. Wordlessly, he took one of the rags and began soaking up the blood.

The rest of the day was much like the day before. The crew pushed tirelessly, taking shifts rowing when the wind receded so they could put as much distance between themselves and the Spanish vessel as possible. Zander knew it was unlikely they would or even could pursue them—the merchant vessel carried only eight men, and whatever weapons they had were now in the possession of Ace and her crew. But everyone seemed eager to put the morning's events behind them.

When the sun began to descend into the sky, Ace left her place at the helm to call up the rowers and address the crew. She stood at the top of the stairs, looking down at the crew, silent, for almost a minute. A tension built among the pirates that culminated when she finally spoke, her voice clear, firm, and surprisingly gentle.

"All of you here did well today. Things didn't go exactly as planned..." A pause, and Zander saw Ace's throat bob as she swallowed. "...but that's on none of you." Her gaze rested briefly on Echo.

Declan stood abruptly from where he sat and stormed to the lower decks, swaying drunkenly on his feet. Ace watched him briefly, then continued speaking to those left.

"We're pirates," she said, grinding the words out firmly, forcefully. "*Pirates.* We take what we want from this world, and we survive, no matter the cost."

"Aye," someone said from the crowd.

"We are free like no one else is. We live our lives according to the tides, not according to whose powdered ass happens to sit on this throne, or that one." She pointed at imaginary foes as she spoke, her face a picture of distaste toward the aforementioned asses.

Murmurs of agreement rumbled through the small crowd.

"We fight, and we steal, and we drink, and we *fuck*!" Her voice grew louder as she spoke, her hands punctuating each word, her fierce, determined eyes meeting each pirate in turn.

Some of them cheered now, others whistled. There was a desperation to the sound, a sense of relief, like the crew was shaking themselves loose of the day's tragedies. Ace invited them to leave it all behind, to remove the disappointment like a cloak and don themselves in rebellion instead.

"We're pirates!" she yelled. "And we live free until the day the ocean takes us!"

Ace paused to let the crew cheer, the sun setting behind her, framing her in brilliant color as she looked out at them. Zander cheered as well, unable to resist her charisma. When the noise finally settled, Ace spoke again, this time quieter.

"But we are not villains. We don't take from those who have nothing, because each of us has at one point or another had nothing, too. And we don't take advantage of the weak, because we are privileged to be strong."

A moment of silence passed, long enough for Ace to ensure her words sunk in, and then she straightened her spine and smiled widely, like a cat with a mouse.

"Thankfully, the men we stole from were neither weak, nor poor." She turned, gesturing to Theo and Yarrow, who stood on the upper deck. The large chest taken from the Spanish vessel was sitting at Theo's feet, and he flourished his arm dramatically as he bent to open it, revealing more gold coins than Zander had ever seen in his life. Excited murmurs rippled through the small crowd.

"I've instructed George to prepare something special for supper with some of those fancy ingredients you all found," Ace continued. "Tonight, we celebrate. Yarrow and Theo will portion you each your share of the gold. As for the wine we took—portion it out yourselves, eh?"

She smiled again as the crowd erupted in a cheer. Zander was the only one who saw the exhaustion return to her face as she turned and retreated to her private quarters.

Zander wished he could follow her. He wanted to wrap his arms around her and never let her go. He wanted to be her solid ground, the way she was for him. He also needed her. The anxiety he felt earlier hadn't entirely abated, and a small part of him still wondered if he was going to hell. But he knew it would have to wait. Perhaps he could find her later, when the crew was drunk and the night heavy enough to veil their affections.

He made to walk to the lower deck, meaning to see if George needed help in the galley.

"Zander."

His head shot up at Ace's voice. She was standing just outside the door to her quarters, looking at him. Her eyes were filled with raw exhaustion and need.

He didn't need her to say it. She simply stood there, waiting for him. Without hesitating, he went to her. He walked past the crew, some of whom stared at him as he went. Others were wholly engrossed in estimating their share of the gold.

When he and Ace disappeared behind her door, a portion of the crew erupted in a swell of cheers and teasing. Ace simply shook her head resignedly, sighing. Zander ignored it, his entire focus on Ace.

"Are you okay?" he asked, his hand gently brushing her cheek. She closed her eyes and leaned into his touch, her hand covering his. She turned her face so she could kiss his palm, then looked into his eyes.

"I'm exhausted," she said. "And I needed you." Her eyes filled with tears. In truth, she had needed him for a long time, far before she ever knew he existed, and he in turn needed her.

Zander pulled her into his chest and held her tightly.

"I'm here," he said. He kissed the top of her head and rubbed her back, his own tears falling silently as she shook against him. "I'm right here, my love."

Ace cried quietly for a while, her arms wrapped around Zander's waist. He felt pieces of himself knitting back together as he held her, like she was a salve for his mental wounds. Then she pulled away, wiping her face. She smiled up at him, the tension from her shoulders and forehead eased.

"Let me get you out of that shirt," Zander said, gesturing toward the blood that still lingered on her clothes.

Ace nodded, allowing Zander to undo the clasps of her vest, then the buttons on her shirt. She watched him thoughtfully as he did so.

"What did you call me?" she said suddenly.

Zander looked up. "Hmm?"

"Just now, when you were holding me. What did you call me?"

Zander's mouth hung open mutely as he remembered what he said, realizing he'd let his feelings slip potentially far too soon.

Well, no going back now, he thought. He undid the final buttons on Ace's shirt and gently slid it from her shoulders, his eyes fixed on hers.

"I called you my love," he said.

To his great relief, Ace smiled, reached her arms around his neck, and kissed him tenderly.

"We should rest," she said. "The crew will be drunk within the hour, and one of us will need to keep watch later. I've asked George to save us some food. Will you stay with me?"

"Of course."

He followed her to the bed, where she collapsed still wearing her pants and boots. Zander removed her boots for her, then his own, and climbed in beside her. She was breathing deeply within minutes, sleeping as Zander held her against his chest. He tucked away the questions he had for her—about that morning, and the merchant captain who had clearly recognized her. They could wait.

But that didn't mean he didn't think about it. His thoughts ruminated over Thomas's slowly falling body, and Ace beyond him, her face filled with disappointment. She killed him. He knew she only did what she had to. Still, his hands shook slightly as he held her.

What would he kill for? He'd never had cause to think about it. Of course, he knew on some level that being a pirate often involved killing. It was a dangerous life, and it belied risks that The Valerian's low-key, morally grey approach to piracy tended to obscure.

Zander was not a pacifist by any means. Growing up poor, one of eight children in a crowded house on an even more crowded street, Zander often had to fight growing up. But he only fought for things that were worthy of the effort. Survival, for instance. Or to protect his family.

What would he kill for now?

Survival? Yes. He'd certainly kill to save himself from death.

Ace? Fuck yes. The surety with which he knew he would kill for her actually scared him a little in its intensity.

Theo? Yarrow? Yes, and yes. They'd acted like family toward him. They *were* family, a fact he'd known deep in his bones since the moment he met them.

And the crew? They were family, too. Perhaps not in the deep, spiritual way he felt Theo and Yarrow were his family, but he'd felt more valued and protected by them in the past few months than he had by his biological family since he was small. In his gut, he knew they would kill for him. And he would do the same.

Realizing this, Zander's heart slowed, his anxiety melting slightly under his conviction. Hell be damned. No God worth his salt would make creatures with such a great capacity for love without expecting some violence. If he was damned for protecting those he loved, so be it.

Zander realized he was holding Ace too tightly—he relaxed his arms around her and began to focus more on his surroundings.

He was in Ace's *bedroom*. The only other time he'd been there was to go over travel plans, and then he'd taken pains not to gawk at her belongings. Now, he took the opportunity to study the room and its many small treasures. A well-worn tapestry with geometric patterns hung on the wall in front of him. Beneath it hung a small charcoal drawing of a naked woman's silhouette—he recognized it as one of Jubal's sketches.

Something near the floor caught his eye. It was letters carved into the wood. The writing was large and unruly—a child's handwriting.

MOM. DAD. ARACELY.

Zander smiled at the tiny time capsule. He had wondered if this sloop was the same one she and her parents sailed when she was a child. He liked knowing this is where she spent her childhood. He found a strange comfort knowing where she'd been, as if her whereabouts had been a question that burned inside of him his whole life.

Then he thought of her kneeling, cleaning up the pool of blood on the deck.

This place was her home. And now, having made the choice of a lifetime—having jumped from land into the cold bite of the ocean in pursuit of love and adventure—it was his home, too.

In that moment, Zander resolved himself to his choice. Perhaps he was playing at being a pirate, he thought. Perhaps this wasn't his adventure at all. But that no longer bothered him, because it was hers.

If his choice was to live alone, each day tedious and predictable, or to sit on the sidelines and watch the woman he loved be the main character in her own adventure, he would choose the latter. Even if death beckoned at every turn.

Unbeknownst to Zander, our hero would soon have an adventure of his very own.

8

The journey to Azores lasted ten days. The stop was brief, much of it focused on avoiding the Portuguese naval ships that filled the waters around the small island chain. The crew found what supplies they could and continued on toward Portugal, a journey that would last six days. After resting in Portugal, they would head South toward Morocco, where Ace promised to find Zander the most delicious tagine he'd ever tasted. Zander had no idea what tagine was, but he was excited to find out.

As they neared Portugal and the promise of several days of rest and recreation, the mood of the crew became considerably lighter. Everyone was eager to spend time on land, and to spend the considerable sum of gold they'd recently acquired. Zander heard all sorts of plans from the men about what they would do. Some envisioned fine tailored clothes and good food. Others daydreamed about brothels and endless cups of wine.

Zander dreamed of nothing but Ace.

As he gazed at her now, her feet up and her eyes focused on the book in her hands, he imagined how luxurious it would feel to have her to himself, no matter how briefly. He'd been staying in her cabin every night for two weeks, long enough for the crew's jokes to die down.

And while he marveled at the fortune of getting to share her bed each night, interruptions were plentiful. He looked forward to staying in bed for as long as they wanted without any pirates barging in.

They would dock in Portugal for four nights—long enough, Ace said, for the crew to unwind "without getting too comfortable." Comfort was a risk she'd seemed particularly concerned about since the raid on the Spanish vessel and the captain who recognized her face.

When he'd asked her the morning after the raid about the captain, she hadn't told him much.

"That man," he'd said to her. "He knew you. And you knew that boat as well."

Ace had taken a deep breath then, like she was bracing herself. For just a moment, something had brimmed behind her eyes, like a wave about to crest over the top of a cliff. But then it was gone, the sudden furrow of her brow pushing it back down from whence it came. When she took his hand and spoke, her voice warbled with the weight of regret.

"There are things in my past I've worked very hard to leave behind," she'd said. "Things I'd rather forget happened. That man knew me during a part of my life I never want to think about again." She'd brought his hand to her heart then, reminding him of the night in the cave. "Someday, I'll tell you all about it. But not today. Today, we sail."

It felt like a promise, and that had been good enough for him. At least, he'd said as much to her.

But the questions he had nagged at him. What didn't he know about this woman he loved so blindly? She already knew more about him than he did about her. She asked questions every night as they lay in her bed. Questions about his childhood, his family, his work. He wasn't sure how much more he could tell her about growing up as one of eight kids, working since he was ten to earn money, his father drinking it away, and his mother sleeping all of the time. Looking back at his past, it all seemed grey in comparison to his life now, like he was finally living in color. Nothing else had ever been real.

When Zander asked Ace questions about her life, she kept her answers brief, always insisting she'd rather hear more about him. If he could find a topic that excited her—books, for instance, or her adventures as a pirate—she'd talk for ages, and he would soak up every bit of it. He lived vicariously through her stories, visiting jungles and forests, palaces and temples, busy markets and abandoned beaches. They were all places she promised to take him.

They talked at length about ideas—what may lay out there in the wide world they hadn't discovered yet, for instance. They talked about religion, government, art. Ace had a subversive approach to so many aspects of life, Zander found himself questioning everything he thought he knew. The world grew larger, more mysterious, and with it he grew as well.

She also read to him. He'd never been good at reading, having only learned to read when he neared adulthood. Right now, she was reading from a book about a man stranded on a deserted island. She sat in her chair, her feet propped on her desk as she read. Zander sat on the bed, leaning against the wall, his eyes closed as he listened.

She reached the end of a passage and stuffed a dried leaf between the pages to mark her place before closing it. She looked at him expectantly, smiling.

"You were right about the story," he said. "I like it."

Ace's smile widened in satisfaction, and she set the book down.

"It's my favorite," she said. "My father gave it to me as a gift shortly before he died."

"Tell me about your parents," Zander said. Ace had a way of avoiding talk about her parents, but Zander felt a sudden urge to ask her about them again.

"They were wonderful," she said. The tension that normally lined her eyes when she mentioned her parents was absent. "My mother was very keen, and almost always working. My father was always making friends with strangers. They were both gentle and good natured. And fun. We had a lot of fun." Ace's smile was wistful. "They would have liked you."

Zander just smiled, hoping she'd continue. After leaving her chair to come sit beside him on the bed, she did.

"They had high hopes for me, my parents. I think they regretted raising me on the ocean. They thought it made me hard when the world expected me to be soft. When we moved to Spain, they tried to correct their mistake by settling down and entering high society. They took on the role of the people we used to sell to. It was almost like a game for them, playing at being respectable, landowning merchants. I got a more formal education, which I loved. But in the end, I just couldn't meet their expectations."

Zander put his hand over hers.

"What happened to them?"

"It was a fire," she said quietly. "They both died in a fire, and within weeks of their deaths I'd run off and become a pirate."

Zander leaned in so he could kiss Ace's temple, then her cheek.

"Quite lucky for me you did," he said softly, squeezing her hand.

A short rap at the door pulled their attention away from each other, and Theo opened the door. "We're approaching land, Captain," he said.

Ace jumped to her feet and retrieved her weapons. Zander followed suit, trailing Ace and Theo to the deck.

Porto, Portugal was nothing but a spot of land in the distance, but the crew were rushing about excitedly as they made their approach. Zander busied himself helping as Ace took her place at the helm, his own excitement growing. As the coast came into view, Zander saw pristine white beaches and sun-bleached buildings with rooftops the color of autumn leaves. The city was a sprawling thing. Zander could feel the buzz of it from here, alive with the promise of something new.

The sloop glided through the water purposefully toward a dock at the city's edge that appeared to be private. Beyond it was a grand house surrounded by trees. As they approached the dock, a man flanked by servants—or bodyguards—exited the home and walked toward them down a long dirt path. He had dark hair, a thick mustache, and he wore a rich orange coat and shorts.

As he walked onto the dock to receive them, Zander could more clearly see the exuberant smile on his face.

"And how are you treating my sloop?" he hollered up at Ace, his voice deep and rich.

"You mean *my* sloop," Ace corrected him, hauling herself over the railing to land squarely in front of him on the dock.

"Yes, yes, you're right," he said with laughter in his voice. "Yours, fair and square. The deal of a century!" He laughed heartily at some joke Zander wasn't privy to, and the two of them grasped each other's hands warmly. "Ah, it's good to see you Aracely," he said, softer now. "You look well."

"As do you, Abilio," Ace said. "Okay if I dock here for a few days?"

"As long as you want," Abilio said. "My beach is yours. It's the least I can do for you. Just as long as your crew keeps their trouble further from shore." He eyed the crew behind her, busily preparing to leave the sloop behind.

"Of course," Ace responded. "They know the rules. You won't see nor smell pirate for the next four days."

Abilio nodded, his eyes surveying the boat appreciatively.

"Well, when you're settled here, come inside for some lunch," he said. "I'll have places set for the three of you." He gestured toward Theo and Yarrow, who waved in his direction.

"Make it four," Ace said.

Half an hour later, the crew had all set off into Porto and The Valerian was being looked after by Abilio's staff. Zander followed Ace, Theo, and Yarrow up the cobblestone walkway toward Abilio's home, where a servant was waiting to open the door for them. Inside, a long ma-hogany table held five settings and a veritable feast. The scent of piri piri peppers, garlic, and warm bread made Zander's mouth water.

Ace, Theo, and Yarrow didn't hesitate to make themselves comfortable at the table. Theo even propped his feet up on the empty chair next to him, stretching luxuriously. Yarrow leveled an incredulous look at him that made him laugh, and the sound summoned Abilio from an adjacent room.

Zander waited to sit until Abilio approached, taking the opportunity to shake his hand before joining his friends at the table.

"And who is this?" Abilio said as he grasped Zander's hand. "A new member of the inner circle?"

"I'm Zander," he responded. "It's very nice to meet you. Thank you for the warm welcome."

"Wonderful to meet you, Zander," Abilio said, gesturing for him to sit as he took his own seat at the head of the table. "Any friend of Aracely's is welcome in my home."

"How is it you know each other?" Zander asked, sitting next to Ace, who already had her plate full of food and was eagerly tucking in.

"I've known Aracely since she was this tall," Abilio said, holding his hand about three feet off the ground. "Her parents were friends of mine, and business associates."

"What is it you do?" Zander asked, curious to know what afforded such splendor, and how Ace's parents were involved.

Abilio shrugged, but he smiled at the other three pirates as if he had a secret. "Oh, some of this, some of that," he said. "But it was tobacco that brought Chandace and Nicolas into my life." He looked from Zander to Ace now, smiling fondly. "Your parents always brought me the best tobacco, and the best stories!" He laughed. "They had more fun together than any couple I've ever known. It was a shame when they retired."

"Aye," Ace agreed. "It was. But they continued having fun, I assure you. It was just…" Ace waved her hands in the air, looking for the word. "…more socially acceptable fun."

Abilio laughed at that and lifted his glass in salute.

"I never thought I'd see you again after your parents sold me that sloop," Abilio said.

He turned to Zander again.

"She showed up at my front door one day with nothing but the clothes on her back and the most beautiful piece of treasure I'd ever seen." He spread his hands apart slightly, as if imagining the treasure in his hands. "A dagger, its hilt *covered* in the most perfect emeralds you've ever seen, and a matching sheath. It was a weapon of such beauty and craftsmanship, I knew right away it was more valuable than anything I owned. And do you know what she wanted in exchange?"

Zander shook his head. "What was it?" he asked.

Abilio pointed his finger toward the back of the house and the bay beyond it.

"Nothing but that old boat," he answered, slapping his knee with the other hand as if it was the funniest thing in the world.

Ace rolled her eyes, but the hint of a smile remained on her face as she interrupted his story. "That boat, and your secrecy," she reminded him.

"Yes, yes," Abilio said. "Of course, my darling! I assume your secrets are safe in present company?" He eyed Zander warily now, apparently wondering if he'd made a mistake.

Ace squeezed Zander's hand over the table.

"They are," she said.

Abilio smiled fondly at the gesture before he continued.

"I had to practically force her to take supplies with her, and a bit of gold. 'There must be something else you want!' I told her. 'I can't let you leave with nothing but a hunk of wood and some rations after what you've brought me!' She thought for a moment and finally said, 'It would seem I'm without a blade now, Abilio. How about that one?' And she pointed to that ivory cutlass you see on her hip, once displayed over my desk. 'A blade for a blade,' she said. As if we were even."

Ace smiled at him and drained her cup. "We *are* even, Abilio," she said as she set it back down.

Abilio shook his head in response. "We'll never be even, little Aracely. We're family."

The four of them left Abilio's home at dusk after a pleasant few hours of food, wine, and conversation. Ace fended off his insistence that he send them into town in one of his carriages, claiming they needed to walk after such a large meal. Zander was grateful for the suggestion as they strolled through cobblestone streets, the lanterns lining them being lit as they went, the smell of grilled sardines filling the air. Theo and Yarrow made quick goodbyes, entering a tavern that seemed to be a favorite and leaving Ace and Zander to themselves.

"Would you like to walk a bit more?" Ace asked him. "Or should we find ourselves a room?"

Zander noticed the way her eyes narrowed slightly when she spoke, how her mouth curved to the side. He pulled her against him so he could nip at her ear before whispering, "Let's find ourselves a bed."

Ace smiled and took his hand, leading him deeper into the city. He lost track of the winding paths as they went, focused only on the way the white feather she'd tied in her hair that morning fluttered behind her as she walked, the way her hips swayed as she dodged moving carts and running children.

They finally arrived at a small inn Ace seemed to know. It was in a busy square, filled with the sounds of laughter, conversation, and the sizzling of food as it cooked. Pop-up eateries dotted the space, and people gathered around them on mismatched stools, eating. It was the most noise Zander had heard in months, and it filled every corner of his head.

Good, he thought. He planned on being very loud tonight.

The bottom floor of the inn was like a microcosm of the noise from outside. Tables filled the empty space, each one crowded with people who ate, and drank, and laughed boisterously. Tendrils of smoke hung lazily in the air. Ace located a woman who appeared to be in charge and arranged for a room, after which they were directed up a small set of stairs to the second floor.

The room was small. The bed, a small table with a single lit candle, and a wash basin took up most of the space. The window was open, a warm breeze wafting in and carrying the sounds of the evening inside. Zander removed his boots and closed it, drawing the curtains tightly.

When he turned back to Ace, the light from the flickering flame was playing against her skin, casting her beauty in an unearthly glow that took his breath away. He wished he could capture this moment. He wanted to engrave it in his mind—everything from the lines of her muscular arms to the thick curve of her brow.

She reached her hand out, inviting him, and for a moment he imagined her edges shifting in the dim light, as if she were an illusion. He let out a breath and closed the space between them, relieved to find she was solid as he placed his calloused hand in hers.

Leaning forward, pulling her close to him, he kissed her tenderly. She breathed in deeply as their kiss deepened, growing in passion. Zander cupped his hands around her face, desperate to keep her right there, right where he could see her. One hand moved to her neck, then her waist. Her own hands roamed hungrily along his back, her fingernails gently pushing into his skin. He lifted her, and she wrapped her legs around him.

He lowered her to the bed, his body covering hers, and she tangled her hands in his hair, pulling hard. He moaned. Pulling his hair was something she did when she wanted more, when she didn't have the patience to wait.

He wouldn't make her wait.

He sat up, his shirt coming off as he did. He tugged at her trousers, pulling them roughly off and tossing them aside. She lay there, spread apart for him, unbuttoning her vest and shirt slowly, and he nearly whimpered at the sight.

Her eyes devoured him as he tugged off his belt, and she sat up to take him in her hands as he pulled down his trousers. He groaned and leaned forward to kiss her, his pants still wrapped around his calves as she sank back onto the bed. His erection rubbed against her warmth, throbbing with need. Trembling, he pulled himself away from her kiss and lowered his body, anchoring his head between her legs as he kicked his trousers off.

The feel of her nails in his scalp urged him on. Her thighs opened and closed against his ears, occasionally muffling her beautiful cries, the centerpiece of the symphony of noise that surrounded them. Zander's entire body flushed with heat when she climaxed, and then she was pulling him toward her, her hand directing him inside, insistent.

He obeyed, burying himself inside her and thrusting desperately, his moans rising in volume until they matched her own. The shaking of the bed against the wall became a rhythmic pulse against the clamor outside, and as he groaned into her mouth, his hands gripping the headboard, he wished he could stay there for the rest of his mortal life.

Later, as they lay happy and tired in each other's arms, Zander imagined what it would have been like if he met Ace under different circumstances. What would have happened if he were wandering the streets of London, lost in his thoughts as he so often was, and he saw her standing there? He imagined her full lips stretched into a wide smile, set against the backdrop of a cold London morning.

"Have I ever told you about St. Paul's cathedral?" he asked her.

"No," Ace said, her voice sleepy. "Something from home?"

"Yes. It's the tallest building in London. I used to beg my mother to walk us there when I was a kid."

"And did she?"

"Only once. But my sister Martha would walk me there sometimes. Looking at that building, it felt like I was in a different world entirely. Like anything was possible."

Zander paused, thinking of his sister as he wrapped one of Ace's curls around his finger. Martha was his dearest friend as a child. She taught him everything—or everything that seemed important as a child, anyway—like how to play huzzlecap, and where one is most likely to find bread that's been thrown out. She married young, and he hardly ever saw her after that. He wondered if she'd dreamt of leaving their life behind when she looked at St. Paul's, too.

"I was standing in front of that cathedral when I decided to leave London. I stood there for an hour perhaps, just staring. I couldn't tear my eyes away from it. The idea of turning around and going back to my life—to the life I was given by my father—it felt like it would kill me. I decided I'd get on any boat, go anywhere, just to be somewhere different than where I was."

Ace looked up at him, understanding on her face. He smiled at her, envisioning her standing in front of St. Paul's cathedral, her trousers and vest replaced by a dress, a silk fan in place of her ivory blade. He wrinkled his nose at the image. It felt wrong somehow, imagining her hair pinned tightly to her head instead of tangled around her shoulders, her gorgeous legs hidden under layers of restrictive cloth.

"What is it?" Ace asked, frowning at his expression.

"I was imagining you in a bodice and skirt," he said.

Ace's face twisted in shock, and Zander burst out laughing at the intensity of her reaction.

"Why in the world would you imagine such a thing?" she asked. She ran her fingernails quickly up and down her arms. "Just thinking of it makes me itchy."

Zander kissed her forehead, smothering another laugh against her cool skin.

"Don't worry, I prefer you in pants. Or rather, out of them," Zander said, stroking her bottom appreciatively. "I was just wondering what it would be like if I met you in London, when I was younger. But the image didn't fit. It was like imagining the ocean resting comfortably in a glass jar."

Zander sighed, running the edge of his thumb against Ace's cheek. "I still feel like that little boy sometimes, Ace. Gazing up at something beautiful, imagining I could be a part of it. Playing pirate and hoping no one recognizes me as the tanner's boy."

Ace sat up. She looked at Zander with a thoughtful expression, then reached out her hand and placed it over his heart.

"I know you, Zander," she said. "I know who you are. The day we met, when you told me that meeting me was possibly the last surprising thing that would ever happen to you—that it would all be downhill from there... I knew you then. I've been there, facing an endless loop of monotony and predictability. I've felt the same desperation to run, to find something, anything, that felt like *me*.

"It wasn't until I was out there on the water, totally free from the expectations of society, that I found myself. You're a pirate, Zander. You may not feel like it yet, but you are. It's written like a treasure map on your skin, in your eyes, in the way that you taste. You're not a nameless little boy, dreaming of adventure. You're free. You're a pirate. You're *my* pirate."

She leaned down and kissed him fiercely then, and Zander almost believed her.

***

Four days later, they sailed away from Porto, Abilio's home shrinking in the distance behind them.

The energy of the crew was markedly different from when they made port. A mix of restlessness and deep satisfaction filled the air as they entered open water once more, heading for new shores and new opportunities. Several of the men wore new clothes, and more than a few looked transformed by ample rest and recreation. The only pirate missing was Declan, who never showed up the morning they left, and whom no one had seen since they docked. A quick search showed he'd taken everything he owned with him. No one seemed surprised. He hadn't been the same since Ace killed Thomas.

As the shore shrunk into the distance behind them, Jubal started to sing. Soon, the crew joined in, and they set out to sea with a shanty on their lips.

Ace stood at the mast, her telescope to her eye and a smile on her face as she gazed out at the water. When she lowered it, she caught Zander's eye and winked.

His stomach flipped as he thought of the last few days, so much of it spent in their noisy room at the inn. A part of him wanted to go back. But he had begun to miss the smell of the ocean air, the sting of the water, the immense task of each new day. He felt relieved to be back on board.

The weight of the raid-gone-sour had finally lifted from Zander's mind. Ace seemed lighter than she had in weeks. Theo and Yarrow were full of smiles, and Zander found he'd missed them more than anything else over the past four days.

For the first time in a long time, Zander was confident that everything was going to be alright.

Once, he roamed the depths of the ocean, hungry and searching for prey. The last of his kind.

The bowels of the sea were his home, the inky black water enveloping him, frigid and unforgiving—as was he.

He knew nothing but hunger.

When the abyss of his home didn't provide the sustenance he required, he followed the promise of food upward. His jaws snapping, tentacles thrashing, he would fly across the expanse of the sea, listening for the telltale sound of a ship upon the water.

And when he found it, he devoured it.

One night, the familiar *cut, cut, cut* of wood on water filled his senses. He propelled himself upward, toward the offensive sound, the promise of a feast waiting—wood, flesh, bone, and metal.

Another sound mingled with the ship's resonance, something that lilted and warbled in a strange rhythm.

Song, something told him.

Food, his body responded.

He pushed harder, the sound filling his mind, his hunger propelling him furiously forward.

The sounds grew louder. *Cut, cut, cut. Warble, lilt, warble.*

Wood, flesh, bone, metal.

He emerged in the too-warm air without stopping, spraying the invading vessel with a barrage of water that smothered the strange melody. He gave no other warning before wrapping himself around his quarry and squeezing. The ship groaned in protest, the last desperate cries of a dying animal. He felt the strangled echoes of its demise in his body. His appetite swelled in response.

He was about to open his jaws, to savor the first taste of a successful hunt, when a piercing cry rang through the air and a blinding pain echoed through his brain.

He caught sight of the small creature just before it attacked again. The tiny stick in its claws was tipped with metal—metal he could crunch between his jaws if only he could reach it. But the creature positioned itself at the edge of the dying ship and leapt forward, weapon in hand.

In the brief moment in which she remained suspended above him, he saw reflected in her small round eyes the same feeling that had driven him throughout the many long years of his life: hunger.

In the next moment, he was blind.

Freeing one of his tentacles from the ship, he whipped it toward his face, wrapping around the tiny creature whose hunger somehow matched his own. He felt the weapon drive deeper before he pulled her away, howling, and the blindness began to numb his other senses.

In a last anguished attempt to defeat his foe, he squeezed, not relenting until he heard the deafening *crack* of the ship, felt the last shudder of its life reverberate upon the surface of the sea before it succumbed.

He was dying, sinking alongside the feast of wood, flesh, bone, and metal. The tiny, fierce creature was still clasped in his tentacle like a prize he would take with him to the afterlife.

With the last of his strength, he brought the prize to his waiting jaws and savored his final meal.

Zander slipped out of bed as quietly as he could, stretching his bare body languidly. Ace still lay in bed, a serene look on her face in the dim light. He wanted to go back to her. But he'd woken suddenly before dawn, and he was restless as soon as his eyes opened. He'd lain there for several minutes before accepting he couldn't go back to sleep.

His clothes were folded neatly by the door. Ace's were thrown haphazardly in a pile nearby. He smirked as he retrieved his garments and pulled them on.

The new outfit he'd bought in Porto still smelled like the inn. He'd been wearing the same two outfits (one borrowed from the previous sailmaker) since he boarded The Valerian. With a pocket full of money and time to kill on land, he'd thought it was time he had something that felt like his own. He looked down at the white shirt, sturdy dark brown trousers, and black leather boots he wore. The boots weren't quite broken in yet, but they were finely crafted and fit him well, the leather hugging his calves comfortably. With Bagu's help, he'd managed to create two small leather sheaths in the inner lining, on the outside of either calf, to store his daggers.

He reached down to retrieve his new coat—an expensive black woolen frock with dark buttons, a silk-lined collar, and long panels that reached to his mid-thighs. He'd seen it in Porto and was immediately drawn to it. If he'd drawn a picture of the pirate he imagined himself to be in his wildest dreams, he would have been wearing a coat like that. But it felt too extravagant, too well-crafted for him.

Ace convinced him to try it on at least. The inner lining contained two hidden pockets of considerable size, and it fit him surprisingly well without alteration. He was just about to take it off and return it to the shop owner when he noticed Ace openly admiring how he looked in it, her eyes narrowed above a promising grin. Without another word, she retrieved a few coins from her pocket and paid for the coat, then pulled him back to the inn so she could peel it off him herself.

Zander buttoned the coat and opened and closed the door quietly, sneaking out to the main deck to catch the first glimpse of the sunrise. It was quiet on deck, save for soft snoring from Jubal, who was supposed to be on watch. The Valerian was still, its sails furled.

Zander walked to the forecastle and looked east, where the first rays of the sun peeked over the horizon. He watched for several minutes before turning his gaze south.

He straightened. There were sails in the distance. He walked quickly to Jubal, waking him as he took the telescope from his pocket, and returned to the forecastle. Jubal sleepily mumbled something Zander didn't hear as he put the telescope to his eye.

It was a ship. A large one, outfitted with serious artillery. It flew a Spanish flag, and beneath it, a flag containing a crest with a prominent eagle in its center. A feeling of foreboding overcame him when he realized it was headed directly toward them as they sat dead in the water.

Zander jogged past a drowsy Jubal to Ace's quarters. The sound of the door opening woke her, and she sat up.

"There's a ship on the horizon," he said, trying to keep his voice calm. "To the south. It's a Spanish vessel, and it's aimed at The Valerian."

Ace went rigid, one hand clutching the blanket at her chest.

"Is there an octopus on the bow?" she asked.

Zander shook his head. "No, but there is a flag with a crest. I can't make out much beyond a large eagle."

Ace's eyes flashed with fear, and the foreboding Zander felt deepened. He fought the urge to go to her, to hold her and kiss her and promise everything was going to be alright. He stood and waited for her orders instead.

"Go get Theo and Yarrow," she said. "Tell them to rouse the crew. Then come straight back to me."

Zander nodded quickly and did as he was told. He rapped quickly on Theo and Yarrow's door before opening it. The couple were laying in bed, Theo's arms wrapped tightly around Yarrow, who had their back to him.

"Rouse the crew," he said. "There's trouble."

When he returned to Ace, she was already dressed and pulling on her boots. She stood as he closed the door, retrieving her compass from atop a pile of papers at her desk. She turned and pressed it into Zander's hand.

"I'm sorry," she said, her voice breaking.

Zander furrowed his brow, bringing his hand to her shoulder as if to brace her. "No," he said softly. "You don't need to be sorry."

Ace blinked back tears, shaking her head in disagreement.

"I'm sorry," she said again, her voice firmer this time. "There's no time to explain. But I need you to keep this. You can give it back when this is all over. Okay?"

Zander nodded and placed the compass in his pocket. He tried to ignore the sudden rattling in his chest, the heaviness in his hands.

Ace took a long, deep breath, closing her eyes as if to steady herself. Then she took another step toward Zander and wrapped her arms around him. He returned the hug, and they stood there for a few seconds in silence, a heavy feeling surrounding them.

When Ace backed away, the vulnerability was gone from her face, replaced with the hard resolve of a pirate captain. She stepped out onto deck, Zander following behind her, and the world became a blur of sound and color in the morning sun.

The ship was closer now, its sails puffed out with a favorable wind that brought it swiftly toward them. The dark wood glowed in the morning sun, giving it an ethereal quality that sent a shudder down Zander's spine. It grew bigger by the second, its enormous size and speed a strange contrast to the calm sea, as if the water carried it forward without a choice, as if destiny itself propelled it toward them.

Ace was shouting orders to the crew, telling them to get out of range, to outrun it. Zander heard her as if through a fog, his eyes locked on that ship. Something inside him squirmed in revulsion, in recognition, like a dog locking on to a dangerous scent.

"MOVE!"

Theo's voice boomed behind him, and the world came into focus again. His feet moved of their own volition, his hands knowing what to do without being told as he joined the other sailors at the rigging.

"Zander, help me out, mate."

Zander turned to see Theo wriggling his arms into a leather contraption that stretched across his torso in the shape of an X. He shifted so Zander could tighten the buckles on his back, securing the strange vest to his body. Upon closer inspection, he realized the leather was adorned with holsters—six in the front and two in the back just above Theo's shoulder blades, allowing him to carry ten guns in total with the two holsters already heavy at his hips.

Before he could ask about the origins of the strange, ominous gun vest, Theo clapped him on the shoulder and jogged away, leaving Zander to return to the rigging.

More than half the crew disappeared below deck, some to row, others to prepare the cannons for The Valerian's defense. Zander looked to the helm as he worked, where Ace was hunched over with a look of intense concentration on her lovely face. Theo and Yarrow stood to each side of her, talking—no, arguing with her, as Theo sorted through a veritable pile of pistols, loading and holstering them one by one.

Ace straightened and said something to each of them, her body language signaling that she was done with the conversation. Whatever she said seemed to pain Yarrow. Ace, her eyes softening, reached out to take one of their hands. They each leaned forward, their foreheads touching intimately. Ace reached out her other hand and pulled Theo toward them, and the three stood with their heads touching for several moments before they parted, Theo joining the sailors and Yarrow heading below deck like nothing had happened.

Zander looked periodically at Ace as he worked, hoping to find some explanation in her eyes, but she wouldn't look his way.

With its sails unfurled, The Valerian began to move. Slowly.

Too slow, Zander thought, willing fate to favor them as it had their pursuer. But with every bit of speed they gained, the ship moved closer, closer. Anxiety riled in his belly. The Valerian could outrun any large ship in the right circumstances, he knew. But it was the circumstances that bothered him.

They weren't prepared. They were caught off guard. They were too far from land, and the mysterious ship was already moving at full speed, angling itself to come alongside. They'd taken too long to steer into the wind and were barely approaching full speed. They would soon be in range of its cannons.

"GUNNERS AT THE READY!" Ace yelled, and Zander stepped forward, needing to be closer to her, just as the first explosion rang through the air.

Zander stumbled, the world beneath him rocking violently. His ears rang. Had they been hit? He looked around—the crew that remained above deck were hunching over, some with their hands cradled protectively over their heads. He realized he was crouching, too. Straightening, his eyes lay on the smoking cavity in the railing where he'd just been standing.

Another shot echoed across the water, this one missing the sloop. Zander moved on unsteady feet toward Ace, who was yelling for more men to help the rowers. They needed to move faster.

Ace gave Zander a look as he approached, gesturing to the helm, and he took over. Without a word she ran below deck, emerging minutes later with Yarrow at her heels.

Wave after wave of anxiety and fear rolled over Zander as he struggled to focus on the task before him. His hands gripped the helm so tightly his fingers ached under the pressure as he kept the sloop pointed Northeast, allowing the favorable wind to carry them away while pivoting toward the land that lay somewhere beyond the horizon. When Ace's hands covered his own, he nearly jumped in surprise.

"We're going to turn 'round," she said, her voice nearly swallowed by the sounds of yelling pirates. "They'll drop anchor soon and try to board us. If we turn 'round we'll be sailing against the wind, but we'll be on the wrong side, and they'll not have time to turn nor reverse sail in time to catch us."

She looked away from him, toward the ship that now loomed close enough that the men aboard were easily visible, as another cannon shot rang out. She looked just as unsure as Zander felt—they would be exposing the side of the vessel to the ship's cannons, like a dragon rolling over and showing its belly. But Ace was right, they'd be on the opposite side, and their sloop could turn 'round faster than any large ship could. They'd be counting on the hope that the ship's sailors had only loaded the starboard cannons, allowing them a small chance of passing by the port side unscathed before they could load those, too.

Calling it risky would be an understatement. But the men couldn't row forever, and the ship was gaining on them too quickly. This was their only chance.

Zander nodded at Ace, ready to escape or sink to the bottom of the sea. Her hands replaced his at the helm, and he rushed to help the sailors at the rigging, where Theo stood poised to direct their movements. Yarrow stood halfway down the stairs, listening for Ace's orders so they could direct the rowers.

The crew collectively held their breath, waiting.

On Ace's signal, the crew acted as one to turn the sloop around. The many hands of the rowers, those of the sailors adjusting the rigging, and Ace's strong hands at the helm worked together with astonishing speed. Zander's heart leapt at the swiftness of the small vessel as it spun.

This is going to work, he thought as they straightened, slicing through the water parallel to the ship. There was no way a ship of that size could turn around fast enough to make up the distance again. They'd likely sail through the day and night, the whole crew foregoing sleep to create more distance between them and their pursuer. All they had to do was get out of range of the cannons.

Ace screamed orders to open fire on the ship, but too late.

A deafening *BOOM* rang across the water from the ship's port side cannons. Then another. Then another. Zander lost his grip on the rigging, the impact of the cannon fire reverberating through his body as it tore a hole in the side of The Valerian. Zander hit the deck as a second shot hit the edge of the mast and ricocheted, leaving a sizable dent. His eyes followed the trajectory of the iron sphere to see its destination, directly in the center of Daniel's chest. He lay lifeless at the foot of a swivel gun.

Zander dragged himself to his feet, stepping over Daniel to take over the gun as Amir threw himself over Daniel's body, screaming. Another cannon ball hit the side of the sloop as he planted his feet and took aim, rocking the small vessel. They were almost past the ship now, but slowing down, either from the shock of the cannons or the holes they tore in the hull, he didn't know. The ship loomed across the water, intimidating in its size and splendor, and far too close. He could hear the men below deck, struggling to load the cannons fast enough, to continue rowing, but the ship had more guns, more men, more everything, and god damnit, they were far better prepared for this attack than they'd anticipated.

His heart sank as he noticed longboats emerging from behind the behemoth vessel, six in total. He leveled shots in the rowers' direction, watching as one, two, three men tumbled into the water. But dozens remained alive, ready to approach The Valerian from every side.

Zander looked over his shoulder and was surprised to see Ace running toward him, abandoning the mast. She took his hand and led him away from the swivel gun, pulling him down into a crouch. Theo quickly replaced him at the gun, and shots rang out across the water from either side, filling the air with deafening noise.

Ace's hand was slick with sweat, her face a mask of desperation.

"Zander," she said, her breathing heavy. "I need you to help me. We need to disable the sails."

"What? Why?" Dread rose from Zander's stomach to his chest, threatening to rise in his throat like bile and choke him. Would they no longer try to outrun the ship?

"Look around, Zander," Ace said, her hands gripping his tightly.

He did.

More bodies lay on the deck—sailors ripped to shreds alongside pieces of the hull, the mast, the rigging. Men were pouring from below deck, swords and cutlasses at the ready, abandoning the oars. Yarrow and Theo stood beside each other at the two swivel guns, their shoulders shaking with effort as they attempted to halt the progress of the long-boats.

The ship across the water loomed like a sea monster, nearly unscathed. The instinct Zander had about the vessel riled in him again, now more desperate than disgusted as the longboats neared.

He looked at Ace again. Her eyes were filled with a sadness that took his breath away.

This is how it ends, he thought. *This is how it all ends.*

Of course, it never *all* ends. But Zander didn't know this.

He squeezed Ace's hands, memorizing the curve of her jaw, the glow of her golden eyes. He was grateful he would die with her instead of alone, in a shack, on an island that was never his home.

"We can't let him have The Valerian," Ace said, cutting into his thoughts. Her words made no sense to him, but the desperation in her voice triggered something intensely protective inside him. "We can't let him take it. We have to disable the sails, make it look like it's not worth his while. Please, Zander."

A tear fell down her cheek. Zander reached to wipe it away, but another cannon shot rang out, zipping above their heads, and he pulled her into his arms instead, cradling her protectively.

"Zander!"

He forced himself to pull away, swallowing his questions. The crew were shooting their pistols toward the water, throwing things overboard, trying to hit the longboats that pulled up alongside The Valerian.

Zander nodded at Ace, ready to do as she asked.

"I'll cover you," Ace said, yelling to be heard over the noise. Just… make them look useless. Make it look worse than it is. Do you understand?"

Zander nodded. Ace took the ivory blade from her hip and held it aloft. Grappling hooks sunk their teeth into the railings.

"Stay with me," Zander said. "Stay right by me, okay?" He couldn't bear the thought of dying without her nearby.

Ace nodded, her eyes filling with tears. "I'll stay with you," she said, her voice breaking.

The first man boarded the ship, his leg swinging over the railing just as his companion was thrown roughly back into the sea by two pirates. His scream echoed through the air as Zander rushed to the first sail and began to climb the rigging, the grip of one of his daggers held firmly between his teeth. When he reached a high enough point, he began cutting at the rope.

When he looked down at Ace, she was daring a sailor in a blue petticoat to approach her. When he did, she disarmed him in three quick moves, then slashed at his face. When he leaned back to avoid the tip of her blade, she ran him through.

Men in blue petticoats were boarding The Valerian from every side, climbing up the sides of the sloop like ants. To say they outnumbered the pirates would be a ridiculous understatement. Whoever orchestrated this attack came prepared for more than a skirmish on the high seas—they came prepared for war.

Adrenaline pumped through Zander's body, pushing him to move quickly and cut deftly, all with one eye on deck. He was careful to ensure ropes or canvas didn't fall on the crew, careful that he didn't destroy the rigging altogether, but kept Ace's insistence in mind that it look unusable.

He glanced down again as he worked the dagger. Ace was fighting off another sailor, but a second man rushed to her side. Zander yelled, and without looking, Ace pushed the man she was fighting into the waiting arms of Yarrow, who slashed his throat. Ace then turned her attention to the second man.

Theo stood beside Yarrow, his arm locked around the throat of a struggling sailor. He used him as a human shield while he unloaded one pistol, then another, and another, at the endless stream of men pulling themselves on board, expertly hitting his mark each time. When he ran out of loaded guns, he used the last pistol to hit the man he held in the temple. Then he pushed his unconscious body into a nearby invader and crouched behind Yarrow to reload his stash of weapons.

The rest of the crew fought frantically, some engaged in swordplay, others attempting to push or cut the men who tried to climb over the sides of the vessel. Saila was slashing wildly with her sword, her body blocking access to the lower decks. Zander saw Aled fall backward as a bullet hit him in the eye. Bagu approached the shooter from behind and killed him with his new daggers, then hefted his body overboard toward one of the half-full longboats and joined Saila in her defense of the staircase.

Zander cut through the rope, allowing another sail to fall pathetically to the side. Quickly scanning his work, he decided it was good enough and began to descend. As he did, he caught sight of one of the invading sailors and was shocked to find them familiar.

So that's where Declan went, Zander thought. Seeing Declan head toward Ace, her back turned to him as she fought off another sailor, he gripped his dagger firmly in his hand and jumped.

He landed on Declan's back, knocking him to the ground. Zander rolled and jumped back up to face him, but Declan didn't stand. The handle of his dagger jutted triumphantly from his back. Zander wasted no time in retrieving it, pulling hard to remove it from his traitorous body.

Ace turned, her eyes landing briefly on Declan's dead body before scanning Zander head to toe. Satisfied he was whole, she took his hand and pulled him toward the bow as a dozen more men boarded The Valerian and began to overwhelm the small group of pirates. Quickly, Zander tucked away his dagger and unsheathed his sword.

He looked out at the scene before him, shocked at how quickly they'd been overrun.

Theo, cutlass in hand, had been pushed back onto the upper deck above the captain's quarters. He parried blows with one hand, pulling his pistols one by one from their holsters with the other hand, and dropping them at his feet when each shot was taken. Yarrow fought ruthlessly at the bottom of the stairs nearby, their sword a blur of motion. Saila had been forced to her stomach, a sailor's boot keeping her firmly on the ground and four more surrounding her, preventing the crew from rescuing her. George was slashing at a pair of men near the captain's quarters, a sword in one hand and a heavy skillet in the other.

A handful of pirates were gathered in front of Ace and Zander—Bagu, Santiago, Sean, Echo—those who hadn't fallen or sank to their knees in surrender choosing to stand their ground with their captain. Invading sailors lay dying on the ground alongside pirates, more of the former defeated than the latter, but they just kept coming. A final longboat pulled alongside The Valerian, likely carrying the ship's captain.

Zander and Ace planted themselves in front of the forecastle, intermittently fighting and maintaining a broken conversation—the last words they would likely ever share in this life.

"Zander," Ace said, slashing at an approaching sailor with her cutlass. "I'm so sorry you got caught up in this." She slashed again, causing the man to dodge within Zander's reach, earning a blade in his side. "I'm sorry anyone got caught up in this."

Zander pulled his blade free from the man's body, wiping sweat from his brow as he glanced at Ace. She looked how he thought he must have—exhausted, scared, heartbroken.

"These past few months were the best"—*slash, slash, stab*—"of my whole life," Zander said. "Don't apologize for them." *Slash, swipe, slash*. He looked at Ace full on, his expression firm.

Ace smiled softly, her arms limp at her sides, the tip of her cutlass dragging on the ground as the man she'd just been fighting fell lifeless on the deck beside her.

"Okay," she said. "Zander—"

Just then, a blood-curdling roar erupted from the main deck, making Zander turn. The roar came from Yarrow, who stood over a dead sailor, their blade still dripping red with the man's blood. Theo was still on the upper deck, separated from Yarrow by a stream of bodies. Theo was surrounded on three sides by men, swinging his cutlass wildly to keep them at bay, his face like that of a cornered animal as he snarled at them. At his feet lay the empty guns he'd discarded one by one, the bodies of the sailors they'd killed scattered nearby.

Zander looked on in awe as Yarrow seemed to inflate to twice their size, their body vibrating with energy as they locked into hyper-focus on their struggling partner. With movements he could barely make out, Yarrow hoisted themselves onto the railing and leapt over the heads of two men, turning to disarm one and then swinging their sword around to cut the knees of one of the men closing in on Theo.

Standing, they pulled a dagger from their belt and threw it over their shoulder at a man approaching from behind; it embedded itself in the man's eye. In the same breath, they ran their sword through the back of one of the men attacking Theo, then used the blade to propel his struggling body in an arc, swinging themselves into place by Theo's side and kicking the man's body away blade in one fell motion as Theo dispatched a third man.

As the sailor's body fell to the deck, a pool of red blooming at his belly, Theo and Yarrow shared a brief but passionate kiss amidst the chaos before turning to fight once more. They stood shoulder to shoulder now, their backs to the sea, fighting the growing crowd filing onto the upper deck.

Zander watched the entire scene in the few moments it happened before launching back into action. He slashed at an invading sailor who'd climbed onto the forecastle, causing him to jump back in fear. He fell straight into the clutches of Bagu, who slammed him roughly to the ground.

Zander felt Ace's hand in his and squeezed, looking over at her. She was looking hopelessly out at the crew, her eyes darting to the approaching longboat every few moments as she surveyed the tragic scene before her. Beyond their temporarily insulated place at the forecastle, her crew struggled to defend the Valerian against a horde of enemies. Half of The Valerian's pirates had fallen or surrendered, and the other half would be out of strength soon. Theo and Yarrow still struggled on the upper deck, blood coating their skin as they continued to fight more than thrice their number.

Ace kept her hand clutched in Zander's as she yelled across the deck.

"ENOUGH!" she hollered, her voice cutting through the noise, her eyes meeting Yarrow's across the tumult. "We surrender. Lay down your arms."

The fighting lulled. Curious, fearful, and more than a few shocked eyes landed on Ace. The pirates standing in front of her looked outraged at the call for surrender. Theo looked resigned. Yarrow looked heartbroken, shaking their head slightly. But Ace's expression was rock hard as she repeated herself, her gaze still fixed on the upper deck. "Enough," she said.

Yarrow's hands rose slowly as they made a show of dropping their weapons. The rest of the crew followed suit, the clattering sound of metal on wood the only sound for several deafening moments. The sailors surrounding them didn't see what Zander did—that Theo used the show as an opportunity to shuffle behind Yarrow, quickly pulling something from the satchel hidden beneath their long shirt. His other hand retrieved a pistol hidden in their belt.

Ace's voice pulled Zander's eyes away from them.

"Zander." She reached one hand up to stroke his face. "It's been a wonderful adventure, loving you."

A shot rang out, followed by a deafening explosion from the upper deck. Through the sudden haze of smoke that filled the air, Zander saw Ace lift the ivory handle of her blade above her head and bring it swiftly down toward him.

Everything went black.

10

Zander lay in his bed, still too exhausted to move from his position on his stomach. He willed himself to open his eyes, but they didn't so much as flutter. He could hear the breeze dancing against the shutters of his small house. Someone yelled just outside—probably someone calling after their children.

The smell of a fresh hide, ready for tanning, filled his nostrils. And something else he didn't recognize. He took a deep breath, surprised to find that it hurt.

No. That's not a hide.

It was blood. The metallic scent became suddenly clearer, as if his nose was coated in it. The sound that filled his ears wasn't the breeze on his shutters, but the waves lapping against the side of the sloop.

And the voice... it came to him as if from a distance, growing louder and clearer as he settled back into his body.

Where is it? the voice called faintly.

Zander struggled to make sense of the question, his head pounding.

Where is it? it asked, louder now, persistent.

As the sound grew clearer, so did the pain.

"Where is it, you stupid bitch?!"

Zander's eyes flew open as a loud *SLAP* followed up the question.

Standing in front of the damaged mast was a man he'd never seen. He was tall, imposing. His jet-black hair was pulled back from his face, revealing sharp, handsome features. His mouth was twisted into a snarl, and his piercing blue eyes were filled with hatred.

Kneeling before him, her hands bound behind her back, was the captain of The Valerian. Ace's head was turned away from Zander, still twisted from the impact of the hit. Zander willed his body to move, to help her, but it wouldn't. He felt his head swimming from the effort alone. Dark shadows appeared at the corners of his vision.

No, he thought. *No, no, no.*

"Have you been chasing me all over the ocean since I left?" Ace said, her voice dripping with sarcastic pity.

The man hit her again. Zander tried with all his might to get up, but he couldn't move a finger, let alone stand. He wanted to throw himself at the man, to wrap his hands around his neck and squeeze until the life drained from him. But he couldn't even groan. His rage only pulled him down, down, further into darkness.

"*Where is it*?" came a sharp whisper in the background of his awareness.

"It never left Antequera."

Ace's words, and the faint image of her back to him as she was marched off deck, bounced around his skull as he drifted once more into oblivion.

***

Zander shot up from the deck, gasping, his nervous system shocked from a sudden and biting cold. He labored for each breath, his heart pounding frantically in his chest. The world was bright and blinding, and he felt as if he should get up and run, but then the dizziness came, and he was once again on his back.

He felt a hand on his shoulder and started, his eyes flying open. Theo was kneeling beside him, his face hovering a few inches above his. Yarrow stood just behind Theo, a bucket clutched in one hand and an expression of concern on their face. They were both sopping wet.

Then it came back to him.

The ship. The compass. Ace. The handle of her dagger, plummeting toward him.

The man.

"They took her!" Zander said, suddenly frantic. "They took Ace."

He tried to sit up again, but Theo gently held his shoulders, making comforting noises, sounds a mother would use to calm her crying child.

"We have to leave, Theo!" His voice broke, the terror of the past several hours rushing through him all at once. They had Ace. They were leaving. He needed to go, to chase them. Why weren't they already leaving?

"Shh, mate," Theo said gently. "We know. You're in no state, trust me."

A sob escaped Zander. Beneath the encompassing panic, he knew Theo was right. The number of shocks his body had experienced in the last few minutes alone rocked through him, almost vibrating in their intensity. But as the frantic energy slowly leaked from his pores, a profound exhaustion took its place.

"We have to go get her," he said. His voice sounded as weak as his body felt.

Yarrow kneeled at his other side. Their face was marked in lines Zander had never seen. They looked worn, sorrowful. They put a gentle hand on his shoulder.

"We know," they said. They looked away, their eyes scanning the sloop, then Theo, then settling again on Zander. "But there's no chasing to be done. Not yet. The Valerian isn't fit to sail, and neither are the three of us. If we want to save our friend, we must tend to our ailments as well as hers." They gestured to the sloop. "We must take a moment to rest. To grieve."

It was then Zander noticed the exhaustion lining Yarrow's face. They looked paper thin.

He took a deep breath and nodded. With Theo's help, he pulled himself into a sitting position.

The devastation he saw around him took his breath away. The mast was badly damaged. Pieces of the shattered railing were scattered here and there. The sails hung limp, lifeless. The edge of the upper deck above the captain's quarters looked like it had opened into a gaping hole. A longer look revealed it wasn't a chasm, but an irregular fissure surrounded by a blanket of charred, blackened wood. And then there were the bodies.

Zander, Theo, and Yarrow were the only living people aboard The Valerian. Bodies—dozens of them, pirates and invading sailors alike—lay sprawled on the deck, their blood running back and forth in small red rivers as the sloop rocked gently on the waves. Zander began to cry as he picked out the faces of the crew, men he'd grown to think of as his family. Jurgen. Raphael. Jan. Abdoul. Jubal. Daniel. Aled. He thought of the rest—those that surrendered—and prayed they were safe and unharmed.

It had never been so quiet on the sea.

As he shifted his weight, his hand landed on something cold and hard. Ace's cutlass. He gripped the ivory handle, squeezing it until his knuckles turned as white as the bone itself. His own sword was nowhere in sight, but he could feel his twin daggers tucked securely in each of his boots.

He brought his attention back to Theo and Yarrow. They were both wounded—Yarrow's arm was bleeding, and their face bruised. Theo was bleeding badly from his shoulder, and he gripped his side in pain. A thin layer of gunpowder coated his fingers. Zander had so many questions, but just one screamed to be said out loud.

"Who was that man? The one who took Ace."

Theo and Yarrow shared a look.

"Who was he?" Zander demanded.

Yarrow sighed. "Her husband."

PART TWO

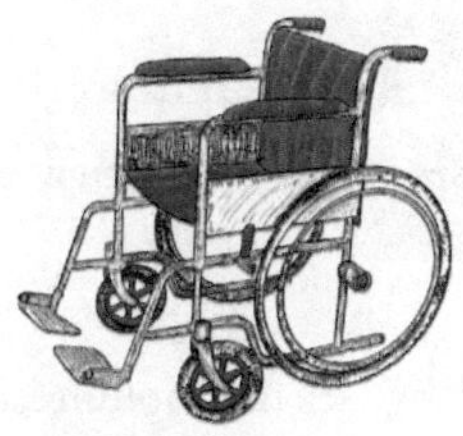

Once, he was dancing.

Fluorescent lights reflected blindingly on the ugly tile floor, blinking and buzzing almost imperceptibly against the music in the nursing home's recreation room.

He'd come here once a week to volunteer since his wife died. It gave him something to do, and in the faces of each resident he saw something that reminded him of her. It was painful, like scratching open an old wound just to see it bleed again, but he found a strange sense of relief in seeing the same confusion and vulnerability echoed on a stranger's face that he once saw on hers.

Alzheimer's was a nasty sonofabitch. It stole her from him, allowing him only glimpses of her vitality toward the end as she struggled to find lucidity. But as she passed from this world to the next, she smiled at him in a knowing way, as if her spirit resurfaced just for a moment in order to say goodbye.

He kept coming here to visit the patients who had no spouse or children to sit by their side each day. It hurt, but also soothed, to know he could provide some sort of comfort.

Today was a special resident event. A dance. It wasn't his usual day to visit, but one of the nurses approached him weeks ago and begged him to come.

"We don't get many older gentleman volunteers," she'd said. "Having you there would give all the ladies a chance to dance with a partner."

So of course, he came. He thought of his Hannah, and how she'd love something like this even if she didn't know the man she was dancing with was her husband.

He was just finishing a dance with Margaret, a little woman who always called him Dave even though that wasn't his name, when the activities coordinator took over the mic to make an announcement. He helped Margaret back to her seat, patting her hand affectionately when she thanked him for the dance.

That was when she caught his eye.

She sat in the corner of the room, hunched over in her chair, her eyes out of focus as they gazed at the floor. Her white hair fell haphazardly over her face in a curtain that obscured one eye. Her fingers fiddled absently with an afghan on her lap. He'd never seen her before, but then again, he did most of his volunteering in the common areas of the nursing home, never visiting rooms unless the staff or a resident requested it.

He thought it was the memory of his wife who drew him to her. She declined rapidly at the end, and the empty look in this woman's eyes was eerily similar to an image of his wife that haunted his dreams of late. But in truth, there was something else about the woman he couldn't quite put his finger on. Perhaps he knew her once, long ago? After 84 years of living in the same town, it wouldn't be surprising to run into someone he once knew here.

But as he approached her, he struggled to find anything familiar about her face. The draw to her came from the inside, as if his very soul tugged him toward her, recognizing something he couldn't see.

Indeed, it did.

He knelt down in front of the woman and gently touched her hand. She didn't respond.

"Hello," he said. Nothing.

From the corner of his eye, he noticed a nurse shaking her head. Her beehive hairdo trembled slightly as she shot him a sad look, like she knew he was wasting his time. Irritated with the look, he persisted, shifting his weight slightly so he was directly in the woman's line of sight.

"Hello there," he tried again, giving her fingers a gentle squeeze.

Her eyes focused then, blinking several times as she took him in. He knew that look of dawning recognition. He'd seen it many times before. He was not, however, prepared for the smile that slowly lit up her features, like a candle melting in reverse. Every inch of her face lifted, brightened, like she was coming back from the dead.

Just then, the music started playing again. Tommy James' voice warbled over the record, "Crimson and Clover" filling the room and igniting his body with a staggering sense of weight as the strange woman feebly squeezed his hand in response.

"There you are," she said softly.

He smiled at her but didn't know how to respond to that. "Would you like to dance?"

"Yes," she answered, her voice surprisingly steady.

As he helped her stand, he noticed how fragile her body was, as if she rarely moved on her own. He easily supported her weight as they moved to the edge of the dance floor and began to slowly sway to the music.

She kept her eyes on him as they danced. They darted around his face like she was learning his features. While he would normally feel uncomfortable under such scrutiny, he found himself surprisingly at ease, even when she leaned into his chest and inhaled deeply. A small sigh escaped the shriveled old woman, and she rested her cheek against him as they continued to sway.

Just as the song was ending, she pulled away to look at him again, the slow shuffle of her feet stopping abruptly.

She was a stark contrast from the huddled, withdrawn old woman he approached only minutes before. She stood up straight, her eyes clear and bright as they roved over him once more.

Her eyes met his with an intensity and longing that shocked him, and as her body softened, her hand brushing along his shoulder in a familiar way, he was filled with a sudden warmth. "Oh, how I've missed you," she whispered.

And then she retreated within herself, her eyes clouding over and losing focus, her shoulders hunching slightly, her feet becoming unsteady.

As he braced her against him to prevent her from falling, he resisted the urge to shake her. A baffling desperation overcame him. He wanted her to come back. He couldn't explain why, but he *needed* her to come back.

A hand on his shoulder pulled him from his spiral—the nurse from before. She moved her arm around the woman's waist to support her, then smiled up at him, her eyes full of tears.

"I've never seen her so alert," she said gently. "You've given her a gift today. I'll take it from here."

He stood there, his arms limp at his sides, and watched helplessly as she took his soulmate away.

11

"Her *husband*?"

Yarrow sighed again, moving to sit beside Theo, who was peeling his empty gun vest from his body. They lowered themselves painstakingly to the ground and gave Zander a hard look.

"Who is Ace to you?" they asked.

Zander looked between Theo and Yarrow in disbelief, his jaw hanging open.

"What the fuck do you mean who is Ace to me?" It was a ludicrous question, like asking his left foot who his right foot was to it. "What is going on, Yarrow?"

Yarrow's expression didn't waver. "Ace trusted us, and only us, with what I'm about to tell you. My gut says she would have told you eventually, and she would likely want you to know now. But I need to be sure you're going to stick around after I tell you. If not, I'd much rather drop you off at the nearest port and do this ourselves."

Zander recoiled at the idea, an unfamiliar rage kindling in his belly at the thought of being left behind—of leaving Ace behind.

"You want to know who Ace is to me?" he asked. "She's the only thing that's ever felt real in my life. She's my heart, my lungs, the sun on my face. I'd pluck my eyes from my head and give them to her if she asked. I'd cut the beating heart from my own mother if she needed it. She's my soulmate. Now *please*, Yarrow, tell me what's happening." His voice felt ragged, breaking under the threat of furious tears.

Yarrow's face softened, and they took Zander's hands in theirs, giving them a squeeze.

"I suspected as much," they said softly. "But I needed to know for sure."

Yarrow looked at Theo, who was leaning against a damaged railing, one arm resting casually on his raised knee. He looked comically like himself—charming, relaxed, poised—a tender smile on his face at Zander's confession. His posture lay in stark contrast to the blood, gunpowder, and saltwater coating his skin and clothes. If Zander wasn't overwhelmed by heartbreak, he might have laughed.

Theo saw Yarrow's look and nodded.

"Let's do this indoors," he said, standing up with a groan. "There's too much... there's *too much* out here."

The three of them went into the surgery to talk. With the door shut, they could almost pretend everything was normal. But evidence of carnage still lay all around them. Bottles and baskets littered the floor, their contents running together in a mix of greenery, glass, and shining liquid. Yarrow set to preserving what they could of the precious ingredients while Theo settled in to tell his story.

"We met Ace nine years ago," Theo began. Zander nodded, remembering. "Her parents owned a small vineyard near Antequera. Rumor had it, they purchased the land from its previous owners for more than it was worth. Word spread, and soon they were rubbing elbows with the richest families in Southern Spain, who all thought they had some vast, mysterious fortune. It was a rumor they allowed to spread. It was smart; it gave them an instant stream of customers.

"Eventually, the rumor reached us. We were docked in Malaga when we heard about the rich couple who'd apparently made a fortune on the high seas. Someone told us they were ruthless pirates. Another insisted they'd plundered gold from the Americas and delivered it to the King, who let them keep a generous share. What interested us was the rumor they were looking for tobacco from Virginia—the same place they used to source their own back in the day, we later found out."

"We ran with a small crew of traders back then," Yarrow explained. "Two of them were Virginians, brothers whose parents settled there from England. We'd come to Spain with crates full of tobacco, among other things, hoping to sell."

"We figured it was our lucky day, and we paid the mysterious pirate couple a visit. That's when we met Ace." Theo smiled fondly at the memory as he spoke. "She was 17 years old, and every bit the woman she is today. She acted as her parents' manager, handling most of the finances and negotiating deals with suppliers and customers." Theo chuckled, wincing in pain as he did. "Her parents tried and tried to get her to stop, insisting she focus her energy elsewhere. But she was so good at it, and so hardheaded, they finally gave up and let her do what she wanted.

"For three years we dealt with Ace, going back and forth from Virginia to Spain buying and selling tobacco. We'd dock at Malaga, send word to the Vidals, and travel to their estate when we heard back. Chandace and Nicolas would always insist we stay a few days as guests. They were like that. But as time went on, Ace started meeting us at the coast more often. She'd spend days at a time with us, lounging around with our crew, taking her time going home. Truth was, she wanted an excuse to be near the sea. In that time, we became very close."

Yarrow took Theo's hand and squeezed, their eyes downcast. Zander knew "close" was an understatement. Theo and Yarrow were connected to Ace in a way he didn't fully understand—not just friends, and not quite parents, but they shared a love as deep as any other.

"It was then we learned the truth about the Vidals," Theo said with a sigh. "Behind all the rumors of buried treasure and storehouses full of gold—rumors Chandace and Nicolas joked about at dinner parties and coyly refused to address outright—the three of them were nothing but an ordinary, loving family. A cunning family, yes, and quite successful both as seafaring merchants and landowning traders. But truly, simple. Parents determined to give their daughter what they never had, and blind to the fact that she didn't want it.

"On one of our trips to Spain about six years ago, Ace showed up in Malaga mere hours after we sent word to her, like she'd run out the door as soon as she saw our message. She arrived with a carriage like always, plus a barrel of wine and a bag of supplies."

"We knew right away something was wrong," said Yarrow. "Ace wasn't herself. She pulled a bag of coins from her pocket and shook it at us."

Yarrow held their hand aloft, shaking an invisible bag of coins.

"She said she needed a holiday. She brought extra coin, and proposed we sail for Ibiza and drink the barrel of wine she'd brought. Of course, a few days getting drunk on a beach sounded fine to the crew, and they agreed. After we loaded the tobacco onto Ace's carriage, she sent her very confused servant away and nearly ran onto the vessel. She didn't breathe until the coast became a distant speck on the horizon."

"That was when she told us about the engagement," Theo said. "Her parents had arranged for her to be married to a viscount. A fucking *viscount*. Newly titled. He'd just taken up residence at a neighboring estate, left to him by his late father. What began as neighborly courtesy turned into a friendship between Ace's father and this man, and when he asked to join their families by marrying Ace, it was an offer no parent would dream of refusing. He was everything they could ever want for her—handsome, charming, rich. *Titled*. He could give Ace, and any children they had, everything they ever wanted or needed. Her parents could rest, could die, knowing Ace wouldn't want for anything."

"Ace was devastated," Yarrow said quietly, their eyes focused on their feet. "She didn't want a title, or land, or jewels. She wanted freedom. It was the one thing a husband could not—would never—give to her."

Zander's heart was no longer in his chest. It was somewhere in his feet, having sunk further with every word his friends said. It leaked out of his toes, leaving him empty as he sat on the ruined floor.

Ace had a husband. *A husband*. He couldn't make sense of it.

"And she went through with it?" he asked.

"She thought about running away," Yarrow said. "We stayed for four days in Ibiza, and she must have changed her mind a dozen times over those four days. She went back, thinking maybe she could find a way out of it. But we knew. There's no way to refuse an offer from a man like that without causing offense."

Zander let out a long breath.

"Not only was he higher in status than Ace's family," Yarrow continued, "but her father had already accepted on her behalf. Going back on his word would have jeopardized their relationship with this man, their business, everything. I think her father likely would have sacrificed all that if he knew it was what Ace really wanted. But in the end, she couldn't bear to ask it of him."

Zander shot to his feet, needing to move. He immediately regretted it. A sudden headache blinded him, and a wave of dizziness overcame him that made him stumble, reach out. His hand grasped the doorframe and he leaned heavily on it, breathing in short bursts to stem a sudden nausea. He felt something touch his arm, then a warm, comforting smell filled his nostrils. The nausea disappeared, and he opened his eyes to see Yarrow. The source of the smell—a small jar filled with oil—was clutched in their hand, which held it to his face.

"Thank you," Zander said. Yarrow nodded and returned to Theo, sitting by him and intertwining their fingers with his.

Ace is married.

Zander reached down and touched the handle of Ace's cutlass, which was attached to his belt. Then he nodded to indicate he was ready to listen again.

Theo continued.

"We weren't sure if we would see Ace again after she was married. It's not exactly common for a Viscountess to oversee the purchase of tobacco. So, we stayed in Spain when our crew set out for the Americas, intending to rejoin them on their return journey. We stayed in Almogia, a small town within walking distance of Ace, and easy carriage distance from her betrothed's estate."

"We wanted to spend as much time with her as we could," Yarrow said. "From everything we'd heard about Lord Sanz, he wasn't the type to socialize with seafaring folk."

"Aye, he sounded like a right prick," Theo said. Yarrow snorted softly, elbowing him. Theo smiled affectionately at them and continued. "Well, you know what I mean. Rich folk." He waved his hands in a vague gesture. "In all the time he'd spent with Ace's father, he never once addressed Ace or even looked at her, like she didn't exist. Suddenly, he wants to marry her." Theo made a disgusted sound, like he had a particularly annoying fly in the back of his throat.

"Over the next few weeks, Ace was tasked with getting to know her new keeper. We had the privilege of hearing every detail after the fact, as Ace would return from her fancy lunches and tea dates, rip off her dress, don her trousers, and rush to the inn we stayed at to get drunk. We got the play by play on *Lord Sanz*. Ignacio." Theo spit his name like it was a curse.

"There was something off about him," Yarrow said.

Her husband.

"Like I said, a right prick," Theo agreed. "But yes, there was something... off. He spent most of their time together asking about Ace's parents, about their life on the sea. He'd gotten it into his head—like most people did—that her parents had some sort of buried treasure, and he was obsessed with it."

"It didn't help that Chandace and Nicolas talked about it as if it were real," Yarrow said.

"Aye, but he never asked *them* about it. He was all compliments and gifts and nightcaps with his new in-laws. But with Ace, he teetered between sickeningly sweet flattery and morbid interest in her parents' secret riches. He asked all sorts of questions about their business as well, feigning interest in her skills as a businesswoman. Even when she acted crass or misbehaved, trying to get him to call off the engagement, he flattered her."

Zander had a hard time imagining Ace being *flattered*. The idea of attempting something like flattery in her presence intimidated even him. Then again, she'd been young.

"Ace wanted to believe him," Yarrow said sadly. "Sitting at the precipice of her whole life changing, she saw a glimmer of hope that her new husband would give her some freedom. Perhaps she could continue working, perhaps he would let her sail. So, she played, ever so little, into his hands. She even alluded to a treasure in their conversations, deeming it her inheritance, hers by right upon her parents' deaths."

"Or it would be given to her husband," Zander said.

"Aye," Theo said, nodding. "Although technically they didn't consummate the marriage."

"Two weeks before the wedding, Ace stopped showing up at the inn," Yarrow continued. "We sent word to her after a few days, but the messenger returned with a response from her fiancé, asking us to come see him at his estate right away."

"His estate was a sprawling thing," Theo said, "surrounded by palms and manicured lawns and security guards. And it was the most uptight goddamn place in the world. No one, not the carriage driver, not the doorman, no one so much as looked at us as they ushered us into a gaudy sitting room, where Lord Sanz was waiting.

"'Sit,'" Theo said, his voice dripping with condescension as he played the role of Lord Sanz. He held out his arm, gesturing in the manner Lord Sanz did, a smug, bored look painted on his face. "So, we sat. 'I wish to speak to you about your tobacco arrangement,' he said. 'We usually deal with the Vidal family,' I told him. 'Have they retired?'

"And without looking up from his perfectly manicured nails, the bastard says, 'In a manner of speaking, yes. They burned to death inside their home night before last. Sad business.'"

Yarrow let out a low, frustrated growl.

"Sad fucking business," they said. "Can you believe that? *Sad fucking business*, indeed. The Vidals were a cornerstone of the Antequera region. A lightning bolt destroyed their legacy, a perfectly timed lightning bolt from a brief summer storm. It was as if Zeus himself had conjured it specifically for that purpose. It was a tragedy."

"We were dumbstruck, mate," Theo said. "For once, I had no words. 'Where is Ace?' Yarrow asked him. Lord Sanz said, 'Aracely is here, in her new home, grieving. And preparing for our upcoming wedding, I imagine.' *Pfft*. Then he moved on with business, telling us he'd be our 'new point of contact' from there on out.

"We asked if we could see her. He ignored us, gesturing to a paper on the table in front of him. 'Here are your new terms. I look forward to seeing you when you have a new shipment of tobacco.' And suddenly we were being ushered from the room again and pushed into a carriage."

"So, what, he was holding Ace prisoner?" Zander asked. The anger burning in his stomach hissed and sputtered with every new revelation.

"Yes," Yarrow said. "Essentially. She was a woman without a keeper; no one would have thought much about her fiancé keeping her close in her grief. But we got word from her that night. Rosario, one of her family's former staff, showed up at the inn with a tiny, scrawled note in Ace's hand. It said the ceremony had been moved up and would occur in three days' time. It also said to meet her the night of the wedding, at midnight, behind the inn."

"We didn't hear anything after that," Theo said. "But three nights later, she showed up on horseback with a knapsack and a second horse trailing behind her. Her hair was flattened on her head with all these tiny fucking... *needles*." Theo pinched his fingers together in the air to demonstrate their miniscule size, his face twisted in frustration at the phantom needles.

"They were pins, dear," Yarrow said.

"They were teeny, tiny torture devices," Theo said adamantly. "You should have heard the noises she made when I helped her take them out, mate. It took ages. I felt like I was torturing the poor thing."

"Darling," Yarrow said.

"Right, well, anyway," Theo continued. "Ace showed up, looking like she's just pulled off a jailbreak."

"She sort of had," Yarrow muttered.

"She told us she was headed to Portugal, that she was determined to live on the sea again, and she hoped we would come with her. Of course, we did. To be honest, we were kind of sick of our old crew, and Ace was family. There was no question. We went."

"You can pretty well fill out the rest of the story," Yarrow said. "We met with Abilio, got The Valerian back, and went about forming a pirate crew. And now... well, Ace's past has caught up with her, as she always feared it would."

Zander let out a long breath. His hands shook, his body still reeling, but his thoughts were coming back into focus.

"And you knew the merchant vessel near Azores was... his?" Zander asked, thinking of the ship with the octopus carved on the bow.

"Not his," Yarrow said. "It belonged to a family friend of Ignacio's, a family he did business with often. The Marins are a seafaring family, while Sanz and his lot are inland folk. Seeing Sanz himself on that ship today... well, that was a shock. As far as any of us knew, the Sanz family didn't own any vessels. Anyway, Ace knew someone on the Marin vessel would likely recognize her. It's why the decision to take it was left up to the crew. Why Ace didn't deal with the captain."

"He knew her," Zander said.

"Yes. He officiated their wedding," Yarrow said. "Ignacio and Ace were supposed to sail away on his sloop the day after the wedding, a sort of coming out tour for Sanz's new wife—a gift from the Marin family."

Theo snorted. Zander looked at him questioningly.

"After Ace met us at the inn, we headed to the port at Malaga and took Marin's boat. We burned it off the coast of Portugal. I'm afraid we're responsible for his dislike of pirates." He chuckled.

"And Declan knew he recognized her," Zander said. "He contacted him somehow when we were in Porto, and word got to Sanz where she was headed."

"Aye," Theo said. "Declan was on the sloop that day, below deck. It's likely he saw something that would have helped him locate the Marin family. The man was a prick, but he was rather smart."

"But why would any man waste all these resources just to chase his estranged wife across the ocean?" Zander asked.

"Because she never told him where to find her inheritance," Yarrow said. "The fabled Vidal fortune."

Zander's head shot up as he remembered what Ace said. "It never left Antequera."

Zander now knew two things for sure. One—he knew where Ace was, or at least where she was headed. And two—he knew he would do anything to get her back, even if he had to defy God himself, before whom Ace had been married.

He had jumped into the sea to chase her once. Now, he'd jump right into the jaws of a monster to find her again.

12

The tale of Ace's marriage and subsequent escape told, the three pirates turned their attention to the ruin that surrounded them.

First, they tended to their wounds. Zander was relieved to find that Yarrow's injuries were mostly superficial—cuts and bruises and quite a few sore muscles. When Theo stripped his shirt off, the injury on his shoulder made Zander's breath catch. Yarrow tended to it with a serious look, their fingers gentle as they pulled bits of debris from the wound, cleaned it, and applied stitches. They'd found enough usable materials among the wreckage of the room to make a poultice, but it was only enough for one application. They checked Theo for more wounds and found none aside from a few broken ribs.

Zander, who'd spent most of the battle either climbing the rigging or lying on the ground unconscious, noted with a sense of bitter regret that he was not seriously injured.

Next, they tended to the bodies. They threw the men Sanz left behind into the sea first, murmuring generic prayers and wishing them rest despite the anger burning in their guts.

With the invaders out of the way, they laid their friends together on the main deck and took their time saying goodbye. Zander looked at each of his friends in turn, tears coating his cheeks as he said silent farewells to all seven of them. He etched their visages in his mind, allowing the horror to build a wall of flaming fury around his heart.

Theo knelt beside each fallen member of The Valerian in turn, resting his hand on their shoulders. He talked to them as if they were still there, telling jokes, reminiscing, openly weeping. Yarrow stood by and looked at the crew members silently for a while, then retreated to their quarters. Moments later, Zander heard muffled screaming followed by the sound of knuckles against wood.

After they'd said their goodbyes, Theo and Zander buried their friends at sea and washed their blood from the deck.

Continuously pushing away thoughts of what he could have done, should have done, Zander went below deck in search of shot plugs and a few spare buckets. They spent the next few hours tending to the most severe damage to The Valerian. When they finished, they were still left with a wreck, but it was a floating wreck, at least.

As evening approached, Zander, Theo, and Yarrow stood gathered in a circle around Ace's desk.

Ace's quarters had been trashed, drawers emptied and shelves wiped clean. Books and other small treasures littered the ground. Zander positioned himself with his back to the bed, unable to look at it without imagining Ace there, sleeping, her arm draped over her face and her foot peeking out from beneath the covers. He couldn't bear to think about it without turning into a sobbing mess.

He tried to stand up straight, taking on the air he knew Ace would have in a similar situation—tough, unbothered, determined, despite the raging sea of emotions running beneath her skin.

"If he thinks the inheritance is still in Antequera, then he'll have taken her back to his estate to get its exact location out of her," Yarrow said. "But if I know Ace, she'll find a way to stall—to survive—until she sees an advantage in telling him. Hopefully, that will give us enough time to reach her... even though, technically, she told us not to come after her."

"An order I'm happy to ignore," Zander said. "She didn't tell me shit, so I'll take the blame if she gets mad." He shrugged.

Theo chuckled at Zander's attempt to lighten the mood. Yarrow gave him a crooked smile and continued.

"The most direct route would be to sail to Malaga and travel North from there, a journey we've made many times." They pointed to Malaga on the map, tracing their finger the short distance North to the region of Antequera.

"But The Valerian isn't fit to sail as far as Malaga," Theo said. "And Lord Prick will likely have lookouts at Malaga's ports anyhow."

Yarrow nodded in agreement.

"We can make it as far as Algarve and find passage from there to Porto," Yarrow said. "Abilio will help us with the necessary supplies. We'll need weapons, at the very least. Horses." Their eyes flashed toward Theo, who was cradling his arm. "Perhaps some medicine."

Zander tried to gauge the distance from Algarve, at the pointed tip of Portugal, to Porto. He suppressed a sigh by biting his tongue. This was going to take forever. He felt time slipping through his fingers like sand. The familiar tug in his chest grew ever fainter as Ace drifted farther away.

Chills ran down Zander's arms from the wind outside, echoing the cold feeling in his gut. The fire damage above deck where Zander had last seen Theo and Yarrow fighting had opened a small crevice in the far wall and ceiling of the captain's quarters. The ocean air drifted in, rustling loose papers.

"Speaking of repairs," Zander said, gesturing to the fissure. "What happened there? One moment Ace was calling for surrender, and the next it sounded as if a bomb had gone off."

"Enough," Yarrow said. "That was what Ace said. 'Enough.' It was a code word meant for me and Theo. Ace knew we likely wouldn't win this fight, and she warned us we'd need a backup plan. She wanted us to get out and take you with us, and she wanted to make sure Sanz left The Valerian behind. She'd rather it sink than end up in his hands."

"What was the plan?" Zander asked.

"A distraction. Something explosive enough that me and Theo could bail overboard and be presumed dead. She was supposed to use it to get you to safety."

"We didn't know she was going to hit you over the head, mate," Theo clarified.

"After that," Yarrow continued, "we'd stay with The Valerian and make sure she didn't sink, or if it fell into the hands of Sanz's men, we'd stowaway and make a new plan from there. She'd hoped there would be a crew left behind as well. She didn't predict he'd take survivors with him."

"And what was the distraction?" Zander asked. "A bomb?"

"A rough version of a grenadier," said Yarrow. Seeing Zander's blank expression, they clarified, shrugging. "A bomb. A small one, usually made with an iron ball and gunpowder, and lit with a fuse. But if you know what you're doing—and I do—anything can be turned into a makeshift grenadier with enough gunpowder and a bit of pitch."

"It can, if you have a partner with excellent aim," Theo said, pulling out his pistol and twirling it playfully in circles. Yarrow winked at him in response.

"I made one shortly after we encountered the Marin vessel. I had a bad feeling."

Zander nodded as the story started to make sense. The item Theo pulled from Yarrow's satchel was a makeshift explosive device. Theo must have thrown it to the ground before shooting at it with his pistol, triggering the explosion. The two of them would've needed to jump first, then set off the bomb in midair.

Zander smirked. "That was risky."

"Aye," Theo said. "But it worked. We stayed out of sight in the water until Lord Prick's men cleared out, then we climbed back on board to find you lying there."

Zander nodded, silent. He tried not to let the fact that Theo and Yarrow were in on Ace's plan from the beginning bother him, but it gnawed at the pit of his stomach, nonetheless. When he found Ace and rescued her, he had some serious questions to ask her about their relationship, secret husband aside.

He looked again toward the crevice in the room—his bedroom, as he'd come to think of it. It felt empty now. Through the broken wood he could see the colors of sunset painting the sky. He wanted to leave now, wanted to never sleep again until he laid eyes on Ace, but his exhaustion was bone-deep. Looking at his friends, he could see they were also at the end of their reserves.

"Algarve it is, then," he said. "At first light we'll tend to the sails and other necessary repairs. Then we'll sail." He looked between his two friends for confirmation. They both nodded.

Zander took several steps backward, plopping down onto the bed with a sigh. Yarrow moved toward him, placing a gentle hand on his shoulder.

"Get some rest, dear," they said.

"You, too," he told them as they made their way out of the room.

When the door closed behind Theo and Yarrow, Zander let out a long sigh. He felt his body and soul sag under the weight of his sadness.

He reached into his pocket and pulled out Ace's compass. He turned it over and over in his hands, his thumb stroking the wood appreciatively. He unfastened the hinges, opening the lid and staring at the dial inside.

"We'll find her," he whispered to the compass. She was his North Star. He had to find her.

He looked again at the destruction around him. The bed where Zander had held his love for so many nights was littered in debris. He couldn't help but think of it in a poetic sense—the soft, warm cushions where he'd spent the most peaceful moments of his life, littered with the wreckage of that comfort as it was torn away from him.

He looked at the floor. Just by his foot was a green seashell Ace brought on board from Azores. A pile of crushed purple petals Zander recognized as a flower she picked in Bermuda lay just beside her desk. Small rocks and pebbles of all sizes slid or rolled back and forth with the soft waves. Her favorite book—the one she'd been reading to him—lay open on the floor, dangerously close to a puddle of water forming nearby.

Painfully, Zander hauled himself up and crossed the room to the book. He picked it up, carefully skimming through the pages, looking for damage. The dried leaf Ace used as a bookmark was still tucked securely between them.

He placed the book gently on the built-in shelf behind Ace's desk. He stooped, retrieving a large piece of dead coral from the ground and putting it back in its place as well. He said a silent prayer of thanks that so much was left behind. Ace's money, a few jewels, even some clothing had all been taken. But the important things—the things Ace truly loved—had been left behind, discarded as trash.

Zander spent the next hour carefully collecting Ace's treasures and putting them back in their places. When his head finally hit the mattress, a wool blanket fastened against the hole in the wall to keep the cold at bay, he was asleep in seconds.

13

"Fuck," Zander muttered, shaking his hand to dispel the pain that blossomed on his fingertips. He resisted the urge to plunge his burning fingers into his mouth to soothe them. They were coated in pitch.

Yarrow made a *tsk*ing noise under their breath, reaching for Zander's hand so they could inspect it.

"I'm okay," Zander said, shaking his head. "You warned me."

"I did," Yarrow agreed.

Zander took a deep breath, resolved to ignore the pain in his hand, and reached for the container of viscous liquid again. He scolded himself internally for not being more careful. He was rushing, his anxiety over getting to shore and finding Ace growing by the second.

The three of them had been awake since dawn. After hauling buckets of water from the bilge that had leaked in overnight, they began work on the sails. Zander made hasty repairs that made him cringe to look at, but the sails were functional. Still, they'd been sailing painfully slow since then. It wasn't yet noon, but Zander felt like time was slipping away from them.

There was not but a light breeze pushing them toward shore, and a heavy fog surrounded them the closer they got to Algarve. Zander anxiously checked Ace's compass every few minutes. Theo, who was at the helm, joked that even if they ran straight into a cliffside in the dense fog, they were moving so slowly it wouldn't feel like much more than a tap.

He carefully painted more pitch over the large canvas ball, his hands shaking. The pitch would soon harden the outer edge of canvas, protecting the store of gunpowder inside. A fuse made of yarn soaked in linseed oil stuck out at one end.

Yarrow had explained the glass bomb they'd detonated with Theo's gun the day before was far more difficult to make. It was meant to be detonated immediately and from afar. They spoke of it as if it was made with a secret formula, and Zander wondered where else they'd used the signature device before.

For the purposes of their impending rescue—namely, making lots of noise, setting a large fire, and snatching Ace in the ensuing chaos—a more basic explosive would work fine.

Their plan had come together in bits and pieces as they worked. Theo seemed confident he could find passage to Porto using what supplies they could scavenge from the ailing sloop. They hoped that in addition to horses, medicine, and weapons, Abilio might send a few men with them as backup, as they expected the Sanz estate to be well-guarded. Ideally, they would use stealth and a well-timed distraction to find Ace, but they would be prepared for a fight, nonetheless.

Zander let out a long breath as Yarrow carefully lowered the finished grenadier to the deck. They'd stretched their supplies to make three fist-sized devices, one for each of them. Yarrow's satchel was air drying over a piece of rigging, having been soaked in the sea, its contents emptied when they jumped overboard. All three would fit nicely in the satchel until they could secure packhorses. Theo's gun vest was already dry and strapped to the pirate himself, though its holsters were empty. Upon asking, Zander learned the vest had been designed by Yarrow, who paid a friend to make it for Theo's 36th birthday.

"Oy," Theo hollered from his position on the upper deck. He had the telescope to his eye. "If I'm not mistaken, that's land up ahead."

Zander released a breath of relief, smiling for the first time since he woke up on deck and realized his life had imploded. He reached over to squeeze Yarrow's shoulder gently as he stood. He retrieved Ace's compass, which was sitting open next to them, then made for their quarters.

His black jacket—the one Ace encouraged him to buy in Porto—was spread neatly on the bed. He donned it, buttoning it tightly around his waist. He attached Ace's ivory-handled blade to his belt. He tucked his daggers securely in his boots, one on each side. In his jacket pockets he placed a flint and steel, Ace's compass, and a flask filled with watered-down wine.

Zander turned, catching his reflection in the small mirror Ace had attached to one wall. He barely recognized the man there. When he'd come aboard, he was every bit the poor tanner's son—strong shoulders, rough hands, and a deep-seated sense of shame. Invisibility was a skill he'd honed well throughout his life, but he'd soon become invisible to even himself, simply floating through life, waiting for something he couldn't quite name.

Before him now stood a pirate. He'd lost the perpetual hunch in his shoulders, the downcast look in his eyes. He stood tall now, his face looking forward at the world, his green eyes lucid and discerning. He still had the same strong shoulders and rough hands, but his body appeared more balanced, more well used. His hair was long now, long enough to tie back, but strands of it always seemed to escape and fall across his face. His face, which he'd always kept clean shaven, now sported a dark brown mustache and beard, which he kept trimmed.

He took one last hard look at himself in that mirror and prayed the man he saw was strong enough to do what needed to be done. He turned, surveying Ace's room again, hoping he'd stand here again soon, Ace's hand in his. Then he left.

When he emerged on deck, Theo and Yarrow had transformed as well. Yarrow's satchel was tied around their waist, their long shirt almost covering it. Theo had a pistol attached to one hip and a sword at the other. He smiled at Zander as he walked toward them.

"You ready to get your girl back, mate?" he said.

Zander smiled, energized by the sight of land slowly coming into view behind his friends. He opened his mouth to answer, but then he saw sails emerge from the fog to the Northwest, and a black flag, and his words were swallowed by terror as a cannon shot rang out across the water.

***

The three of them hit the deck at the same time, covering their heads. Theo's arms went around Yarrow, cradling them protectively. The cannon shot hit the water just to the side of them—too close.

Zander looked again at the ship. It was big, much larger than theirs. A cursory glance showed it was well manned; at least sixty men were gathered on deck.

"Where is the white flag?" Zander called to Theo and Yarrow.

"There!" Yarrow yelled, pointing to a corner where they'd piled debris the day before. He crawled toward it on his belly. Another shot rang out, this one closer. His hands closed over the flag, and he tore it from its place amid the rubbish. Theo was at his side now, and he took the flag roughly from his hands, holding it high above his head and waving it desperately in the air.

The ship was right in front of them now, and longboats were already being lowered into the water. They seemed to have seen the flag, as they were no longer firing, and Zander could hear laughter ringing out amongst the crew. Zander stood and walked to where Yarrow stood, warily watching the ship.

Yarrow looked up at him, their mouth set in a thin line.

"Take a deep breath, love," they said. "Steady yourself. These are the pirates you've heard stories about."

A chill ran down Zander's spine.

"Once we board, we do what we can to survive," Yarrow continued. "We look for resources that can be of use to us. We aren't friends, any of us, alright? Better them see us as castoffs, easily controlled and manipulated, not a group of unified outsiders."

Zander nodded, swallowing. The plans they'd made just this morning drained from his head like so much blood, leaving him lightheaded.

When the men boarded the ship, Zander knew immediately Yarrow was right. He knew it had been too much to hope for, that these pirates would be fair and benevolent like Ace's crew. Rather, it seemed they'd stepped right out of a fantastical story.

They reeked of rum and sweat. Their clothes were dirty and torn, as if there weren't enough to go around. They shoved one another roughly as they climbed aboard, shouting, more grunts than words. Zander, Yarrow, and Theo were already on their knees, their hands up, but they were each shoved to the ground anyway and quickly disarmed. Ace's cutlass was taken, but tentative relief snaked through Zander when they failed to notice his inner pockets or check his boots.

The pirates spread across The Valerian like rats looking for cheese, and Zander winced when he heard their fruitless search turn to wanton destruction, the frustrated men breaking anything they could find.

Zander heard more than a few English accents among the crew, including one from the captain, who stood at the helm of his vessel, shouting orders for the captives to be brought aboard. The ship was close enough Zander could see the captain clearly. His face was marked by deep wrinkles that resembled the grooves ocean waves sometimes carved in the sand. They snaked across his skin, which was bright red and blotchy. His eyes were narrowed as he grimaced at the damaged sloop, assessing it. He wore fine clothes, a stark contrast to his men.

A hand roughly grabbed Zander by the elbow, hauling him up from where he knelt on deck. "You heard 'im," said the sailor, who had a thick Irish accent and a mess of tangled red hair. Ace's blade already hung from his belt.

Zander heard Theo cry out in pain as a scrawny pirate with a length of canvas tied around his head in a makeshift eyepatch grabbed him by his injured arm, pulling him up to stand.

Yarrow stood automatically at the sound of Theo's cry, earning a punch to the head from a large man with wild blonde curls. Zander stifled the urge to scream as Yarrow's body fell limp to the ground, unconscious. He saw a flash of panic in Theo's eyes as he watched his lover fall, but he showed no other reaction as the men marched him away, Zander and the Irishman following in their wake. The large pirate who'd hit Yarrow stooped down and hauled them up, throwing them over his shoulder like a sack of flour.

Upon boarding the ship, the captives were brought before the captain. Theo and Zander were forced to kneel by their captors; Yarrow was dropped roughly to the ground at his feet. One of the longboats was still at The Valerian, the men remaining likely still looking for loot, of which they would find precious little.

The captain stood in front of them, his hands on his hips, his feet spread apart and his pelvis thrust forward. He looked down his nose at them silently for a few moments before speaking.

"It appears someone got to you 'fore us," he said. "So, I'm left with only you three as a reward. Convince me why I should keep you aboard my ship when I could kill you and be rid of three extra mouths to feed."

Theo spoke right away, mercifully saving Zander from responding.

"I'm an expert marksman, and my previous vessel's boatswain," he said. He nodded his head toward Zander. "He's a sailmaker. That one there,"—he angled his head toward Yarrow's unconscious body without looking at them—"makes the best rum punch you've ever tasted in your life. But between you and me, Captain, both of them are a right pain in the ass."

The captain looked dubious, his eyes dancing between Zander and Theo as he assessed them both. "A sailmaker we can use," he said. "And the small fellow can scrub decks as well as anyone, I'm sure." A rumble of quiet laughter sounded behind him from a few crew members, who were eyeing Yarrow with a mixture of amusement and malice that made Zander's skin crawl. "As for you," he said, his gaze returning to Theo. "You expect me to believe you're an expert marksman?"

Theo flashed a smile that reminded Zander of a snarling dog. "Give me back my pistol and I'll prove it to you," he said.

"Ha!" the captain scoffed, then gestured to two men on his right. "Put this one in the brig for a few days," he said. His voice turned to a low growl. "Leave some scars on 'im first. Stuff the other two in the orlop and give them something to do." He turned on his heel abruptly and walked away.

A large man with a snake tattoo covering one arm shoved Theo in the direction of the brig, a vicious smile on his face. Another man followed, carrying Yarrow's satchel in one hand and twirling a small blade in the other.

Before he disappeared below deck, Theo looked back at Zander, a meaningful look in his eyes.

Zander knew what the look meant. *Survive*, it said. *Both of you, survive.*

Zander carefully picked up Yarrow's body, draping his arms under their back and knees, and headed below deck to the orlop. He would survive, and he would get them out of this mess, and they would find Ace if it was the last thing he did.

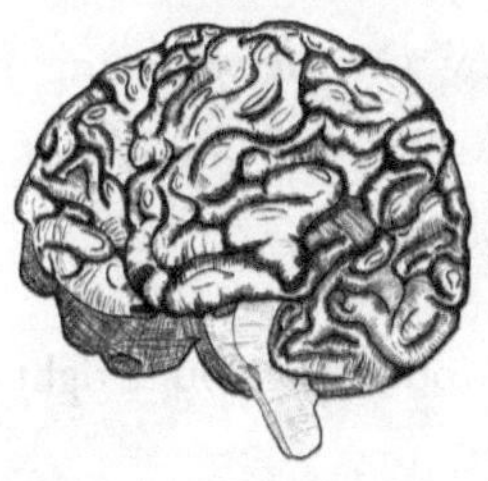

Once, he was in between. On one side of the liminal space in which he existed was the world beyond forms, where it seemed that only moments ago, he'd been whispering soft promises to his love. On the other side was a world with which he was familiar, but within which he did not, at present, belong.

For she had been swept away again on the tides of the universe, and this time, they did not let him follow. This was *her* lesson. But he slipped in between anyway, and he stayed with her.

She lived a lonely life, devoid of the warmth she deserved. She had no one to which she could turn, no one to talk to who truly understood her. Sometimes she would cry out to him, and he would throw himself against the barrier between their worlds, trying to reach her. And though she could not see nor hear him, his thrashing against the insidious wall that separated them seemed to calm her down.

She began to believe, deep within her soul, that someone was coming to save her. She didn't realize he was already there.

When she talked out loud to herself, he talked back. They carried on conversations like this quite often, and even though her ears couldn't hear what he said, he found ways to whisper to her that went deeper. Eventually, she knew what he was going to say before he said it. Sometimes she would stop in the middle of a sentence and laugh, anticipating what he would say.

"I know, I know," she would say. "You're right."

She called him her "imaginary therapist." She wondered at times if she was mentally unstable, carrying on conversations with someone who didn't exist. The strange thing was, she felt more heard by the fictional character in her head than she ever had from a real person.

Sometimes, she would talk to him in her head, and he would talk back. They'd run through her anxieties together while she sat listening to a lecture, and he would calm her down. She'd tell him jokes while she did the dishes, and she imagined him laughing and telling her how funny she was. And when she scolded herself for being pathetic, telling jokes to a fake person inside her head, he would tell her she had been many things in their lives, but she had never been pathetic.

And when she laid in bed at night and cried, wondering where her true love was, wondering why he hadn't saved her, he tried to call out to her from the space between worlds.

I'm here, he would say. *I'm right here. Hold on.*

Eventually, his words would sink in, and she would fall asleep. The next day she would wake with renewed hope that her life would someday be filled with love.

But years went by, and no love came. Hope, like a balloon, drifted higher and higher until it ran out of air, and came drifting down.

No one ever came to save her. No grand love unfolded before her like a stage upon which she could dance. And eventually, years of loneliness and rejection made her fold in upon herself and give up.

In the last years of her life, a faint presence kept her company. A voice without sound, a shoulder without substance, a kiss without breath. And she grew comfortable with what she perceived to be her perpetual instability—perhaps, the reason no one ever gave her the love she desired.

But one day, when her body was weary and old, he found the barrier between them growing thinner. It thinned until he could push his way through, reaching across to take her hand.

And then he saved her.

When she awoke on the other side, she found the love she'd always dreamed of, waiting.

14

Zander was in a state of hyper alertness as he scrubbed the orlop deck on the strange new pirate ship. Yarrow lay nearby on a spare piece of canvas he'd found, still unconscious. He registered every breath they took, heard it even over the sounds of Theo being beaten just over their heads. They'd brought him to the gunner deck, where a small cell lay in one corner. Zander passed by on his way to the orlop just in time to see the man with the snake tattoo throw the first punch.

His heart beat wildly in anger and fear. Adrenaline coursed through his body, begging him to move, to do anything at all. But he was hopelessly, infuriatingly stuck.

The orlop of the new ship was much larger than The Valerian's tiny storage deck, as he'd expected, but it was not well looked after. Thick layers of grime coated the corners of the deck, and some of the wood seemed to be rotting away. It was a maze of crates and barrels, some of them seemingly empty, and others that smelled as if they were filled with rotten fruit, or dead mice. A thick, musty smell overwhelmed him and made him sick to his stomach. The man guarding them either didn't notice or didn't mind it in his seat near the stairs.

A sharp intake of breath alerted Zander to Yarrow's consciousness. He made his way to them quickly and quietly, mindful of the guard, whose eyes had drifted closed a few minutes prior. He put his finger to his lips when Yarrow opened their eyes, his other hand cradling their head comfortingly.

"Welcome back," he whispered. "Don't sit up yet. You got a nasty knock to the head."

Yarrow's blue eyes darted back and forth, silently taking in their surroundings. After a few moments, they carefully lifted themselves onto their elbows.

"How long have I been out?" they said, their voice soft.

"Not quite an hour. How do you feel?"

Yarrow's hand trailed to the back of their head, and they winced as they touched the point of impact. Their short blonde hair stuck up in odd places, parts of it barely matted from blood.

Zander held out his arm and Yarrow gripped it, pulling themselves fully upright.

"Where is Theo?"

"In the brig. I heard the men talking when we came down here. We're sailing to Cadiz."

Yarrow's eyes grew sharper. "Then we're headed in the right direction."

Zander nodded. They were sailing away from Porto and Abilio's aid, but they were headed in the direction of Ace. Cadiz was on the way to Gibraltar, and past the strait was a clear shot to the port of Malaga, just South of where Ace was being held. It was unlikely the pirates planned on crossing the strait, which would be teeming with Royal Navy ships. That meant they needed to get off this ship in Cadiz somehow and travel overland to Ace.

"Do you have anything of use?" Yarrow asked.

Zander patted his boot. "They didn't check these, nor my inner pockets. I have my daggers, flint and steel, and Ace's compass."

"The satchel?"

"I saw them carry it to the brig when they took Theo. It's probably been ransacked by now."

Yarrow nodded. "Likely so. Anything promising down here?"

"Not really," Zander admitted. "There's much to explore, though."

Yarrow nodded resolutely. "Much to explore, indeed. Take care, love. I'm going to do some prospecting of my own."

Before Zander could object to being left alone in the damp, smelly dungeon of the orlop, Yarrow hollered to the pirate meant to be guarding them.

"Oy!" they said. The man's eyes shot open. "Don't suppose you have a surgeon on board, do you? I believe I would benefit from a looking over." Yarrow gestured to the wound on the back of their head, pasting a smile on their face Zander had never seen them wear before. It was innocent, almost... dainty.

The pirate at the stairs grunted and stood, gesturing for Yarrow to follow him. Yarrow made a show of standing up slowly, groaning slightly with each step they took.

"You," the man said, pointing to Zander, "stay here and don't fucking break anything. I've gotta take a leak."

Zander nodded and watched them disappear upstairs, wondering what in this disgusting mess he could possibly worsen. When they were out of sight, he rushed to the stairway and looked up to ensure no one was coming, then began to frantically search the orlop.

The adrenaline still coursing through Zander's body seemed to rise to the surface, thrilled to have a purpose other than clearing grime from the rotting floorboards. His fingers shook as he opened crates and peered inside barrels, his ears listening for the sounds of the wooden stairs creaking. He gagged as he found the source of a particularly sour smell, a barrel filled with oranges covered in a thick layer of green mold. Fruit flies emerged in a small cloud as he lifted the lid, then quickly replaced it, his arm covering his mouth as he struggled to hold on to the contents of his stomach.

He moved on, picking up a pile of canvas scraps atop a nearby chest and tossing them aside to open it. As the scraps fell to the ground, Zander heard a *clunk* that gave him pause. Picking up a bit of material, he grinned at what lay beneath: a needle made of thick bone, about as long as the distance from his wrist to his fingertips and curved in a semicircle. A sailmaker's needle.

Heavy footsteps sounded on the stairs. Zander reached for a scrap of canvas and wrapped it tightly around the needle, shoving it inside his boot with his dagger. When the pirate meant to guard him returned, he was already on his knees, scrubbing more grime.

***

Zander scrubbed the orlop until the pirates summoned him to the main deck. When he emerged, the smell of the sea rushed over him, and his knees almost buckled in relief. He felt as if he hadn't breathed real air in hours.

Second only to the smell of saltwater was the smell of cooking food. His stomach grumbled loudly. When was the last time he'd eaten? The sun was low on the horizon. It must have been quite a while ago.

Someone bumped roughly into him, nearly knocking him over.

"Watch it, scrub," came a rough voice. Zander looked up to see a pirate looming over him, his long hair in locs. He snarled at Zander as he walked by, a small group of pirates trailing behind him. Zander tried to keep the surprise off his face at seeing Yarrow among the group, acting chummy with a sailor whose head was shaved close to the skin, revealing a long, deep scar across his skull.

"Yah, watch it," Yarrow told him roughly. Zander watched the group pass, smirking to himself when Yarrow turned and winked at him.

"Grub," said his guard, jutting his chin in the direction of a line of men waiting to approach a large pot that'd been brought from the galley. The smell grew stronger as he approached. Normally, it would not have been an appealing smell—something of a mix between pickled herring and burnt beans—but he was hungry enough that it made his mouth water.

Zander found what appeared to be the end of the line, just behind a short, squat man wearing a leather cap. His eyes scanned the deck, noticing the sailors who stormed The Valerian alongside dozens of new faces. The red headed sailor who now wore Ace's blade at his hip was eating from a wooden bowl a few paces away. He gave Zander a sour look upon noticing his gaze and spat on the ground at his feet threateningly. Zander looked away.

"Move," said a deep voice behind him before a pair of hands pushed him to the side, knocking him to the ground. Zander looked up to see a skinny man with stringy brown hair and pale skin leering over him. The two pirates with him laughed as they followed him to Zander's place in line.

Zander took a deep breath as he stood and silently took his place behind them, his hands clenched into fists.

He had his place in line taken three more times before he finally got food. It was a thick stew of questionable color and uncertain ingredients, scraped from the bottom of a giant pot. A hard piece of bread was shoved into the wooden bowl, jutting out from the measly portion at a sharp angle, unmoving.

Zander carried his bowl to the far reaches of the main deck, away from the crowds of men. He guessed there was a mess area below deck for eating, but he preferred to stay in the cold, crisp air as long as he could.

He tucked the bread into his jacket, unsure of whether Theo would be fed in the brig or not, and brought the bowl to his mouth. The sludge advanced slowly from the bottom of the dish to his mouth, and despite his hunger, he struggled to swallow it. He thought of George and his clever ways of stretching ingredients and sent a silent prayer of safety his way.

He took a second gulp of his stew before a hand swatted the bowl from his grip, spilling most of the thick sludge down the front of his clothes.

The redhead with Ace's blade laughed loudly, clutching his stomach like a child who'd played a particularly funny trick. A few men on deck chuckled at the scene.

"Better pick that up," he said. "And hurry. Captain wants you in the brig overnight."

Zander frowned but kept his lips sealed. The brig would do fine. He was sick of these goddamn pirates.

When Zander arrived below deck to be locked away in the brig, he found Theo laying atop a pile of straw tucked into the corner like a makeshift bed, his uninjured arm draped over his eyes. The pirate who escorted him downstairs unlocked the creaking door and shoved him inside, locking it behind him and quickly turning to go. He nodded toward the pirate keeping watch over Theo and pulled a pipe from his pocket, gesturing. The guard nodded and stood, following him out to the main deck and leaving Theo and Zander alone.

Theo raised his arm, peeking from beneath his elbow at Zander.

"Fancy seeing you here," he said.

Zander let out a sharp breath. Theo was in awful shape, bruises and gashes covering his face, his shirt soaked through with blood where his shoulder injury reopened. His left eye was so swollen, it was a wonder he could open it.

"Theo," Zander breathed, walking to kneel next to him. Theo made to sit up, and Zander offered his arm to help. Once he was upright, Zander took his hand and squeezed, a silent apology.

Theo smiled slightly at him. "I'm alright, mate. Been worse."

Zander offered him the bread from his pocket and Theo took it grate-fully, tearing off a small bite with his hands.

"We're sailing to Cadiz," Zander said.

Theo nodded, making a noise through the bread in his mouth that indicated he already knew.

They sat in silence for several minutes, Theo chewing and Zander slowly spiraling into the depths of despair and anxiety. Eventually, they heard Yarrow's voice approaching.

"Next time, next time!" they said. "I'll make you the best rum punch you've ever tasted. Tomorrow. That's a promise."

They were ushered into the room by two pirates who seemed less like guards than fans, trailing behind Yarrow good-naturedly and then locking them in the brig with an air of apology, as if they were em-barrassed at the inconvenience they were causing. Yarrow waved them off, yawning dramatically and making a big show of sitting as far away from Theo and Zander as possible. They waved goodbye to their new friends, who disappeared above deck and into the cacophony of what sounded like brawling.

Their guard returned a moment later and took up his position by the door, putting up his feet and drinking deeply from a flask.

It took over an hour for the guard to drink himself to sleep, in which time Zander and his friends struggled to remain awake, desperate to talk to one another. The noise above deck was only beginning to die down when they had their chance.

Once they were satisfied the guard slept soundly, Yarrow pulled them-selves across the small space in the brig and clutched Theo's hands like a lifeline, bringing them to their lips and kissing each one of his fingers. They brought one hand to his face, gently caressing his wounds.

"Who did this to you, my love?" they whispered, their voice fierce, their tender gaze sharpening into hard lines. A dangerous promise lay in their eyes.

Theo leaned forward and pressed his forehead to Yarrow's. "In time, my fortune," he said.

The two stared into each other's eyes, communicating silently for several moments, before they turned to Zander. The three of them shared a moment of heavy silence before Zander spoke, softly, so as not to wake their guard.

"So, we'll abandon ship in Cadiz and make our way to Antequera."

Theo nodded. "Aye, seems like our only option." He looked to Yarrow to confirm, then said, "You two have any luck today?"

"Some," Zander said. "I was scrubbing the orlop most of the day, but it wasn't entirely fruitless." He nodded toward the satchel laying at the other side of the room, partially obscured by Theo's gun vest. "I suppose Yarrow's satchel has been picked clean by now."

"Aye, it has," Theo said, turning to lift the straw behind his back. Tucked beneath the top layer were the three grenadiers.

"How did you get those?" Zander asked, surprised relief rushing through him.

Theo produced a small metal pin seemingly out of nowhere. "Picked the lock," he said. "These pirates are idiots. They were too busy hitting me to remember the satchel, for one. Then they left me unguarded at dinnertime."

"That's good," Yarrow said. "They don't see us as a threat. After all, why would they?" They gave Theo a pointed look, smirking. "I, for example, am harmless—not good for much but making *rum punch*." Then they plunged their hand into their pocket, pulling it out to reveal a fat handful of coins they'd stolen from their new pirate friends.

Theo struggled to contain the laughter that bubbled out of him, his hand clutching his stomach as if it would keep the noise inside his body.

"You heard about the rum punch comment, then?" he said through his laughter.

Yarrow nodded, pocketing the coins again and leaning forward to give him a kiss. "You make it too easy, my love."

"Aye, well, it's been some time since you've gotten to play," Theo said. "So, we have coins and grenadiers. What else?"

Zander pulled the dagger from his left boot, careful to keep the sailmaker's needle in its place.

"One of you should take this," he said, offering the blade handle-first. "I have my other one, and a sailmaker's needle as well."

Yarrow nodded at Theo, who took the dagger and tucked it in the side of his own boot.

The three of them planned to lay low the next day, blending in, help-ing, finding supplies they could steal or weaknesses they could exploit for their escape. They just had to bide their time, to earn a bit of trust. By the end of the day tomorrow they'd be in Cadiz, and if they could only remain unwatched for a few moments, they could escape and begin the long overland journey to Antequera.

Zander slept fitfully that night, dreaming of Ace. A monster pulled her to the depths, a monster he couldn't see, and Zander couldn't swim fast enough to reach her.

15

Blending in proved much easier for Yarrow than for Zander.

He was doing his best to be helpful, industrious, invisible. But he seemed to have somehow lost his natural talent for invisibility over the past few months, a fact he was both proud of and frustrated by. These pirates were fucking assholes, and it took every ounce of willpower he had to keep himself from smashing the nearest sailor's face against the mast.

The ship was crowded, noisy, and stinking. At every turn waited the sweat-slicked face of some pirate ready with an insult or a slap. The conversations he overheard made him sick: tales of violence and licentiousness that made his stomach writhe in hatred, the men who told them daring him to challenge them when they saw the disgust on his face. Zander briefly wondered at the chances he'd joined the only good pirate crew in existence when he swam to Ace's sloop.

At least Zander's inability to blend in served as a distraction from Yarrow's work. They donned an air of harmless amiability, acting as lackey to the largest pirates here and there while simultaneously feigning ignorance about anything to do with sailing, and thus avoiding any real work. They flattered, they sneaked, they slipped out of sight into the infirmary or the crew's quarters, showing up minutes later to laugh at someone's joke while detaching the gun holster at their side and emptying their pistol of bullets.

Zander covered for them more than a few times, to his great embarrassment. Once, he spotted Yarrow slipping a flask from the pocket of the red-haired pirate who took Ace's cutlass, clearly pushing their luck now. He caught their eye, his brows furrowing in a manner that said, *Really? Do we need that?* They simply smiled back at him.

When Zander noticed the pirate begin to turn in Yarrow's direction, the flask still halfway out of their pocket, he panicked. He did the only thing he could think of and yelled loudly to get the pirate's attention.

"Hey!" he said, his voice coming out in an angry growl. The red-haired pirate stared at him incredulously as Yarrow slinked into the background and out of sight.

He narrowed his eyes at Zander, his hand resting menacingly on the handle of Ace's blade. Zander wished he could cut his fingers off to prevent him from touching it again.

"*What,*" he said sharply.

Zander said the first thing that came to his mind. "You've got bird shit on your head."

The pirate's face wrinkled in confusion. He stood and he walked away, his hand leaving the blade's handle to casually touch his head, testing. Zander sighed loudly, ignoring the snickers from those nearby.

The hours dragged on, and Zander remained the pirate crew's favorite new target. By late afternoon he had bruises forming on his arms, his face, his ribs. He was starving, having been barred by the captain from eating because of the mess he'd made on deck the night before when his food was knocked from his hands.

"Sorry about earlier, love," Yarrow whispered to him later on. It was nearly evening, and they were approaching Cadiz swiftly. They stood with their backs toward the men, each feigning interest in the horizon as they stood several paces away from one another.

Zander shook his head. "Don't worry about it. Seems you've had a productive day."

Yarrow nodded, giving Zander a careful sidelong glance.

"Are you alright? You've taken your fair share of shit today."

"I'm okay," Zander said, meeting their eyes as much as he could without fully turning his head. "How is Theo?"

"He's alright," Yarrow said. "He'll be alright." Then, seeing one of their new friends approaching, Yarrow loudly yelled something in French at him and walked away in a huff.

Zander stifled the urge to chuckle and looked at the horizon again. He hoped Theo could convince someone to let him out of the brig before they docked. If not, they'd have to sneak him above deck before making their escape.

Later, as they approached the narrow peninsula on the Spanish coast that was their destination, Theo emerged from below deck, his eyes squinting against the sun as it sank low in the sky. He gave Zander a quick nod, subtly patting the pocket of his jacket and the bulge beneath—one of the three grenadiers. Zander and Yarrow had been carrying theirs all day; he wondered how Yarrow's clothes hadn't gotten heavy enough to fall off by now, with all the things they'd com-mandeered since that morning.

The captain, whom Zander had seen very little of since their capture, was directing several men as they carried heavy-looking crates from his quarters onto deck. The men strained under the weight of the boxes, walking carefully under the threat of the captain to cut their ears off if they damaged the goods inside.

The shore loomed. Zander could see a swath of whitewashed buildings in the distance. A single, long wooden dock sat unused on the shore, allowing the large ship to make berth and open the gangway. There were no other ships, only a company of men and several carriages waiting on the beach. Zander could see a rough path on which the carriages had traveled, leading up over rolling hills, largely bare of trees. In one spot, large boulders broke up the beach, leading away from the water and providing the only potential cover for their escape.

Zander thanked his lucky stars it was nearing evening, providing them the additional cover of darkness in the relatively open plain beyond the shore.

He was veering toward the port side of the ship, where Yarrow stood. Theo was making his way there as well, casually drifting behind a thick crowd of sailors, when the captain called out.

"You there!"

Zander didn't turn around, though he knew somehow the call was di-rected toward him. A hand gripped his shoulder, turning him roughly around to face the captain, who was pointing at him.

"You," he said again, "and your friends. Seems I've a use for you after all. You'll carry these crates to shore when we dock and bring back the payment. Chuckles here will go with you." He gestured to a large man wearing a menacing snarl on his pockmarked face, who Zander presumed to be Chuckles.

Zander nodded mutely and walked forward. Theo and Yarrow approached as well, careful not to look at one another. Zander could almost feel the relief of the men who'd carried the crates out of the captain's quarters at not having to carry them any further. Whether that was because of their weight or the several dozen armed men waiting for them on shore as they docked was unclear.

As they released the gangway, the armed men formed a path leading to a central carriage, where a man waited next to a single wooden chest. Zander couldn't help but feel expendable as he leaned down and took one side of a crate across from Yarrow; Theo and Chuckles picked up the other. He walked sideways down the gangway, on to the dock, and toward the two lines of guns pointed at them, using every modicum of self-control he had.

His eyes scanned the landscape as he walked. This shouldn't be happening. They should be escaping right now. The entire crew stood motionless on the ship, watching this scene play out. They could be climbing down the ratlines on the other side of the ship, unnoticed, to run for the rocky shore. Instead, every set of eyes on land and sea were glued to them as they carried god-knows-what at gunpoint through a tunnel of fierce-looking men.

When they reached the end of the line, the man nodded silently toward the ground, indicating they should set the crates down in the sand. Instantly, they were surrounded by people as the crates were pried open and the insides inspected. Once he was seemingly satisfied with the contents, the man gestured for the lids to be closed again and the swarm of men parted, allowing Theo and Zander to lift a chest containing payment and carry it back up the dock, to the gangway, and onto the ship.

The sun was just above the horizon now, threatening to set on the day and on their chance of escape. All eyes remained glued to Zander and Theo as they walked on deck and brought the chest directly to the captain's quarters. He looked around briefly when they entered. It was a disgustingly extravagant room.

When they emerged, the gangway was being removed, and the pirates eagerly prepared to set sail under the captain's promise to break out a new barrel of rum once they were on open water.

Zander's body threatened to crumble under his emotions, frustration begging to brim over in the form of tears, or a guttural scream. He held it inside, scanning the ship for any sign of a chance to bail without being noticed. Yarrow had been pulled aside by a group of jollier-than-normal pirates jeering about that rum punch they promised, one of their arms around Yarrow's neck in a firm but friendly grip. Theo was being prodded back toward the brig—he protested that he needed to piss before he went, his eyes scanning the ship for an escape, but to no avail.

They were sailing south. *South.* The worst direction they could possibly go, away from Ace, away from Spain, across open water and toward another continent entirely. Zander stood, frozen. He was unsure of how long he simply stared at the land shrinking in the distance before he was making his way to a deserted corner of the forecastle. He needed to do something, anything, *now*.

Reaching the corner, he tore off his jacket and hung it on one shoulder, using it to shield his hands as he dug the grenadier and the flint and steel from his pockets. His hands shook as he positioned the grenadier between his boots, bending to strike the flint against steel, willing the sparks to catch on the exposed fuse.

His logic screamed at him to stop what he was doing and think for a moment. He'd never handled an explosive before, not in this life. He would likely kill himself doing this, or kill his friends, or blow off his hand at the very least. He wasn't Theo the expert marksman, or Yarrow the inventor, or Ace the fierce pirate captain.

But if there's one thing that's true about Z, it is the power of his persistence. This would not be the first nor the last time he surprised himself with his tendency to find a way when there seemed to be none.

And right now, the woman he loved was in trouble. In fact, she may already be dead. And he was out of options. It was with a sudden rush of excruciating clarity that he realized the simple choice that lay before him. He would make this ship turn around, and he would find Ace, or he would die.

Perhaps, he needed to die... or at least appear to.

The fuse lit. Zander straightened, suddenly and painfully aware of the danger he was in. His coat fell from his shoulder, landing on the ground nearby. He held the hissing explosive before him.

Now what?

Zander rushed across the forecastle and toward the other side of the ship, as far from Yarrow as he could manage and away from the general area of the brig. He stayed as close as he could to the railing, holding the lit bomb awkwardly at his side, trying to obscure it from view as he rushed past pirates who looked after him in confusion, their nostrils flaring. He counted under his breath, praying Yarrow was right about their estimate of the time they'd have between lighting the fuse and the modest explosion—about thirty seconds.

"Fifteen, sixteen, seventeen…" He ran into the redheaded sailor with Ace's knife, knocking him off balance, and continued to rush onward, his eyes glued in front of him. He started leaping over obstacles, stepping on feet in his haste. "Twenty one, twenty two…"

He made it to the upper deck, climbed atop the railing, and turned around to look at the crowd of pirates before him. Yarrow's gaze was fixed on him from the other side of the ship, their eyes wide in shock. A few of the pirates stopped to notice him. The sparks from the fuse burned his hand, and as he brought the grenadier in front of him to see the fuse nearly burnt to its end, realization dawned on several men nearby and they sprinted away from the now-visible flare.

Zander took one deep breath, knowing it may be his last, and looked out at the crowd of men he'd grown to hate in so little a time.

"You're all a bunch of fucking assholes," he said, and dropped the bomb on deck just as the fuse burnt down to the gunpowder inside.

By some miraculous stroke of luck, Zander's feet slipped on the damp railing just as the grenadier exploded. He had meant to say more—that he hated their guts, that he would curse them from beyond the grave so their socks would always be wet and their ale always turn sour, but he slipped before he could say them, the words swallowed in a gasp as he fell backward at just the right moment, avoiding the impact of the blast.

He hit the water feet first, his body straightening into an arrow on instinct as he fell (he did a lot of falling into the water his first month on The Valerian). He sunk below the depths, the murky darkness surrounding him in a cold embrace.

He sank, his arms unfurling from his chest and opening wide to the water. He surrendered to it, and the sea cradled him like a mother holding her child.

And then he heard it. A small voice, whispering in a language he didn't know, a sound he heard more with his chest than his ears. Time seemed to slow as the water whispered to him, wrapping around his heart in a familiar tug. He knew then that Ace was alive, as sure as he knew the sky was blue. And he was going to find her.

He swam, propelling himself upward until he reached the hull of the ship. He emerged near the stern, careful not to gasp too loudly for air, and grabbed for a straggling rope just before it drifted out of reach. He clung to the rotting ratline and waited. His companions were likely scanning the water for signs of his body, but in the growing darkness they would quickly give him up for dead and move on—which is just what he wanted.

The ship was drifting steadily south, moving slowly in the light breeze. Still, Zander's legs threatened to flail behind him as he clung to the rope. He reached for a nearby ratline, this one still securely attached. His arm strained, his muscles stretching, freezing water splashing in his face. His fingers finally found purchase, and with great effort he pulled himself forward against the force of the water, tucking his arm inside the interconnected ropes, hoisting himself out of the water, and holding on for dear life.

He wiggled his right foot, which rested precariously on a shot plug jutting from the hull, feeling his remaining dagger still tucked securely in his right boot. His other boot jutted awkwardly out to the side, the measure of canvas and the needle inside pressed against his heel.

The darkness deepened with every breath. He just needed to hold on for a little while longer, and then he was going to turn this goddamned ship around.

16

Zander clung to the side of the ship for nearly an hour, his limbs tucked behind sections of rigging to take the pressure off his aching muscles. The sounds of a celebration drifted from the upper deck, laughter mixing with the clash of swords and merry singing.

Zander wanted to kill them all.

He was still wet, for despite the bit of air rushing past him as the ship slowly moved across the water, it splashed high enough to soak him again before he dried. He was freezing, every muscle in his body tensed to avoid falling, his right arm and shoulder numb from the rope cutting off his circulation.

For the first thirty minutes he clung to the rope, his ears strained to hear a gunshot, a splash, something indicating he'd doomed his friends to the depths in his haste to escape the ship. He hoped their feigned hatred of him gave them some protection, yet he ruminated on their possible deaths anyway, anxious and filled with preemptive rage.

By the time he decided to move, he wasn't sure if his ears had simply grown accustomed to the noise, or if it really was getting quieter above deck. Deciding he couldn't hold on any longer without overfatiguing his muscles, he began to climb.

He went slowly, testing each rope he clung to, his ears straining to hear any noise, his muscles protesting against his own weight. When he reached the top of the stern and peered through the gaps in the railing, he saw a single pirate standing lazily at the helm, their arm draped over it and their chin resting atop their forearm. There was a large hole in the ground near his feet where Zander's grenade had landed, the char marks around it wet with seawater to prevent a fire from spreading. Zander held his breath as he pulled himself up and over the railing, wincing at every sound he made, until his feet landed on solid wood.

He didn't allow his tensed muscles to relax, didn't give himself time to take a breath. He pulled the dagger from his boot, took three great strides toward the pirate, and reached his arm around to cover his mouth as he slit his throat. He then lowered the man's body gently to the ground.

He was marginally aware of his body starting to shake. A mix of rage and adrenaline rushed through him, screaming for him to move, to run, to kill the rest of them before he collapsed of exhaustion. He forced himself to move slowly instead, crouching behind the helm and looking down at the main deck.

It was strangely quiet for the hour, the sounds of celebration from earlier now absent. About a dozen men lay sleeping on the main deck, a normal occurrence given the number of pirates on board and the modest size of their sleeping quarters. A few were still awake at the forecastle, playing a game involving dice. Zander could tell from their slurred speech they were all quite drunk.

He pulled off his wet, sloshing boots, then his socks. He took the sail-maker's hook from its canvas wrap and held it firmly in his left hand, the dagger still clutched in his right. He crept quietly down the stairs from the upper deck. He scanned the bodies of the sleeping pirates, then continued, crouching low as he approached the forecastle.

When he reached the bottom of the stairs, he took a deep breath and then sprinted up, taking the five men playing dice by surprise.

The first man had his back to him. Zander buried his dagger in his side as he jabbed the sailmaker's needle into the neck of the man on his left, then pulled it swiftly free. A man to his right stood and reached for his weapon, but Zander pulled his dagger free and swung, the blade slicing across the man's throat before he threw it straight ahead, burying it in the eye of a fourth man.

One pirate remained, a small fellow Zander had once overheard bragging about abducting a girl from her home and forcing her onto the ship. He blinked up at Zander, confusion, fear, and strong drink clouding his eyes.

Zander reached down and wrapped his hand around the man's neck, lifting him with strength he didn't know he had, and hurled him roughly over the edge of the ship.

He stood there for a moment, panting, his left fist coated in blood where he'd torn the sailmaker's needle through the second man's throat. He pulled his dagger free from the eye of the fourth man and turned around just as the red-headed sailor reached the stairs, having woken from his slumber on deck.

Zander was renewed by rage at the sight of Ace's blade in the man's hand, and he bent over, propelling himself into his adversary's legs. The pirate fell forward onto his stomach, Ace's blade slipping from his grasp. He reached for it, but Zander turned and thrust his dagger into the center of his hand, pinning it to the deck. He screamed. Zander picked up the cutlass and silenced him with a hard knock to the back of the head.

That was much louder than I planned, Zander thought, bracing himself to turn around and see the rest of the pirates waking. He was surprised to see all except one of them still asleep. The large pirate with the snake tattoo on one arm was awake, and he was charging at him, a terrifying grimace on his face.

Zander readied himself, but the man stopped suddenly, his eyes wide. He plummeted forward like a felled tree, revealing Yarrow, their hand still in position from throwing the knife now jutting from the back of his head.

Something between a laugh and a sob escaped Zander at the sight of Yarrow. He looked again at the rest of the pirates on deck, who slept on, no sign they'd heard the commotion aside from a few men sleepily rolling over or mumbling to themselves.

"What in the world's gotten into these ones?" Zander asked.

Yarrow smiled. "Rum punch," they said, pulling a couple of small, brown bottles Zander recognized as laudanum from their pocket.

The relief that rushed through Zander's body brought him to his knees, and he gave himself fully over to hysterics, his body shaking with maniacal laughter. When he looked up, Yarrow stood above him, a concerned look on their face. Zander sighed, wiping stray tears from his face, and took their hand when they offered it, standing.

"You think the three of us can turn this ship around?" he asked.

Yarrow scanned the deck. "We'll have to dispatch this lot," they said. "I'm quite sure the men downstairs will sleep soundly through the night—I tucked them in myself." Yarrow winked. "But we can't sail and keep our eyes on them at the same time."

Zander nodded once, then turned to retrieve his dagger from where it remained stuck in the Irishman's hand. He realized he still had the sailmaker's needle clutched tightly in his left fist. He dropped it and pulled the blade free with a sickening crunch, then slit the pirate's throat before he could wake from the pain. Then he and Yarrow walked carefully amidst the rows of sleeping men on deck, killing them one by one, a horrifying deed that Zander registered with vague, numb awareness.

They then headed to the brig. Yarrow informed Zander the man guarding Theo was likely the only one on board who didn't partake in the rum punch, opting to drink from his own flask instead. They crept carefully toward the entrance to the gunner deck, where they could hear Theo talking loudly in his telltale storytelling voice.

The guard was visible from beyond the doorway, leaning forward on his haunches, enraptured with whatever Theo was saying. Zander recognized the man's white-blonde hair and broad shoulders, but he hadn't interacted with him. As Zander and Yarrow crept closer, a noise came from below deck that sounded like voices. Zander looked at Yarrow, who pointed to indicate they would take care of the men downstairs while Zander dispatched the pirate guarding Theo.

Zander rushed onto the gunner deck, making a beeline for the guard.

"Mate!" Theo exclaimed, and the excitement in his voice made Zander pause for a moment to smile at him. The guard stood, and Zander raised his sword arm, but Theo cried out again.

"Wait!" he said, standing. He swung open the unlocked door to his cell and strode out, his hands held up in a conciliatory gesture.

The guard looked in confusion from Theo to the brig, dumbfounded.

"Don't kill this one, mate," Theo said. "Me and Andrew are friends."

Andrew continued to stare, his mouth hanging open, clearly wondering how long the cell door had been unlocked.

"No hard feelings, mate," Theo said to Andrew. "We're going to leave. I'm going to have to tie you up, though. You know, appearances and all." He waved his hands in the air, shrugging apologetically.

Andrew looked from Theo to Zander and his shoulders dropped, his decision made.

"Naw," he said, and charged at Zander, his hand moving to draw his sword.

One moment he was charging, and the next he was on the ground. Theo stood above him, Zander's second dagger gripped in his first, the handle of which he'd used to hit him on the back of the head. Theo looked down at Andrew's unconscious body with a look of profound disappointment.

"I thought we were friends," he said.

Yarrow, who'd appeared in the doorway sometime during the exchange, clucked their tongue and gave Theo a sympathetic look. "We can still tie him up, dear. No need to kill him."

Theo turned fully toward Zander and scanned him from head to toe. His shoulders dropped in relief, and he walked forward, his arms out for a hug.

"You're not dead," he said, his arms wrapping tightly around Zander's shoulders. Zander hugged him back, grateful they were all alive.

"I told you he was alive," Yarrow said.

"Yes, well," Theo said, pulling away. "Sometimes you're a damn liar, aren't you?"

This made the three of them laugh, the tension breaking like a sheet of glass. Theo's laughter released several waiting tears from his eyes, and he winced as he wiped them from his bruised face.

"I'm glad you're alright," he said. He offered Zander's dagger to him.

Zander didn't know what to say. He nodded, clapping his hand gently on Theo's good shoulder with one hand and taking the dagger with the other.

"You okay to sail?" he asked Theo.

"I'm always okay to sail," Theo answered.

"And below deck?" Zander said, looking to Yarrow.

"All's quiet," Yarrow said. "Let's turn this bitch around."

Sailing a large ship was an entirely different beast than sailing The Valerian. The sloop was fast, versatile, and didn't require many hands. The ship was a slow, uncooperative thing. Yarrow manned the helm. They held Ace's compass; Zander had found his jacket right where he left it, the contents of the pockets untouched. Zander and Theo painstakingly tended to the sails.

Zander wished he had six more hands to make the work easier. Instead, he and Theo rushed back and forth, each doing the work of three men. Theo stayed on deck, not able to climb the rigging due to his arm. Zander stayed above ground, leaping from one part of the rigging to another like an ape, coordinating his movements with Theo on the ground as they adjusted the sails, pouring every ounce of their will into making the ship turn 'round and head Northeast.

Zander gave little thought to rest. His eyes were on his hands, on Theo, on Yarrow, on the stars above their heads that pointed his way home. He wouldn't sleep until he found her if that's what it took.

A part of him knew he was pushing his body to its limits. But his muscles had stopped aching soon after boarding the pirate ship once more. His body was numb of all feeling, lithe and ready, as long as he didn't stop moving.

And below his still bare feet, the crew slept, the sounds of the ocean lapping against the hull filling their ears, fueling their drug-induced dreams.

They didn't head back to Cadiz. They veered farther east instead, aiming sloppily toward the Strait of Gibraltar. They wouldn't be able to sail across the strait—in addition to a greater naval presence, the winds in the strait were notoriously difficult to sail in.

They would end up somewhere on the Spanish shore just shy of the strait itself. Precision was not achievable with so many sails and so few sailors; all they needed to concern themselves with was finding a piece of shore they could make berth—or run aground, more likely—and run east.

When the sight of land appeared distantly on the darkened horizon, Zander's hands were aching. His clothes were finally dry, the wind having whipped the wet material against his skin for the past few hours. His boots, still drying, remained on deck. When they were satisfied with their trajectory toward a long stretch of shore that appeared abandoned, he climbed down from the rigging and donned his wool coat.

The three then wordlessly prepared themselves to abandon ship. As Theo and Yarrow began attaching long climbing ropes to the bow, Zander put his hand gently on Yarrow's shoulder.

"The captain," he said. "Did he have any of your rum punch?"

Yarrow nodded, smiling. "Plenty. He let me lead him into his room like a small child who'd stayed up past their bedtime."

Zander chuckled. "I'm going to sneak in and take a look around. I'll bind the door behind me." He picked up a spare piece of rope Yarrow and Theo weren't using. Yarrow nodded and turned away, and Zander headed to the captain's quarters, still barefoot.

Creeping inside, Zander allowed himself a more careful look at the opulent room. It was larger than Ace's quarters, decorated in garish reds and golds, as if the captain thought himself some sort of king. The captain himself was snoring loudly in his bed, draped atop a velvet blanket with his clothes still on. A familiar chest—the one he and Theo had carried inside only hours ago—sat at the foot of his bed.

Zander crept carefully forward and tested the lid—it was locked. He looked around, and when no key was found sitting on a table or hanging on a hook labeled "important keys," he tiptoed toward the captain. He carefully inspected his pockets—a pipe, a flask, an apple core, its sliminess making Zander shudder and toss it across the room like it meant to bite him.

Finally, he found a key inside an inner pocket of the captain's red coat. He slept soundly through the frisking.

The chest opened with a loud yawn, but still the captain slept. Inside was more gold than Zander had ever seen before, far more than the sum they'd taken from the dreaded merchant ship weeks ago. Zander quickly filled his pockets, then closed the chest and made to leave.

Something caught his eye before he reached the door. Sitting on a small table near the bed was a crystal about the size of a guava fruit. Its base was a thin rock in layers of black and brown. Towering atop it were small mountains of purple all clustered together, their tips dark, growing lighter the further down they went.

Smiling, Zander thought of Ace and her collection of beautiful things. He took the crystal and placed it in an inner pocket, where it would be safe.

Zander left the captain's quarters with significantly heavier pockets. Outside, he tied the rope tightly around the handles of the double doors leading to the captain's quarters, preventing them from being opened from the inside. The thought crossed his mind that he ought to have just killed him, but Zander had done enough killing for the day. His shoulders felt heavy with death.

He looked behind him—the shore loomed closer. Theo and Yarrow emerged from below deck, each fully outfitted with weapons and supplies. Theo's gun vest was filled with a new collection of stolen guns. Two pistols hung from the holsters at his belt, along with a sword. Yarrow carried their own sword, taken back from whichever pirate had it, along with a dagger, and their satchel, which was full with god-knows-what.

Theo was wiping his hands on a piece of cloth when they emerged. Blood stained the rag, but there were no wounds on Theo's hands—the blood was someone else's.

"Trouble?" Zander asked, looking pointedly at the rag.

Theo shook his head. "Just taking care of a problem."

One of Yarrow's eyebrows shot up. "He wasn't exactly a problem. He was asleep."

"He punched you and knocked you unconscious, my heart. Him continuing to breathe was a problem."

Zander smirked at the reluctant smile on Yarrow's face and walked past them to find his damp socks and boots. He accepted a spare pistol when Yarrow handed it to him, shoving it roughly in his outer pocket. Ace's cutlass hung from his hip, and he tucked his twin daggers back into his boots. He'd become accustomed to feeling them there.

Remembering the coins he'd taken, he split them roughly between him and his friends, and the three of them approached the bow of the ship.

They would run aground in roughly a minute. The ship wasn't exactly going fast, but it was moving quickly enough they'd have to brace themselves. Then they'd climb down the ropes Theo and Yarrow had fastened and run for their lives before the rest of the pirates streamed out onto deck. The plan was to head east, following the shore as closely as possible while maintaining cover, and get far enough from the pirates that they wouldn't bother pursuing them.

Zander looked at the sky, then checked Ace's compass. He had the faintest idea of where they were. He guessed it was around one o'clock in the morning. He was at least partially confident this plan would work, that they wouldn't be caught or killed in the midst of it. He was almost certain his body would continue to carry him forward once they were free from immediate danger.

He was only completely sure of one thing as the ship barreled toward the shore—he was going to find Ace again if it killed him.

But you and I both know that even death can't interrupt this particular love story.

Once, he was living his life in precisely the way he ought to. And it was 4:23 p.m.

4:23 pm was when he first saw her. It was at this very intersection, on this very patch of ground, just beneath the neon lights that signaled when to walk. He'd left work that day at exactly 4:06 pm, and upon seeing the telltale blue lights that meant the city enforcers were waiting on his normal route, he decided to take a different path home.

He was assigned to the tall, crystalline office building, its pale blue walls rising up in identical fashion to those surrounding it, upon finishing his education. His education had also been assigned to him, as had his area of study, his apartment, his roommates, and his path home from work.

But that day, he saw the blue lights of the city enforcers as they buzzed over the heads of the crowds, and something in him said,

No.

It was the first time he'd ever taken a different route home. Perhaps, his first authentic refusal.

He went in the opposite direction, taking a route home that would end up adding exactly 11 minutes to his walk. At some point during those 11 minutes—at this very intersection, on this very patch of ground—he felt a sudden compulsion to look to his right.

And there she was.

She marched forward, one of a dozen other people, all wearing the same shade of soft blue denim that made up his own three-piece suit. Black curls bounced beneath her hat, framing soft features. She had brown eyes, a long nose, and her face was devoid of expression, just like everyone around her. Just like him.

She crossed the road and walked right past him, going the other way. And for the first time in twenty-one years on his afternoon commute, he stopped and turned around. People jostled into him, murmuring confusedly at the sudden obstacle in the flow of foot traffic. He stood still as a statue, watching her walk away. He could have sworn that for a moment, she slowed and almost turned. Then she was swallowed by the crowd.

That was 34 days ago. It is 4:23 pm.

The crowd of people has grown accustomed to him by now. For 34 days, he has stood in this exact spot at 4:23 pm. Every day, he has stood still for exactly three minutes, slowly turning in place, looking. The crowd, whether because it consisted of the same people every day or because it held some sort of collective muscle memory, had adapted to his presence for those three minutes. He was now simply another given, an ordered and predictable part of a carefully planned existence. In fact, he thought, when he stopped this strange tradition, the crowd would probably still ebb around the place he stood, people tripping and jostling one another at his sudden absence.

Would that be what it was like when he died? His death nothing but a momentary lapse of function, quickly filled in and forgotten for mindless routine?

That may be so. But for 34 days, he'd held a slightly greater significance. Not a cog in a machine, but a pebble in the hinges.

His greatest pleasure had become standing in the flow of people at that intersection, like a stubborn boulder amidst a stream, unwilling to succumb to erosion, forcing them to deviate from the plan for mere seconds a day. And always, looking for her.

He was surprised he hadn't been caught. He'd heard of people being hauled off to re-education centers for less.

A nudge at the corner of his mind.

Turn right.

He turned, and there she was: to anyone else, simply another point in a sea of blue. But to him, she held an aura of distinction. Something in her skin called to him. The air around her swirled a different color, held a different weight. She was an enigma, and she called to him.

And then—it was as if the heavens parted and a chorus of fabled angels sang—she looked at him, and her mouth parted slightly, as if she had gasped.

It was only after she'd passed, her eyes never leaving his as she walked, that he realized he'd been smiling. His cheeks hurt.

The next day, a miracle: she appeared again. Again, she looked at him. This time, her lips stayed pressed together, but they crinkled in a way that could have been the beginnings of a smile. The day after that, her fingers lifted from their place at her side, wiggling at him in a covert wave. He longed to reach out and grab them. The next day, she smiled wide enough that he could see her teeth peeking from behind her lips—they were gangly and crooked, the most wonderful teeth he'd ever seen.

On the fifth day, he waited for her in tense anxiety, his plan set and ready to hatch.

As she approached him, her brow furrowed, perhaps noticing the strange way he stood, like a man readying himself to jump across a chasm. He angled his body suddenly, wedging himself between her and another man, who huffed loudly at the incursion, and became one with the current.

They walked side by side for several minutes, neither of them daring to do so much as look at the other. He had never walked in this direction before. The pale blue buildings that rose up around them had a slightly different hue, as if the sun hit them differently here.

They came to another intersection and stopped to wait their turn, and he looked at her. Her chest heaved up and down, and her cheeks pinked where before they were pale and colorless. She looked up at him, and he noticed she had a dimple on her right cheek when she smiled. It was soft and subtle, like it hadn't had much use.

And then he saw it—blue lights.

The city enforcers buzzed up ahead, the small black drones zipping back and forth across the street, scanning citizens. The blue lights made his head hurt when they scanned him, put sparkles in his eyes for the rest of the day, but unless he was out of place, he wouldn't be stopped.

And he was out of place.

He looked back at her, his heart beating frantically. Her eyes were wide, searching him, as if she were trying to memorize his face.

What he did next was the least orderly thing he would ever do. He leaned down, his face level with hers, their breath mingling for mere moments, and he kissed her. He kissed her like he would never see her again, for indeed he would not—not in this life, anyway.

When he broke away, he still tasted the salt of her tears on his lips. And when the city enforcers swooped down and carried him away to be re-educated, he didn't regret a single moment of the last 34 days, six minutes, and 24 seconds of his life.

17

Zander's bones rattled with the vibration of the ship running aground. Despite bracing themselves for impact, the three pirates were still thrown forward onto their knees. The ear-piercing crack of wood hitting stone indicated a rocky shore, and Zander grimaced, wondering how much damage they'd done to the hull.

Then he remembered he hated those assholes, and his concern vanished.

As soon as the ship came to a standstill, the three of them rappelled down the side. They hit the ground running, sprinting east across the wet sand, heading for a line of trees near the shore. Once they got just inside of the tree line, Zander stopped and looked back at the ship. In the black of night, he could make out the silhouettes of a few drunken pirates, their forms barely illuminated by the light of a lantern.

He spared them only a glance before he turned to follow his friends.

The three companions continued in an all-out sprint for what felt like ages, jumping over stones and fallen branches, putting as much distance as they could between themselves and the ship. The sea lay to their right, the waves a comforting roar. To their left were miles of rolling hills and trees, free from any sign of civilization.

Eventually, they slowed to a jog, and finally, they walked, their breathing loud and labored over the sound of their footsteps. They walked like that, without speaking, for over an hour. Zander was beginning to agonize over the slowly encroaching exhaustion he felt when the distinct shape of low stone walls came into view up ahead.

As they neared, Zander realized they were ruins. Eroded stone walls outlined the shape of what looked to have once been part of a town. Pieces of the walls made with discolored brick stood higher here and there, and one open square contained the remnants of around a dozen stone pillars. As they approached, Zander could barely make out the delicate lines and whorls that decorated their tops.

Theo sat roughly on the ground next to one of the pillars, throwing his arms out against the wall at his back as if he were lounging on a feather bed.

"We should rest here," Yarrow said, sitting atop a low stone wall. "I'll take first watch. We'll leave at dawn and keep heading east."

Zander opened his mouth to protest, meaning to take first watch instead, but Yarrow silenced him with a look. "*Rest*," they said, pointing at the ground like they were commanding a dog to lay down.

Ever the loyal companion, Zander obeyed. He was asleep almost as soon as his head hit the stone pillow.

***

Zander woke to the first rays of dawn peeking over the low stone wall above his head. The smell of smoke burned his nostrils. It took several seconds for him to remember where he was, and when he did, he shot up from his place on the ground and looked frantically around him.

Yarrow knelt nearby, smiling at him, a small fire growing in a stone circle near their feet.

"Morning," they said and held up a skewer of mushrooms in greeting.

"Morning," Zander said. "Why didn't you wake me to take watch?"

"There was no need," Yarrow said. "I couldn't have slept if I tried."

Zander looked over to find Theo still asleep on the ground, his cheek smashed against the stone and his hair covering his eyes. He gave Yarrow a look of concern, but they waved it off.

"Truly, I'm fine," they said. "Times like this, I find it works better for me to stay awake. Besides, I found breakfast." They positioned the skewer over the fire. Zander noticed several more resting on a nearby stone. "And I had enough time to gather plants to make a poultice for Theo's arm."

Zander stood slowly, stretching his aching muscles, then leaned down to take Yarrow's hand and squeeze it in silent thanks. They squeezed back, smiling briefly at him before turning their attention back to the fire.

After wandering off to relieve himself, Zander returned to find Theo awake and eating roasted mushrooms. Yarrow offered him one as he approached, and he took it gratefully. The three ate in silence, then Yarrow cleaned Theo's wounds and applied the poultice, wrapping his shoulder carefully in his used bandages. Then the three pirates gathered their things and continued to walk, sticking to the hard packed ground beyond the sand, the sea close enough to smell but far enough they could walk easily.

A chill hung in the air as they set out that soon dissipated as the sun drifted upward from the horizon. Spring was in full bloom on the Spanish coast, summer peeking its head, and Yarrow stopped occasionally to pick herbs or flowers that they carefully placed in their satchel.

They came upon a small fishing village shortly after setting out, where they purchased smoked fish to carry with them and refilled their flasks with fresh water. Theo spoke with the man they bought the food from and ascertained they'd landed about a five hour walk from Tarifa, a trade center that Theo seemed confident would supply more effective transportation than their aching feet. They thanked the man and continued east.

When Tarifa emerged on the horizon, the sun was high in the sky. Zander's feet ached, and his body was sore from clinging to the side of the pirate ship the day prior, but he didn't complain. He just took one heavy step after another, the image of golden eyes filling his head.

It had been three full days since he last saw Ace. And while he no longer worried she was dead, he couldn't stop running through the other sinister possibilities in his head. With one step, she was tied to a wall, her hands strung above her head. With the next step, she was beaten within an inch of her life. With yet another step, she had moved back in with her husband and agreed to start wearing dresses and serving tea.

Zander loosed a long sigh, kicking at a rock near his feet.

"Doing alright, mate?" Theo asked, slowing to walk beside him. Yarrow was up ahead, scraping sap from a tree.

Zander gave Theo a grateful smile. "I'm... anxious," he said, feeling the word wasn't altogether sincere. Really, he was scared. Over the last three days, his fear had lain dormant under layers of adrenaline and anxiety. Now, with hours of silence and nothing to do but walk and think, it was free to bubble to the surface, whispering all the most horrible possible outcomes to Zander.

Theo nodded and continued walking next to Zander for several minutes, looking at his shoes as if they held the answer to some unspoken question.

Finally, he said, "Did I ever tell you about Tortuga?"

Zander shook his head, mentally cataloging the locations of Theo's many stories in his head. "I don't think so," he said.

"It was about four years ago," Theo began. "We made port in Tortuga on the cusp of a storm. The crew found refuge in a lively tavern, where we all intended to drink ourselves under the table and ride out the rain. It was a good time at first. Ace was deep in her cup, singing, dancing, and generally making a ruckus. That is, until she noticed a barmaid with a black eye and rope marks on her wrists. Fatima was her name.

"Ace made a big show of flirting with her. Tipping her with gold coins, complimenting her, and eventually, calling her over to the corner of the tavern to sit on her lap. Away from the big ugly fellow who had been keeping a close eye on her all night, the one she skirted around to avoid being roughly grabbed at. Ace whispered in her ear. To anyone watching, it was nothing but a pirate staking her claim on her nightly entertainment. But Ace wasn't whispering sweet nothings in the maid's ear. She wasn't gripping the woman's waist as an act of dominance. Her hand hovered just above her hip, not touching her, as they conspired together.

"It was no surprise the woman wasn't there willingly. She was taken from Morocco and eventually ended up in Tortuga, working in that tavern, under the supervision of the ugly oaf, a former pirate himself from what I understood. Ace asked her to come with us, but she refused. Apparently, the man had her brother too. He was being held somewhere under lock and key. They kept him locked up in the evenings while she worked, to prevent her from running. And during the day they tied her up while he labored, to prevent him from running."

Theo's face twisted with disgust, and he spat on the ground, as if ridding his body of the very mention of the insidious manipulation.

"That's horrific," Zander said softly.

"Aye, it was," Theo agreed. "And all too common a sight. But Ace, she's never been one to look the other way. She waited until the rain started to die down and the crew was good and drunk. By the time night fell, she was sober. She told me and Yarrow to get the crew back to The Valerian, and to make sure the girl was with us. 'Come find me after,' she said, and settled into her seat, staring down the man across the tavern with all the vitriol she could muster.

"Well, he noticed the stare, and he didn't like it. As he walked over to Ace, Yarrow and I shuffling the crew out the door like a bunch of drunken geese, the barmaid hidden in their midst, it was like watching a rhinoceros approach a tiger. Big, lumbering, overly confident. And she just sat there, waiting, ready to strike. I lingered just long enough to watch him haul her across the tavern and into a room in the back, where he closed the door and latched it behind them.

"I was terrified, Mate. I'd seen Ace get into and out of plenty of sticky situations, but that was the first time I'd walked away and let her do it alone. Yarrow and I herded the crew to the ship at a run, and once we came in sight of the dock I put the barmaid's hand in Yarrow's, told her everything was going to be alright, and sprinted back to the tavern, convinced Ace was already dead. When I got there, I went around back, sneaking through the mud, my ears straining to hear any sign of Ace over the gentle patter of rain."

Theo tiptoed across the sandy ground in demonstration, his hand cupped at his ear.

"Then I heard a man yell, and Ace's voice hollered out, clear as a bell, 'FUCK YOU, YOU OVERGROWN GALLIWASP!' and a loud *WHAM!* followed, like someone had hit the floor. I burst in through the back door, guns blazing, ready to kill every fucker in the place, and you know what I found?"

Theo looked at Zander expectantly, having stopped in his tracks, his raised hands in the shape of phantom pistols.

"What?" Zander said, thoroughly engrossed in the story.

"I found Ace, in the center of a large room, her hands bound above her. She hung from the ceiling, the tips of her toes just barely scraping the floor. Blood ran down her face like she'd been hit, and at her feet lay the rhinoceros man, unconscious. She looked at me, one eye closed to keep the blood out, and smiled." Theo smiled widely in imitation of Ace. "'Right on time!' she said. 'Cut me down. I know where her brother is.'

"Mate, in the time it took me to usher the crew away and sprint back, Ace had goaded the awful man into telling her every horrible thing he'd ever done, including exactly where he was keeping Fatima's brother and where the key was to unlock the door. She was beat up, yes. But she didn't break. Every time his fist landed on Ace, it broke away a bit of his own resolve, a layer of inhibition, and Ace found out just what she wanted to know. And as soon as she knew it, she likened him to a fat lizard and hoisted her feet up off the ground, knocking him out with a well-placed kick to the head.

"And that's the story of the last time we ever docked in Tortuga, and our first ever trip to Morocco." Theo placed his hand on Zander's shoulder. "You see, mate, Ace very seldom walks into a situation without an escape plan. I'm willing to bet she's been steps ahead of Lord Sanz since the moment we spotted those sails on the horizon. We're well on our way. She'll be alright."

Zander smiled and reached up to place his hand atop Theo's. His eyes glistened with emotion he wasn't yet ready to express. "Thank you, Theo," he said softly. Theo nodded, and they continued on.

***

Tarifa was a sprawling mix of permanent buildings and large tents. An ancient stone castle stood like a watchman to the North, the Spanish flags positioned at its turrets a stark contrast to its dull grey facade. Vessels of all sizes, from rowboats to giant ships, were docked at the harbor. People of all shapes and colors mingled at the edge of the beach where locals and traveling traders offered their wares. Zander heard African dialects and various versions of English interspersed with Spanish, and his weary mind was tempted to get lost in the myriad of sounds, smells, and sights that confronted him at the busy trade port.

Zander spotted a woman selling clothing and stopped to buy a pair of socks to replace his still-damp ones. Theo acquired wrappings from another merchant for his injuries, and Yarrow traded some of the herbs they'd foraged for a small bottle of oil, which they made Zander rub on his blistering soles before he wrapped his feet and swapped his rancid socks for the new, dry pair. As he pulled on his boots, he noticed a small pile of leatherbound journals stacked nearby on an artisan's blanket. With Theo's attention focused elsewhere, he bought one small enough to fit in his coat's outer pocket. Once this was all over, he'd give it to Theo as a gift, so he could begin writing his book.

All that remained was to purchase food and passage to Malaga, the port that lay South of the Sanz estate, and Ace's old home. On a regular merchant ship rather than a pirate ship, the three would be able to disembark without drawing too much attention from potential spies for Sanz.

Zander was feeling refreshed, hopeful even, with dry feet that smelled like grass and a full stomach, as they turned their attention to the line of vessels at the shore.

"With as much gold as we have, we should be able to charter one of these to Malaga and get our girl," Theo said.

Yarrow nodded, pointing at a sailboat where a few men were unloading their wares. "That one looks promising," they said. "The crew is young, but they look experienced. I imagine they wouldn't be averse to leaving right away."

As Theo and Yarrow debated the merits of the sailboat against other nearby vessels, Zander's eye caught on a far-off ship he hadn't noticed before. He stood staring at it, the many people milling about crossing in and out of his line of sight, occasionally brushing against his black jacket. It was so far off he couldn't be sure, but it appeared to have black sails.

"What do you think, mate?" Theo asked.

Zander opened his mouth to reply, intending to tell them he didn't give a damn which boat they took as long as it sailed quickly, when a broad-shouldered man with blonde hair that was nearly white emerged from the crowd. Upon seeing them, Andrew's eyes widened in recognition.

He couldn't hear the pirate's voice over the crowd, but his lips curled into an unmistakable '*You!*' as he pointed at the three of them. That's when Zander noticed the dozen or so other pirates with him.

"Zander?" Theo said, snapping his fingers in front of Zander's face as if to wake him up. Zander looked at him, then back at the pirates, his eyes wide.

"Run!"

They took off into the crowd, the pirates screaming curses behind them. Zander dodged carts and donkeys, leapt over steaming cauldrons of food, and slipped between tents, mindful of Theo and Yarrow's presence like shadows as he ran. They moved further inland, zigzagging through the crowd in an attempt to lose the pirates, canvas tents and clouds of spices blocking their vision as they ran blindly away.

When they came to the edge of the crowd, Tarifa's commerce district flattened from tall tents and administrative buildings into squat houses and farmland.

"There!" Yarrow said, pointing ahead of them to a large stable.

They continued to run, and as they got closer, Zander looked behind him to see nearly a dozen pirates emerge from the crowd and look around, their weapons unsheathed.

"Go!" Yarrow said, pointing to Zander and Theo, then to their left and right, signaling for the men to split up and circle around the back of the property. Zander did so wordlessly, turning left and making a wide arc around the fenced property while Yarrow approached the man at the main gate, wailing loudly and speaking French.

While the bewildered man tried to calm down the seemingly hysterical person at his gate, Zander met Theo at the back of the stables. They nodded at one another silently, then slipped inside, where they knocked two young men on the back of the head and another across the face, leaving them unconscious on the straw-covered floor before securing three horses. Zander dropped a handful of gold coins on the ground near the front door as they bolted out of the stable toward Yarrow, who pushed the unsuspecting man to the side to save him from being trampled by his own livestock.

Then, like a vision from the pages of a storybook, Yarrow crouched, balancing on the balls of their feet, before jumping up and grabbing the reins of the horse Theo led beside his own, swinging themselves expertly into the saddle. The whole thing happened in a matter of moments, and Yarrow was spurring the horse forward before it even had time to slow down.

The three pirates rode past the open gate at a furious pace, veering North, away from the ocean. Zander looked back to see the pirates chasing them reach the edge of the fence surrounding the stable. They drew their weapons, but before they could shoot, Theo had turned himself around in his saddle. With the calm focus of a man standing at a shooting range rather than riding backward on a stolen horse, Theo drew the pistols from his vest one by one, ringing out seven shots in the direction of the pirates. One by one, seven pirates fell to the ground.

Theo shot until they were out of range, whereupon he holstered his pistols and turned himself back around on the horse like a trained acrobat. Zander marveled at him. His mouth hung open slightly as he beheld his two remarkable friends, riding proudly side by side against the glorious backdrop of rolling Spanish hills, like two gods among men. Theo, fully aware of the aesthetic appeal of he and his partner's many talents, looked sidelong at Zander and winked.

<h1 style="text-align:center">18</h1>

Zander didn't remember horseback riding being such a literal pain in the ass.

It had been years since he rode a horse, the last time being when he was sixteen, just after his sister Martha was married to her husband, Philip. Philip had a stretch of land in the countryside, and one day a carriage showed up unannounced and took him to visit his sister. As it turned out, her husband had left the country for several months, and Martha used his absence as an opportunity to steal her brother away from the city for a few weeks.

His father had been furious when he got back home. Zander's explanation as to why he'd failed to show up to his apprenticeship was met with a belt, but he didn't care. He'd spent two weeks with his favorite sister, drinking wine and riding her wealthy husband's horses across his lush estate in the countryside. It was two of the best weeks of his life, and the last time he ever saw Martha.

Now, having ridden hard and fast along the coast for nearly an hour, then veering North, he didn't feel like a carefree teenager. He felt like a crotchety old man with a severely chapped ass—perhaps due to the distinct lack of expensive wine.

He was grateful when Yarrow found a spot they deemed suitable to begin the off-road portion of their journey, announcing they'd be venturing into the forest up ahead instead of remaining in the open. He longed for shade, the afternoon sun having made him drowsy enough to nearly fall off his horse.

He occasionally glanced at Ace's compass as they traveled, but it was more for comfort than function. He truly had no idea where they were without a map, and he'd only ever learned to navigate on the water, by the stars. But Yarrow seemed to know what they were doing, and they were undoubtedly more well-traveled than he, so he followed Theo's lead and trusted Yarrow blindly as they entered the thick wall of trees.

The horses picked their way slowly through the dense forest, and Zander passed the time with a mix of sightseeing and crippling anxiety. The open countryside they'd ridden through provided beautiful scenery—rolling hills, flowers in bloom, and the occasional group of wild pigs—but he couldn't shake the feeling that each time he turned around, he'd see someone chasing them. Here in the forest, the sights were squished into smaller spaces—insects, fungi, tiny birds—at first, he felt relatively safe in the cover of the trees.

That is, until he saw a spotted cat the size of a bloodhound with pointed ears and long patches of fur that hung down on either side of its face like jowls. It lay prostrate at the base of a tree, its legs flexed as if to pounce, its long teeth peeking out of its mouth as it snarled silently at the passersby. A chill ran down Zander's spine at the sight of the beautiful animal. It was unlike anything he'd ever seen, and he was glad to put distance between himself and it before they stopped for the night.

They made camp in a clearing next to a stream with enough room for the horses to graze before they slept. A small waterfall, tucked behind a tangle of trees and bushes, fed the stream.

Once they'd all drank their fill and settled the horses, Theo announced he'd be walking the perimeter to ensure they weren't near any predators' dens or other unforeseen dangers. Yarrow began removing various herbs and flowers from their pockets, then got to work on their satchel, from which they produced a veritable abundance of green things. Zander had no idea how they fit so much in that little bag.

"Well," Yarrow said, crouching over the materials laid out before them and assessing their merit, "it's not much. At least, nothing filling. But we could scrape together a decent broth. I've got a sturdy leather pouch we can string up to boil water in, courtesy of our former captors." They looked up at Zander and shrugged. "We'll be hungry come morning, but at least we'll be able to sleep with something in our bellies."

Zander nodded, then looked at the stream behind them. His stomach rumbled loudly, and he put a hand against his torso as if to quiet it.

"Maybe we could catch some fish?"

"We could try if you fancy spearfishing. I don't have anything to fashion as a hook."

Zander mentally scolded himself for not taking the sailmaker's needle from the pirate ship with him. He imagined himself trying to spear fish out of the stream, and in his exhaustion, he almost laughed out loud.

"Perhaps it would be easier to find some mushrooms or roots. I can help you look."

Yarrow nodded and stood, and Zander followed them into the trees. For the next several minutes, Zander listened as Yarrow pointed out various plants, explaining their use in remedies or recipes, occasionally warning him against a poisonous variety using some version of a rhyme or acronym, usually in French. When they came upon a large patch of watercress, Zander busied himself gathering the leafy green vegetable while Yarrow cleaned the dirt off a handful of thick roots in the stream.

"Where did you learn to forage?" Zander asked. "You're quite wonderful at it."

"My mother," Yarrow said, smiling. "She was a healer of sorts. Not officially, but that's what people knew her as. Every time someone had a cut, or a rash, or a bump on the head, they came to my mother. She used to take me and my brothers out with her to forage for medicinal plants, but we always came back with dinner, too. She believed the land would always provide what we needed to live."

Zander's stomach growled again, and he hoped their dinner of wet salad and herb broth would be enough to keep the three of them alive long enough to find Ace.

"That sounds like a nice way to grow up."

"It was," Yarrow agreed. "She did well, my mother. Raised us well. But once I'd grown, a quiet life in the country wasn't enough for me."

"What came next?" Zander asked, eager to know more about his friend, who rarely talked about their past.

Yarrow looked sidelong at him, and Zander thought perhaps they wouldn't answer. Finally, they smirked and continued talking.

"I went to Paris. Spent a year or so being young and reckless. Drinking, sleeping around. Then I met Nicolette. My first love."

Yarrow gazed at the stream as they spoke, as if Nicolette's face was projected on top of the water. Zander stayed silent, waiting for them to continue, his hands frozen midway through tearing away a handful of watercress.

"Nicolette opened up a whole new world to me. She was part of an underground group of intellectuals. They became my friends."

Yarrow paused, then looked at Zander. When they didn't go on, he made an impatient gesture with his hands. "Well, go on. You can't just casually mention some underground society and not tell me more."

Yarrow chuckled and continued scrubbing at the roots. "They used to meet in secret in the back of a tavern. It was a dark, smoky room filled with the greatest minds I'd ever encountered. Poets. Philosophers. Scientists. They would gather and talk of revolution. Of progress. Some of them had traveled across the world. Others sat in the halls of kings. Still others made dark inventions—some for the pursuit of justice, others for their own amusement." Yarrow's mouth tilted up at one side.

"I learned much from my new friends. But I soon grew sick of talking about ideas in the back of a dingy tavern. I wanted to spread my wings, to apply my new skills elsewhere. There was something else out there, something calling to me. I could feel it in my bones."

"What was it?" Zander asked.

Yarrow looked up and smiled, shaking droplets from the now-clean roots grasped in their hand.

"It was Theo."

A gunshot rang out, then another, and the two of them shot to their feet in alarm. Yarrow took only a moment to ascertain the direction of the noise before they took off running. Zander followed close behind.

When they found Theo, he was clutching two dead rabbits in his fist, a wide smile on his face as he walked casually toward them.

"I found dinner!" he announced, lifting his hand to show off his catch. Each one had been shot directly through its head, leaving the rest of the meat intact.

Yarrow's shoulders visibly relaxed, and Zander chuckled in relief knowing Theo was safe, and that he wouldn't have to live off watercress and broth for the night. He held out his hand, gesturing for Theo to give him the carcasses.

"I'll take care of those," he said.

As he hunched over the rabbits a little while later, his dagger making quick work of the soft hide, Yarrow tended to a fire. His mind ruminated once again on all the horrible scenarios they might encounter when they found Ace, in part to avoid reliving the very real violence of the past few days. He paused, taking a deep breath to keep his hands from shaking.

Theo was busy sharpening sticks to skewer and roast the meat. He nodded at Zander, his eyes casting down at his blood-stained hands.

"You're rather quick at that," he said.

Zander nodded, his catastrophic line of thought momentarily ceasing. "Well, tanning was the family business, but we didn't stick to cow hides. Me and my siblings used to catch rabbits all the time. My dad taught me to skin them so we could preserve the hide with the fur still on. They caught a decent price at market if you had enough of them. We ate a lot of rabbit stew growing up."

Zander winked, his crooked smile a welcome sight to Theo and Yarrow, who'd traded several silent glances during their journey pertaining to Zander's well-being. Alas, the two of them had watched him pull himself apart many times in the pursuit of his soulmate, in many different lives, though they didn't remember that now. Still, on top of the deep worry they felt over Ace's well-being, they shared a growing dread that should they fail to save her, Zander would unravel yet again.

After Zander skinned and cleaned the rabbits for cooking, he used his dagger to scrape the hides, rinsing it after every pass in the stream. As he sat on the ground by the water, the sun quickly dropping toward the horizon, he watched the water jump from the rocks up ahead, falling in a long wave to the stream below. He could make out the miniscule droplets that crested the top of the waterfall from where he sat, leaping outward before falling to the stream below. They looked like tiny little people jumping from the edge, waiting to see if they would fall or fly.

When he was satisfied with the hides, he cleaned off his dagger and moved to sit by the fire. He wasn't sure what he'd do with the rabbit hides, but there was no use in wasting them, so he laid them out on a large stone near the fire to begin drying overnight. As he sat, Theo handed him a skewer of rabbit meat. Zander accepted it gratefully, then took a handful of watercress and stuffed it in his mouth.

The three companions ate quietly for a while.

"We'll make it to Almogia tomorrow," Yarrow said eventually. "We can gather supplies there, and information about Ignacio's recent comings and goings." Yarrow looked at Zander. "If Ignacio has returned home, he'll have docked in Malaga, then passed through Almogia on the way to his estate. When Ace's parents were alive, they did a lot of business in Almogia. I have an idea of who to talk to. If we're lucky, we'll make it to the Sanz estate before they have a chance to settle."

And before they've had a chance to hurt her, Zander thought hopefully.

Yarrow tossed their empty skewer into the fire and tented their hands, their elbows on their knees.

"From Almogia, we'll cross the limestone valley, keeping away from the main roads leading to the Sanz estate. We can camp in the valley until it's late enough, then approach from the south, where there are no roads leading in. There's a hill behind the estate that will serve as a lookout point until we're ready to strike. From there, we'll need to split up. There will be at least one servant entrance in the back, on the south side. The stables lie to the east, and storehouses to the west. Our best chance of escape will be to the northeast, on the main road leading in. We'll need to find a way to position the horses near the road if we're going to flee fast enough."

Zander looked at the ground near Theo's feet, where he'd drawn a rough approximation of Yarrow's instructions in the dirt using his empty skewer. "I thought you'd only been there once?" Zander asked, looking at Yarrow in disbelief.

Yarrow looked at him as if the question was completely irrelevant. "I have."

Zander looked at Theo, who shrugged as if he was used to Yarrow memorizing the exact layout of every place they'd ever been to. The firelight threw the bruises on his face into stark relief. Zander didn't fail to notice how he winced when he shrugged, nor that he'd been clutching his shoulder since they sat down to eat. Worry churned in his gut, but he made a note of it and set it aside. There wasn't much he could do for Theo now.

"What else should we expect from Lord Sanz?" Zander asked.

"One of two things," Yarrow said. "One, he'll be so wrapped up in the victory of finding Ace, so focused on extracting from her the location of her parents' famed treasure, that he won't expect us to come save her. If he's as arrogant as I remember, this is likely. It should make it easy to cause a distraction and get her out of there. Two, he's grown up slightly and realizes Ace is capable, as are her friends, and he will be prepared for us. In that case, our job will be more challenging."

"The last time we saw Sanz, his estate was crawling with servants and guards," Theo said. "You'd think he was a goddamned prince or something. By the looks of the ship he arrived on to fetch Ace, he's given into the delusion and built himself an army. There's a chance his men sailed away after they brought Sanz home. Maybe they're looking for treasure, or small children they can steal candy from. Or, perhaps, they're surrounding his estate as we speak."

Zander heaved a great sigh, tossing his empty skewer in the fire atop the other two. He looked up at the dark night sky as if the answers to his questions were twinkling in the blanket of stars above his head. Seeing no revelations, he looked back at his fellow pirates.

He was tired, frustrated, in pain. The last few months had felt like years. He'd grown and changed in ways he didn't know was possible. He'd found an enormous well of strength and determination inside him he didn't know existed. He'd learned how to sail, how to sword-fight, and how to rob a crew of merchants on the high seas without firing a single shot. And on top of all of that, he'd fallen deeply in love with a person he felt like he'd known for lifetimes, only to discover he barely knew her at all. He'd found a family, only to lose them.

If the last few months had felt like years, the last three days had felt like months. The pain of loss weighed on him, threatening to drag him into an abyss. But the absolute miracle that was Yarrow and Theo kept him going. He would not lose them, too.

Looking at them now, Zander could see the same heartbreak he felt in their eyes, the same bone-deep exhaustion. The same dogged determination.

"We'd better get some rest," he said finally. "I'll take first watch."

Instead of protesting, Yarrow nodded, seeming to have finally succumbed to the need for sleep. Zander gazed into the fire as they slept, thinking about all of the ways he was going to make Ignacio pay for what he'd done to his family.

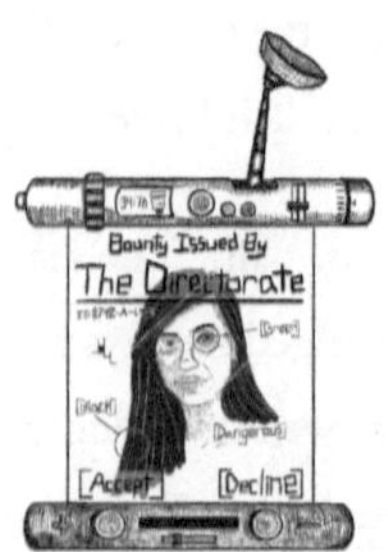

Once, he was a hunter. And she was not only his prey—she was the bane of his existence.

It had been years since he started chasing her. Every other bounty hunter in the galaxy had long since given up on her capture, elusive as she was. But not him. Not his team.

It was the three of them then—Zed, Teshva, and Yuna. It had been the three of them for decades. At one point they did this job for the money just like everyone else. They did it to survive. But somewhere along the way, finding her became like a calling, a quest that would define the purpose of their lives.

For him, it became an obsession.

They lived in an endlessly frustrating cycle of pursuit, moving from place to place in their starship, working small jobs. Without fail, they questioned the criminals they brought in for bounty, bargaining or threatening to gain hints as to her whereabouts. The tips were sometimes credible. But for years, every good tip brought them to her doorstep only for the trail to suddenly go cold, like she disappeared into thin air as soon as they entered the planet's atmosphere.

He could see it was wearing on them. She had the biggest bounty on her head in The Directorate's history. Catching her would change their lives forever. But it was more than that. It was like some invisible force connected them, pulling them across the universe behind her. With each near miss, the tension receded, then snapped painfully back into place when she escaped. It ground them down, breaking off bits and pieces of their souls like wind eroding stone.

Yuna and Teshva were nearing their breaking point. He could see they wanted to give up. The mission required them all to sacrifice things, to give up normal lives. They became the job. But they, at least, still had each other. They had something to live for, should they leave this life behind. He didn't know who he was without the job.

He didn't know who he was without her.

He sat looking at his partners across the table. They pushed their food back and forth across their plates, their eyes unfocused. Years ago, they would have been full of talk. The three of them would sit for hours after getting a tip, drinking and trading ideas about what their next step should be. It was like a game.

Today, it felt old. Stale. They could smell the looming disappointment.

Desperation curled around his torso like a snake as he thought of them leaving him.

"Maybe we could fix the ship," he said.

Yuna and Teshva looked up at the same time.

"Hmm?" Yuna said.

"Maybe we could be faster. I could replace a few things, give her a tune-up. You never know, it could be just the edge we need."

Teshva shrugged. "Tinker away. It can't hurt anything."

Yuna's mouth turned up slightly at the corner. "I don't know about that. You remember Okshvos, don't you? The hyperspace booster?"

Zed rolled his eyes as Teshva's shoulders shook with laughter.

"You're never going to let me live that down, are you?" he asked Yuna.

"Spending our money on a defective heating coil someone painted and called a hyperspace booster?" Yuna said. "No, no I'm not, Z. Never."

Teshva was doubled over in laughter now. "It improves jump speed by up to fifteen percent!" he said between laughs, mocking Zed.

"Ah, knock off, the both of you," Zed said, grinning. He stood. "I'm going to start poking around and see what needs to be replaced. And then the two of you can go to Lfthos Market and spare me the trouble."

"You mean spare you the embarrassment," Yuna said. Zed pushed them playfully as he walked by, ruffling their hair in mock anger.

The ship's engine room was normally loud and hot. Now, idle as they sat parked on one of The Directorate's outpost planets, it was cool and quiet, bathed in a soft red glow from the reserve lights lining the ceiling. Zed retrieved his data pad and started taking notes.

As he came to the maze of tubes that directed water, coolant, and lubricant to various parts of the ship, he paused. He set the data pad down and wedged himself inside the recess in the wall where each tube emerged from the floor, snaking up to various openings in the wall. Where each tube emerged, a label identified their purpose. Zed sank to his knees to getter a close look and realized each one was also labeled with miniscule instructions on how and when to flush them. He grimaced as he realized most of them were overdue.

"Well, add that to the list," he mumbled to himself.

As he stood, his eye caught on something wedged in the back corner of the small space. He leaned forward to get a better look and his heart nearly stopped when he recognized the device.

"Tesh, Yuna!" he called as he ran back into the common space. He skidded to a stop when he rounded the corner and almost collided with them both.

"Woah there," Teshva said. "What is it?"

Zed presented his open palm in response, a look of fierce excitement in his eyes.

"Is that…?" Yuna began.

"Yes," Zed said. "A proximity alert. I found it hidden in the engine room. It's probably been there for years. This is how she knows we're coming! This is why she's always gone when we show up!"

"Well, fucking hell!" Teshva exclaimed.

"Give me that," Yuna said, snatching the device from Zed's hands and rushing to their work station.

"Can you use it to find out where she is?" Zed asked.

"You fucking bet I can," Yuna said, their eyes and hands focused on the device as it rested atop their computer's scanning pad. "And I can disable it before it alarms. She won't know what hit her."

A rush of energy filled Zed's body as he realized how close they were to the end. He was finally going to catch her.

Then what? said a small voice in the back of his mind. He quickly squashed it.

19

The next morning brought a breakfast of broth and watercress salad, and the three pirates traveled on toward Almogia.

After hours of steady riding, the town emerged, a bright spot amidst the rolling hills of brown and green. As they approached, Zander saw white stucco buildings with terracotta roofs. Gardens and orchards dotted the landscape surrounding the town. They rode in on packed dirt roads lined with people chatting, cooking, and doing business. Zander took a deep breath, the smells of food and fire filling him with hope—they were almost there.

They dismounted and walked their horses to a set of stables, where they paid for them to be fed, watered, and looked after until the afternoon. Then they walked to a narrow path lined with stunning mosaic tiles, at the end of which lay an inn. Inside, two men played guitars. Most of the tables scattered around the room were empty, but a handful of people ate or drank. There was a pleasant hum of chatter beneath the lively music.

Yarrow approached a woman behind the bar when they walked in. Zander hung back with Theo, who was looking around and smiling appreciatively at the place, a nostalgic smile on his face.

"Is this where you and Ace used to meet?" Zander asked him.

Theo nodded. "The very place." He pushed a quick sigh through his pursed lips. "Never thought I'd be back here."

Yarrow returned and pushed a key into Zander's hand.

"I got us a room for a few hours. We could all use a chance to freshen up, and I need a place to tend to Theo's wounds. You go up first, Zander. There will be a fresh water basin and some food waiting. Theo and I will talk to a few people here first."

"You're sure you don't want to go up first?" Zander asked.

Yarrow shook their head. "I already see some people I want to talk to. I'd rather get it out of the way before they leave. Besides, I need to purchase fresh bandages before I can tend to Theo. You go on, love. Eat. Get cleaned up. Put some more of that oil on your feet."

Theo nodded in agreement. "Take a few deep breaths before the plunge," he said, clapping Zander on the back.

Zander made his way past the dining tables and musicians to a narrow set of stairs. Upstairs, a narrow hallway led him to a door marked with the number two, the same number painted on the key's filigree.

He unlocked the door and pushed it open to find a bed, a table with a full washbasin, and a plate containing something that looked like an omelet stuffed with potatoes. He obeyed his stomach first, sitting down on the edge of the bed and devouring the tasty meal. Then he removed his boots and stockings, followed by his jacket, pants, and shirt. He took the cloth from the edge of the basin and dipped it in the water.

As he worked the cloth over his skin, wiping away days' worth of dirt, sweat, and blood to reveal bruised and battered skin, Zander thought of nothing but Ace. His fingers itched, as if he could reach out and touch her.

He could feel that she was alive. Something taut in his chest grew looser with every inch he progressed in her direction, like a chain connecting their hearts.

But once they saved her, would she still want him?

Her face flashed in his mind, the scene of a raging battle behind her on the deck of The Valerian. She'd said she loved him. She'd also knocked him unconscious with the handle of her blade, albeit to disguise him as a dead body. Still—if that wasn't mixed signals, he didn't know what was. Despite the growing surety with which he felt their connection, he couldn't help wondering now, at the precipice of her rescue, whether he'd only imagined she felt the same.

What if she'd only said it because she thought she'd never see him again? If so, chasing her across Spain with a trail of bodies in his wake would seem rather desperate. He didn't want to be just another man who sought to win her, to control her. He didn't want her to feel stuck with him, or even worse, indebted to him.

He knew what he wanted. He wanted to cut his chest open and lay his heart bare. He wanted to offer himself up like a sacrificial lamb, every dark secret open to her scrutiny, every desire transparent to her gaze. He couldn't carry on with her as they had, a mountain of secrets between them, and with it, an ocean of doubts.

But would she want the same?

Having cleaned himself, Zander opened the shuttered window by the bed and leaned out, his bare torso welcoming the fresh air as he bent down and beat his clothing against the side of the building. Clouds of dust escaped and blew away on the breeze. When he was satisfied, he dressed, emptied the water from his basin, and made his way downstairs. Not seeing Yarrow or Theo, he returned the key to the woman at the bar and asked if she'd give it to his companions when they returned.

He wandered through the quaint streets of Almogia for a while, debating whether he was proficient enough in Spanish to ask any of the people he passed about the comings and goings of Lord Sanz, until he heard a familiar voice up ahead.

Theo was speaking animatedly with a stout man who appeared to be in his sixties. His short, dark hair was painted with thick grey streaks, and his muscular arms were folded as he listened to Theo speak, a serious expression on his face. Seeing Zander approach in his periphery, Theo gestured to him and spoke rapidly in Spanish. Zander couldn't make it out, but he deduced that Theo was explaining who he was. The man gave Zander a friendly smile and held out his hand to shake.

"Zander, this is Hugo," Theo said, nearly breathless with what sounded like relief. "Hugo Vidal, Ace's uncle."

Zander's grip on Hugo's hand tightened, as if he could feel Ace's blood running through the veins beneath his skin.

"It's good to meet you, sir," he said. "My name is Zander."

Hugo nodded, looking appraisingly at Zander. He felt suddenly self-conscious.

"Hugo and I were just filling each other in," Theo said. "You know how I said Ignacio moved the wedding up after Ace's parents died? Well, Hugo came down from Aviles to handle his brother's affairs after the fire—"

"And take care of my niece," Hugo interjected.

"And see to Ace," Theo agreed, nodding. "But when he showed up, the wedding was already underway." Theo leveled a questioning look at Hugo. "I didn't expect you to still be here. I thought you would have gone north by now, back home."

"I had reasons to stick around," Hugo said. "This is home now. But I can tell you about that later, along with everything else I know. Come inside. There are some things you should be aware of."

Theo nodded, then smiled as he looked behind Hugo. Yarrow was approaching swiftly, a look of purpose on their face as they made their way toward Theo. But upon seeing Hugo, their face lit up and they sped into a jog. The two embraced, and Hugo laughed and rubbed circles on Yarrow's back affectionately.

"Hugo," Yarrow said emphatically as they broke away. "What a pleasure to see your face again. What the hell are you doing here?"

"I'll tell you," Hugo said. "But first, come in for some food. There is much to talk about."

The three pirates followed Hugo into a quaint white house with a row of yellow flowers in the front. Inside, the simple, cozy home was decorated in warm colors. Hugo gestured to a sitting area and began busying himself arranging a variety of food on a large, wooden platter.

Zander sat and looked to Theo and Yarrow, who were sharing a significant look, hints of smiles on their faces. They both looked at him at the same time.

"Ace's uncle, huh?" Zander said quietly.

Yarrow nodded. "Nicolas's brother. He used to come visit from Aviles, where Nicolas was born, quite often. He would stay for weeks or months at a time. Sometimes he would buy things from our crew to bring back home. He never had children, but he loved Ace like she was his own."

"I would have mentioned him to you, mate," Theo said, "but I didn't think it was relevant at the time. I figured he'd gone home after Ace left and that was that. Apparently, he stayed at Ignacio's estate for a while, after Ace left. That's all he said before you two showed up."

Just then, the door opened, and a man walked through holding a basket of vegetables. He froze upon seeing the three pirates, his hat in his hand and his mouth open, like he had something on the tip of his tongue just before he walked through the door, but now had lost it. He was tall and wiry, with thin dark hair and hazel eyes.

"Hello," he said tentatively. Hugo approached the group with a platter of ham, cheese, olives, and bread in his hands. He placed it down on the table in front of them and turned to kiss the newcomer on the cheek.

"As I said before, I had reasons to stick around. Friends, this is Cristian. Cristian, this is Theo, Yarrow, and Zander."

The group exchanged pleasantries, and Hugo took the basket from Cristian to set on the counter before returning. The two of them sat down across from the pirates, and Hugo let out a long sigh.

"You're just in time," he told Cristian. "These are Aracely's friends. Ignacio has her, mi amor."

Cristian's face took on a steely tone.

"Then it's good I'm here," he said, straightening. He looked at the three of them with new eyes, like he was sizing them up. "I was Lord Sanz's household manager for 25 years."

Yarrow snapped their fingers as if they'd solved a puzzle.

"That's where I know you from!" Theo exclaimed. "You were there when Sanz told us about the Vidals."

Cristian nodded somberly. "Please, allow me to explain. I first worked for Ignacio's father. I entered the household when Ignacio was fifteen. I never understood what happened to that boy to make him the way he is. His mother passed when he was young, and his father was stern, but not unkind. Ignacio, however, was a spoiled, selfish young man. He was greedy, manipulative, and cruel. When his father died, I continued in his employ for the sake of the family businesses, which had come to feel, in part, like my own. But I soon found his approach to business... unpalatable."

Cristian swallowed, glancing at Hugo, and continued.

"After we moved into his current estate, I began making preparations to retire with the money I had saved. I originally come from Madrid, same as Lord Sanz. But I've always enjoyed this part of the country and imagined myself settling down here. That was shortly before Ignacio became acquainted with—obsessed with—Chandace and Nicolas."

"Obsessed?" Zander interjected.

Cristian nodded. "He wanted what they had. Not just their business, or their wealth. He wanted the goodwill they had, the respect, the aura of mystery and danger. He watched how people acted around them and it made him sick with jealousy. He became their friend, but privately, he spoke of them like they were an obstacle to his own greatness. Then he offered marriage to their daughter, and I... well, had I known..." He trailed off.

Hugo took his hand and nodded encouragingly. Cristian continued.

"The day Chandace and Nicolas died, Ignacio sent a carriage to retrieve Aracely for dinner. When the carriage left the estate, it bore two men: the coachman, and one of Ignacio's personal attendants. When it returned, only the coachman and Aracely came with it. That evening, the Vidal estate burned to the ground with Chandace and Nicolas inside. According to the servants who survived, when the fire started, they were sitting in the loggia with a bottle of wine, given to them by the coachman as a gift from Lord Sanz. It was there that the fire started."

"Wait," Theo said, a hand in the air. "The fire started in the loggia?"

"What's a loggia?" Zander asked.

"A partially enclosed room," Yarrow answered. "The Vidals' spanned the length of one side of their house, with large open arches leading to the garden."

"That doesn't make any sense," Theo said. "There was a goddamn *pond* just outside the central arch, for god's sake. How could that kill them? Unless the lightning hit them directly?"

Hugo nodded slowly, leaning forward onto his haunches. "Tell me, Theo. How does a room with six open doors trap two people inside to burn to death?"

"Are you saying what I think you're saying?" asked Yarrow. "Do you think Ignacio was responsible for the Vidals' deaths?"

"I didn't believe it at first," Cristian said. "After the fire, Ignacio offered Aracely refuge. He also hired the servants from the Vidal household as part of his own staff. He was charming in those days following the fire... doting."

Cristian shivered, as if the sight of Ignacio doting on someone was akin to watching a kelpie shed its human skin just before it pulled you to the depths.

"He proclaimed they should perform the wedding ceremony sooner than planned, so he could act as Aracely's protector in the absence of her parents. He feigned concern over her reputation, living in his home without being wed. I still viewed Ignacio as a spoiled little boy, a schoolyard bully—not a killer. A part of me believed he was sincere, and that perhaps taking a wife would temper him. That was my mistake. I now believe, as Hugo said, that Ignacio had something to do with the Vidals' deaths."

A shiver ran down Zander's spine. Yarrow buried their face in their hands with a loud sigh. Theo, his face a mask of cold fury, placed his hand comfortingly on their back.

"Ignacio may have been doting in those first days following the fire, but he was also very controlling," Cristian continued. "He kept Ace confined to her room most of the time, and when she left, she was under his direct supervision. He wouldn't allow her to visit her ruined home. He was concerned over her safety, he said. He wouldn't allow any of the Vidals' former staff to see or speak to her. The poor girl was... well, she was trapped. Her home burned to the ground, her parents dead, and not a familiar face in sight."

"Until the wedding," Hugo said. "When I arrived."

"Did no one tell you they'd moved the date of the wedding?" Zander asked.

Hugo shook his head. "I suspect Ignacio thought it would be over before I arrived. He wanted to lay claim to Ace's inheritance before anyone could interfere. But when word reached me of Nicolas and Chandace's deaths, I left Aviles the same hour. I showed up during the reception to find my Aracely sitting at a banquet table, wearing a wedding dress, tears of grief running down her beautiful face. Her expression when she saw me... it broke my heart. It was relief. But Ignacio's—it was irritation I saw there. Like I'd interrupted something.

"But it was only a flash across his charming exterior," Hugo continued. "He welcomed me, calling me family, insisting I stay as long as I needed while I sorted through the ruins of my brother's life. Unfortunately, the pomp and circumstance of the wedding made it nearly impossible to get Aracely alone. I had but moments with her—to hug her, to hold her—mere moments to share our grief at the loss of our family. I thought we'd have all the days following to grieve together, to celebrate this supposedly happy union. But I only had the chance to tell her I loved her before I was ushered to a seat, given food and wine. Before I knew it, Ignacio was drunkenly announcing his intentions to take his wife to bed, and I was being ushered to a guest room. The next morning, she was gone."

Hugo wiped his eyes, which were glistening with tears.

"There was something in her eyes when we parted. I didn't know it then, but it was goodbye."

"Yet you stayed," Yarrow said.

Hugo nodded, settling back in his chair. "When it was discovered Aracely had left, Ignacio tore through the house in a rage. He accused me of making her leave. He demanded to go through my things. It was only when Cristian intervened that he left me alone. But Cristian stayed, and he told me where my Aracely was."

"I was the one who helped her flee," Cristian explained. "Days before the wedding, I visited her room. When she asked me to get a message to you two"—he gestured to Theo and Yarrow with his chin—"I gave Rosario the note and made up an excuse for her to go into town. But before I did, I read the note. I knew she wouldn't be able to get past Ignacio's guards by herself, so the night of the wedding, I waited at the bottom of the stairs until I heard her sneak out, and I showed her how to escape without being noticed."

"And how was that?" Zander asked.

"There is a small system of tunnels beneath the Sanz estate," Cristian answered. "They were originally built so servants could move about the estate without being seen. At some point, one of the tunnels was lengthened so that it led beyond the house. The tunnels were no longer used by the time Ignacio was born, and he never knew about them. But the kitchen staff used to use them to sneak out to the storehouses and smoke cogollo.”

“Cristian told me everything he knew,” Hugo said. “I couldn’t go home then. But I couldn’t stay under Ignacio’s roof either. So, Cristian offered to let me stay here, in the house he’d bought.”

“I retired weeks later,” Cristian said. “Together, Hugo and I sorted through the rubble of the Vidals’ home, salvaging what we could. Then we worked on keeping the Vidal estate and all of its businesses out of Ignacio’s hands.”

Hugo exhaled sharply, his face contorting with frustration.

“I beseeched anyone with power I could find, trying to convince them Ignacio had no claim to the estate of a wife who’d abandoned him the night of their wedding. But Ignacio paraded witness after witness to the court who’d attended the wedding, each of them claiming to have knowledge the marriage was consummated.”

“I suspect he also bribed the officials,” Cristian said.

“In either case, we weren’t successful. Ignacio inherited Nicolas’s vineyards, his tobacco trade, and his land. And I never saw Ace again.” Hugo was silent for a moment, sullen. Then he looked to Cristian, and the two smiled tenderly at each other. “Cristian has soothed my aching heart all this time. But it has been difficult, living here in the shadow of Ignacio’s victory.”

Cristian nodded. “Ignacio’s hunger for power and riches has only grown. We are able to live quiet lives here in Almogia, unbothered by him. Despite being so close to the Sanz estate, Ignacio has no reason to spend time here. But word of his activities circulates all the same. And word is, Ignacio's obsession with the Vidal legacy has spread beyond Spain."

"That's what I was coming here to tell you," Yarrow said, looking at Theo. "Ignacio abandoned the tobacco trade shortly after Chandace and Nicolas's deaths. He's become a privateer, and he and his crew—the crew that boarded the Valerian—have been roaming the Mediterranean for years, terrorizing ships, even ransacking villages. He's becoming a fucking pirate."

Theo slapped his hands against his knees, suddenly outraged. "Of course, he had to go and *copy* Ace!" he yelled. "What a fucking fake, playing pirate with his fancy little crew." He sat back in his chair roughly, angrily folding his arms. "Fucking *privateer*," he muttered.

"I'm surprised you hadn't heard of his activities, given your current line of work," Hugo said, raising his eyebrow at the three of them.

"We never sailed the Mediterranean as a rule," Yarrow said. "We stayed in the Caribbean most of the year, and we stuck to the West side of Gibraltar when we came this way. Ace always feared he'd find her somehow."

"And now he has," Cristian said, sitting up straighter. "And I'm going to tell you how to get her out."

20

Zander, Theo, and Yarrow were silent as they rode across the limestone valley toward Antequera. Even the horses seemed quieter than usual, as if they knew they carried their riders into the mouth of a beast.

The three pirates were armed to the teeth, having procured more supplies in Almogia before leaving. Each of Zander's boots hid a dagger, and in addition to Ace's ivory cutlass, a loaded pistol hung from his belt.

Zander reflected on everything Cristian told them as he passed beneath the shadows of the large limestone formations that surrounded them.

"Ignacio is not just playing at being a pirate," he'd said. "He's sought out professionals, and he's paid them well to help him achieve his fool's dream. He's squandered enormous amounts of resources—resources I helped build when his father was alive—in pursuit of Aracely and whatever treasure he believes she'll lead him to. The men he's hired—former pirates, mercenaries, and soldiers—have a reputation for being cruel and reckless."

"Reckless is good," Yarrow had said. "Reckless people are easy to beat. Reckless people never see people like me coming."

Zander looked up to see an Ibex standing on the ridge of one of the rock formations. The limestone beneath the creature's hooves puddled in large, flat wafers that piled on top of one another in columns, each pillar connecting at the bottom. Lone columns dotted the landscape as well, tall and proud, looking out over the valley like ancient guardians.

Dusk settled in and Zander watched the sky turn shades of pink and purple, a stunning backdrop against the dramatic stone figures that dotted the landscape.

Yarrow brought their horse up short, and Zander and Theo flanked them. They lifted their hand, pointing at the ridge ahead of them like the grim reaper staking its claim.

"The Sanz estate is just over that ridge," they said quietly. "We'll leave the horses tied here and approach on foot. We'll observe as long as there's light." They squinted upward, as if ascertaining how much time they had left. "We passed a semicircle of stones a while ago, barring any view from the north. That would be a good place to make camp and wait for the deep night."

Wordlessly, the three dismounted their stolen horses and attached the leads to a nearby tree. Then they walked.

It took twenty minutes to reach the ridge and scale it. They dropped to their hands and knees near the top, inching forward until the Sanz estate loomed before them, a sleeping giant nestled in the sprawling valley beyond.

The bone-white building that housed Ignacio and his stolen bride was constructed in a large central circle that was two stories high.

Single-story wings lay to the west, east, and north, rectangular appendages jutting from the circular center. The north wing led to a large open square dotted with palms, and the main road leading in. From their position, Zander could see signs of a garden in the circular open courtyard in the center of the house. Just as Yarrow said, stables lay to the northeast of the building, and storehouses to the west, with acres of vineyards stretching into the distance beyond.

In the front square, a fire burned, and eight uniformed men stood or sat around it, drinking and laughing.

"Ignacio's privateers," Yarrow whispered.

"Fake pirates," Theo corrected them under his breath.

"Why would he bring any of them here?" Yarrow wondered. "Why not leave them on board the ship, or put them up in Malaga? They're ruining his lawn." There was a touch of humor in Yarrow's voice.

Zander scanned the grounds. "I don't see any other guards," he said. "Could he be using his new crew as a replacement for them?"

Theo nodded slowly, his eyes darting back and forth. "Aye," he said. "It's possible. If Cristian is right and he's been hiring mercenaries, he may have run through his resources faster than he anticipated."

"I imagine he thought he'd find Ace and the Vidals' mythical treasure much sooner," Yarrow said. "No matter. It appears as if he's left the rest of them aboard the ship. I'll take a dozen fake pirates over well-trained guards any day." They winked at Theo, and he smiled back at them.

Just as Cristian told them, two entrances marked the south side of the building, each attached to the narrow junctions between the central structure and its opposite wings. The one on the right led to the kitchens in the east wing. It was well-used. As they watched, half a dozen people walked in and out, tossing scraps into a compost pile or emptying pails of water. The one on the left led to the west wing.

"The west wing is deserted," Cristian had told them. "Ignacio's father used to stay there. I've never seen him step foot inside it."

That's where they would enter.

"Ignacio is a creature of habit," Cristian had continued. "Just as he kept the west wing preserved, he kept Aracely's room untouched. The bed has not even been made since the last time he kept her there. It's a monument to his failure. That is where he will keep her again. She will be on the top floor in the central part of the building. The door faces southeast. Two doors down, facing southwest, is Ignacio's room."

As they lay there looking at the estate, Zander's eyes kept wandering to a particular window on the top floor, the curtains drawn. He knew it was her window, because it was the only one with bars.

The plan was to lead the horses to where the tunnel let out, hidden behind a copse of trees near the storehouses. After the horses were secured, the three pirates would split up. Yarrow would head to the stables, where they would release the animals inside and use one of the remaining grenadiers to create a fiery distraction. The second bomb was a backup, in case things went wrong.

"One explosion means everything is going according to plan," Yarrow had said. "Two explosions means I had to improvise."

The distraction would draw Ignacio and his privateers to the stables, allowing Theo and Zander to find Ace. They would enter the central part of the building from the abandoned west wing, and Theo would pick the lock on Ace's door while Zander kept watch or cleared a path of escape, depending on how effective the distraction was. Once they had Ace, they would find the tunnel entrance, which Cristian informed them was in the kitchens.

"No one should bother you, if they are even awake" he'd said. "No one is loyal enough to Ignacio to put themselves in harm's way."

As Zander looked out over the estate from his elevated vantage point, he ran through Cristian's instructions once more in his head, trying to match the descriptions with reality. As he'd said, the central part of the building housed rooms that opened to the garden. The terracotta roof sheltered the tile walkways connecting the rooms and leading to each covered wing, as well as the stairs that led up on either side of the garden. Large columns surrounding the garden supported the overhanging roof. The garden itself was exposed to the sky, and even in the failing light, Zander could see it was overgrown.

The tether in his heart gave a small tug. He was close, so close.

Hold on, Ace, he thought. *I'm here.*

They watched until the darkness fell like a blanket, then they carefully retraced their steps to where the horses waited. They led the horses back to the semicircle of stones, and as Theo fed them carrots from their saddlebags, Zander helped Yarrow make a fire. Then the three of them sat around it, eating cold croquetas.

All there was left to do was wait. With just three of them against Sanz and his men, they would need to rely on surprise and confusion. A distraction was more effective against men who'd been shocked out of sleep, so they would wait until the hour was late before they made their move.

Theo finished his food and sighed contentedly, wiping his hands together to free them of crumbs. He looked at Yarrow and Zander, who were gazing silently and seriously into the fire, a pair of statues. In contrast, Theo could barely sit still. He repositioned himself a few times, first leaning back on his elbows, then hunched forward with his legs folded. He made little noises with his mouth. He drummed his hands on his knees. He tossed bits of grass into the fire, then poked at them with a stick as they burned. Finally, he shot to his feet and held his hand out to Yarrow.

Yarrow looked at him, an eyebrow raised.

"I can't take the silence anymore," Theo said. "I'll die of boredom before we rescue Ace. Dance with me, my fortune."

Yarrow smiled, but their expression was dubious. "You want me to dance with you?" they said. "Now?"

Theo's smile widened, and he nodded.

"There is no music," Yarrow observed.

In response, Theo reached down and took Yarrow's hand in his, pulling them up gently. "Oh, there isn't yet," he said.

"Theo," Yarrow groaned. "This is not the time for serenades."

"I disagree, my heart," Theo said, pulling Yarrow close to him and kissing them tenderly on the nose. "We are on the precipice of a great battle."

Theo put his hand on Yarrow's hip and turned them around gracefully. "We will march to war in mere hours, risking life and limb to save our friend, our captain."

He carefully dipped Yarrow, and their left foot popped up gracefully as their head tilted back, a reluctant smile on their face. Theo gazed into their eyes. "And here I am, still in love with you. There has never been a better time for a serenade."

He lifted Yarrow and they fell into an easy sway as Theo began to sing:

Yarrow, Yarrow

Won't you come grow in my yard? Oh,

I won't do you any harm, no

Come relieve me of my sorrow

Yarrow, Yarrow

In the mornings if you'd greet me

Promise that you'll never leave me

I would love you so completely

Zander watched Theo and Yarrow dance beneath the glow of the nearly full moon above their heads. Theo's rich voice filled the ring of stones around them, punctuated by Yarrow's occasional laughter as Theo spun them in circles.

Zander's anxiety was soothed by the tender sight. It felt familiar, like a piece of home. He'd seen them dance together on the sloop, but the sense of comfort he felt ran deeper, as if he'd been seeing Theo and Yarrow dance all his life. And indeed, if one took all the moments from the many lifetimes he had lived in which he saw some version of this dance, they would likely fill up a lifetime all on their own.

As he watched his friends, waiting for the predetermined hour, Zander thought about their final moments with Hugo and Cristian. Hugo had grasped him by the elbow, pulled him close, and given him a look that pierced his very soul.

"You go get her," he'd said. "You tell her I love her. You keep her safe." His voice softened. "And please, come visit. All of you."

21

When Theo and Zander parted with Yarrow, the night was deep and still. They tethered their horses to a tree on the west side of the property, far enough from the storehouses they wouldn't be noticed, but close enough for a fast getaway when Zander, Theo, and Ace emerged from the tunnel exit nearby.

Before they parted, Theo and Yarrow pressed their foreheads together, their hands on one another's faces.

"Be safe, my love," Yarrow whispered.

"I am never safe," Theo answered. "But I will return to you whole." He kissed them, and the three pirates parted ways.

Zander and Theo crept quickly and quietly toward the back of the house, where the door to the west wing stood unguarded. A tug at the handle showed it was locked, and Theo retrieved the pin he kept in his sleeve to make fast work of it. Upon hearing the satisfying *click* of the lock giving way, the two entered the abandoned west wing and closed the door behind them.

Inside was a foyer of sorts, decorated with lavish rugs and tapestries. The Sanz family crest, featuring the eagle that hailed The Valerian's doom the morning Zander first spotted it, took up the wall in front of them. To their right was a door, and beyond it, the inner courtyard and its overgrown garden. To their left was a long hallway lined with closed doors. Faintly glowing oil lamps dotted the walls, illuminating more extravagant décor.

"If this wing is abandoned, why are the lamps lit?" Theo wondered aloud.

Zander, having wondered the same thing, was already creeping forward down the long hallway. He stopped several paces in, listening to the faint cacophony surrounding him. When he finally recognized it as the distinct sound of snoring echoing from multiple rooms within the giant hall, he whipped around, looking at Theo in alarm.

"It's not abandoned," he whispered, just as a loud explosion sounded from the stables.

Zander and Theo rushed into the room closest to the foyer, which was mercifully unlocked. Inside, they found two men rubbing the sleep from their eyes, one wrapped in the covers of a large bed and the other sleeping in a pile of blankets on the floor. The second man shot up upon seeing the two pirates, but Theo quickly ran him through. He then swung his blade so the tip quivered at the throat of the second man, still wrapped in his covers, frozen in fear.

"How many men sleep in this hall?" Theo growled.

The man, who appeared no older than twenty, sputtered wordlessly. Theo pushed the blade so the tip pierced his neck, red blooming on his skin.

"How many?" he repeated.

"Not quite thirty," the man said, his voice coming out as a squeak. "But there are at least two dozen more sleeping in the stables."

Theo's eyes widened, and he twisted the blade almost imperceptibly against the man's throat.

"Why are there so many of you?" he demanded. "Aren't you supposed to be privateers or something? Why aren't you on your ship, pretending to be pirates?"

"L-Lord Sanz needed help guarding the prisoners," the man said.

"Prisoners?"

"Yes, the ones we took from the boat whence the lady came. The p-pirates. They were being held here, until yesterday morning when some men came to retrieve them. They paid a bounty for each one. Lord Sanz promised us each payment after..." The man's lower lip trembled, and he squeezed his eyes shut.

"After what?" Zander demanded, taking a step closer.

"After he was... done... with her," the man blubbered. Upon feeling Theo's blade dig further into his neck, the man's hands shot up, and tears streamed down his face. "Please," he said. "I don't wanna be here. I have no other prospects. I'm just here for the money."

"And the rest of your friends?" Theo said. "Do they have any loyalty to Sanz beyond his coin purse?"

The young man attempted to shake his head, but Theo's blade made him think better of it. "No, sir. I don't believe so, sir."

"Good," Theo said. "I suggest you get the hell out of here then, once you wake up."

"Wha—"

Theo took a step forward before he could speak again and grabbed the side of his head, slamming it hard into the bedframe. The young man slumped over. Zander winced, thinking of Theo's injury. It took a surprising amount of force to knock a man out by hitting him, Zander had recently learned.

Muffled voices sounded from the hallway, soldiers waking from the sound of the explosion.

"It's a fire!" Zander heard someone holler. "I can see it from my window!"

A loud *thud* from the foyer indicated someone had entered the west wing from the central courtyard.

"Get dressed, you idiots!" a man yelled. "We're under attack!"

The muffled voices turned to the urgent patter of feet upon the ground.

"Fuck," Theo muttered, his voice shaking. "We've just sent dozens of men out there to find Yarrow."

Zander peeled back the curtains to look outside. The stables burned like a lit torch, sending sparks shooting into the night sky. Zander wondered if dozens of men and horses burned inside it, or if Yarrow had managed to free the innocent beasts before lighting the fuse.

Zander turned to see Theo with his ear pressed against the door, his sword sheathed but his hand hovering near one of his pistols. Footfalls sounded more heavily from the hallway now, the men's boots stomping urgently toward the door at the end of the corridor. Zander held his breath, hoping no one would notice two missing men.

Neither man moved as they waited for the wing to clear out. Theo's jaw was rigidly set, his lips a thin line. His hands shook.

"You should go to Yarrow," Zander said.

Theo's head whipped toward Zander, and he stood straighter. "I can't leave you, mate. Besides, you need me to pick the lock on Ace's door."

"Go to them," Zander insisted, knowing what he'd want if he were in Theo's place and Ace was just outside. "I'll figure something out. Between the two of you, maybe you can keep all these men distracted a bit longer until I do."

Theo was silent for a moment, staring intensely at Zander. Finally, he sheathed his sword and strode across the room, wrapping Zander in a hug. Zander returned the embrace, the smell of gunpowder and the sea enveloping him.

When Theo pulled away, his expression was hard. "It's quiet out there now. I'll cover you while you get to the central wing's entrance. Then I'll go out the way we came. Be safe, Zander. Get our girl."

Zander just nodded, unable to say what he wanted to say. The urge to fit a thousand words of gratitude into the moments they had left flitted up through his body and escaped in fright. Zander hoped his eyes said something like, *Please don't die, you wonderful bastard.*

Zander pried the door open slowly, and Theo stuck his head out, a pistol in each hand. When he nodded, Zander slipped into the hallway. He made his way past the foyer and to the door leading to the central courtyard, Theo following behind him, spinning as he walked, guns drawn. When Zander reached the door, he looked back at Theo and nodded.

"Check it's not locked," Theo said, gesturing toward the door with his chin.

Zander gently turned the handle.

"It's open," he whispered. "Go."

Theo nodded once, then disappeared.

Zander was left alone then, standing in the dim hallway, his hand still clutching the handle of the door. He could hear the soft rumble of voices from beyond. He turned the handle slowly until it unlatched, then opened it ever so slightly, holding his breath as if it would prevent the wood from creaking. When a sliver of moonlight shone through the crack in the door, he stopped and listened.

Suddenly, a voice boomed across the courtyard that raised Zander's hackles. It was a voice he'd heard before, from the edge of unconsciousness aboard the Valerian. *Where is it?* he'd said before he slapped Ace—before he *hurt* his love. Ignacio's voice was filled with the same lilting condescension now as he spoke to the men gathered in the central courtyard.

"You!" he yelled. "Take a third of the men and put out that goddamn fire before it spreads. You—what's your fucking name? Bruno." He sighed dramatically, as if reaching around in his empty brain for the man's name was extremely inconvenient for him. "Round up another third to come with me to the storehouses. No, you can't have him! Not you, Bruno. YOU! That one's in my group, he's the best shot."

Zander rolled his eyes so hard he nearly passed out. He listened to the shuffling of feet around the courtyard as the men determined who went with which group. It took an absurdly long time, and Zander thought a group of schoolchildren could likely form teams faster than these fools. He smiled in satisfaction when he heard Ignacio let out a growl of frustration and bark at the men to move faster.

"You lot leave through the front. I'll go out through the study in the west wing. The rest of you, stay here, and don't let that fucking woman out!"

Zander darted quickly behind the door, plastering himself to the wall just before it swung open. Nine men rushed across the foyer and down the hall, heading for the double doors at its end. Ignacio was positioned in the middle of the line, four men in front of him and four men behind, a cushion of safety for his precious, pampered ass as he ran away from the fire and toward whatever treasures laid in his storehouses.

Zander watched silently, his view partially obscured by the door as they entered the study at the end of the hall and exited through a door on the west side of the building. Then, all was quiet.

He took a few steadying breaths and stepped out from behind the door.

Zed, Yuna, and Teshva landed on the desolate planet of Carthosi, just outside the abandoned city of Nurk. The signal Yuna detected hailed from the center of the city, near the only structure left standing among the ruins: a temple, its twisting, spiral corners stretching into the blackened sky. Most of its grand turrets had crumbled away, but the sacrificial altar jutting from its peak remained, a gruesome relic of the city's past.

The three hunters emerged into the barren landscape silently, breaking apart in a formation each knew by heart. Zed took the lead, heading for the temple as his partners flanked him on either side like ghosts. He held his gun aloft, ready to shoot on sight—she was wanted, dead or alive.

As the temple loomed closer, Zed could hear a gentle melody drifting toward them over the landscape. As the shadow of the grand building enveloped them, he realized it wasn't a musical recording like he initially guessed. She was singing.

He didn't know why, but it unnerved him. He'd never thought of her as someone who might sing, or dance, or appreciate art. To him, she had always been a criminal, a number with a payday attached. Over time, she'd morphed in his mind into a monster, all shadow and teeth and noxious poison.

But the woman he saw before him was no monster.

She sat at a makeshift table of fallen rubble in a large open-air receiving area lined with columns, the dark temple rising behind her. Her feet dangled from a wooden stool, her black hair falling in sheets on either side of her face as she tinkered with something. Wrinkles around her eyes showed her focus, but she sang like she hadn't a care in the world. It was beautiful.

Zed forced himself to put one foot in front of the other, fighting a strange, infuriating urge to stop and stare. But then she looked up, and their eyes met, and despite himself he stopped.

"You," she said.

A gunshot rang out from the right. Yuna's shot flew past her head, so close her curtain of black hair whipped around her face, obscuring it. She bolted. Zed followed. In moments, his companions were running alongside him.

"Where is her ship?" Yuna hollered.

"I didn't see it," Zed said, leaping over a fallen boulder as he ran. Their quarry zigzagged between pillars and ducked behind barriers, but her destination was clear: the staircase at the back of the open room, leading upward, curving out of sight and into darkness.

"We need to find her ship before she does," Teshva said. "Yuna and I will split up and find it. Zed, continue pursuit."

Zed nodded silently, his eyes still fixed on the woman before him as his partners broke off. He could hear her breathing heavily as he ran up the spiraling staircase, but she remained just out of sight. Frustration rose in him, not at the pursuit, but at his inexplicable desire to see her face again.

Eventually, they emerged into blinding day at the top of the temple. There was nowhere else to run.

She's mine now.

But she didn't stop. She ran across the open roof toward the sacrificial platform. Would she jump? It would make his job easier if she did, but the thought disturbed him for some reason, and he choked back a cry of fear.

"AMAYA!" he yelled as he approached her. She was standing at the edge of the altar, looking down. "It's over, Amaya. Surrender."

She whipped around to face him. Her pale skin was flushed, her chest heaving from exertion. From where he stood, he could see the striking green color of her eyes. Like emeralds.

"Why are you chasing me?" she asked him, her voice level despite the fear in her eyes.

"You know why," he answered, still closing in, his gun trained on her. "You've done terrible things."

"The only terrible things I've done were to terrible people."

Zed's breath came in short bursts as he advanced. A strange, heavy feeling descended on him. He felt his hand drop a fraction of an inch, as if gravity itself was begging him to put the gun down.

"You don't know me," she said. "You don't know anything about me."

"Oh, yes I do," Zed countered. "I know you placed a proximity alert on my ship."

"I just want to live in peace."

"So do I," he said, and raised his gun to shoot.

As he prepared to pull the trigger, Zed looked into the eyes of the monster he'd hunted all these years. She simply stood there, her hands limp at her sides, her hair swaying in the wind. She looked sorrowful. Defeated. Resigned.

He'd seen that look before. It nagged at him, somewhere deep in the recesses of his memory. It was too familiar, too intimate. It crawled beneath his skin, and instead of the victory he thought he'd feel with her life in his hands, he felt like he was being torn apart from the inside. He inexplicably felt that if he pulled that trigger, his own life would end there on the altar, a sacrifice to the gods of The Directorate.

In shock at his own hesitance, he lowered the gun, and the two enemies stood at the sacrificial altar in silence, a strange sense of comradery hanging in the air between them.

Then she nodded at him, a silent thanks in her eyes, and stepped off the edge.

He gasped, his hands reaching out to the empty air. Something inside him shuddered, threatening to break—until he saw her float upward from beyond the ridge. Her right arm gripped a buzzing drone that carried her away toward wherever her ship was hidden.

She looked back at him, and he barely heard her words over the wind.

"Goodbye, Hunter."

Zed watched her disappear, his gun discarded on the altar at his feet.

22

Zander crept silently around the door and peered outside. A stone walkway circled around the courtyard. To the right were the stairs leading to the upper floor. The overgrown garden obscured his view of the other side, but he could see three guards positioned against the walls: one just outside the door, to the right; another farther right, smoking; and a third to his left near the entrance to the north wing, his eyes fixed on a position upstairs where Ace's prison would be.

Zander closed his eyes for a moment and imagined Ace—no, felt her—above him, waiting for someone to save her, and it gave him the steel he needed to face the men waiting just outside.

Zander pulled the dagger from his right boot and stepped quickly outside, burying the blade in the neck of the first man, his left hand covering his mouth to prevent him from screaming. With his hand still on his mouth, he removed the blade and turned, throwing it at the guard on his left, pushing the stunned man backward with a dull *thud*.

As he removed his hand from the first man's mouth and let his body slide to the floor, he slipped the dagger from his left boot and threw it at the smoking guard to his right. He was running toward him before the knife landed, knowing from its trajectory it would be a nonlethal blow. The man's hand went to his shoulder just after the knife buried there, and his mouth opened to yell, but Zander was already on him. He took the man's face in one hand and swung down hard, going onto one knee as he slammed the back of the man's head into the ground. There was a sickening crack, then silence.

Zander pulled the dagger roughly from the man's shoulder and retreated, making to retrieve the second blade. As he ran, a shot rang out from above him. The bullet whizzed past his head, and he ducked into the garden, rolling onto the ground and looking up, trying to see where the shot came from. Voices rang across the courtyard as the remaining guards tried to ascertain what was happening.

From his position behind an unruly fern, he spotted the shooter at the top of the stairs, his face illuminated by a torch positioned on the wall behind him. He appeared to have been guarding Ace's door, but was now aiming his pistol blindly into the darkened garden.

Just then, another explosion sounded from outside, this one to the west—Yarrow's second grenadier. The man looked toward the sound, and Zander used the opportunity to stand, firing at him from a better vantage point. His second shot landed in the man's stomach just above his belly button. Zander threw himself to the ground again as the man slumped to the floor.

He stayed low, reaching up to pop the collar of his black coat so it obscured part of his face. Strands of his brown hair hung in front of his eyes as he darted past a walkway leading down the middle of the garden, making for the other side of the courtyard.

He could hear the labored breathing of a person behind one of the columns supporting the roof as he approached the east side. He moved silently around the column, emerging to find a single guard positioned at the wall, the rest having moved to examine the dead men. The guard clutched his pistol with two hands, his eyes focused on the veritable jungle in front of him. He didn't notice Zander approaching until it was too late. Zander dragged the edge of the knife across his throat and lowered him gently to the ground.

Hearing footsteps behind him, Zander rushed into the garden again, relying on the darkness amidst the overgrown plants to shelter him. He looked up at Ace's door, which was now unguarded, from his crouched position. He took several deep, shaking breaths, attempting to calm his frantic heart. He tried to focus on the voices around him, to count how many men were left in the central courtyard. He'd need to kill them too, before he saved Ace. Lord only knew how long it would take him to pick a lock. He hoped the dead man at the top of the stairs had a key.

He'd counted at least three distinct voices when a loud crashing noise sounded above his head. Suddenly, Ace's door exploded off its hinges, and a stunning pirate barreled out after it, shoulder first. Without stopping, Ace hopped onto the guardrail and leapt into the garden below, aiming for a tall plant with long, narrow leaves jutting out from a thick cane.

Zander heard the remaining men yell from three directions as Ace wrapped her arms around the stalk of the plant, steadied herself, and fell on her ass on the garden pathway. He darted from his hiding spot toward the other end of the walkway, emerging in time to see her rise from the ground and whip around to face him.

Time slowed down as Zander was taken back to a jungle in Barbados, where he first laid eyes on his beautiful pirate captain. Like then, she wore her favorite red vest over a white shirt. The shirt was torn and dirty, and a button was missing from her vest. A large shard of glass from a mirror was gripped in her hand, a length of material wrapped around one end in a makeshift handle.

Her eyes held the same wild excitement they did the day he met her, a fire that suddenly sputtered, then cooled, upon seeing him there. His heart beat wildly, and a smile spread across his face. Then she threw her knife at him.

Zander jumped as the mirror shard flew past his head and landed square in the cheek of the man sneaking up behind him. He whipped around and punched the man in the throat, then buried his dagger between his ribs before turning back up to look at Ace. *Now* she was smiling at him. He let out a quick sigh of relief, then unsheathed her ivory cutlass as the bushes to her left began rustling.

"Catch!" he yelled and hefted the blade in the air. She reached up and caught it just in time to cross blades with the man who barreled out of the tangle of leaves at her side. Zander turned his attention toward the final man, who had been standing several yards behind the first, watching the scene unfold from the safety of the shadows. Seeing he had no choice now but to flee or fight, he ran at him, jumping over the body of his comrade and swinging a sword wildly at Zander.

Zander, whose daggers were currently buried in the torsos of two dead men, threw all of his focus into footwork as he dodged the man's wide swings. He waited until the man paused, reaching for the pistol at his hip. He ducked low, sliding beneath his arm, then stood and swung his fist into the back of the man's head. As he fell to his knees, Zander retrieved his pistol and shot him once in the back of his head.

Ace's opponent dropped at the same time, and the courtyard was suddenly silent, save for the two pirates' heavy breathing, and a lone cricket. Zander replaced his weapon and turned to look at Ace.

For a moment, she didn't say anything. She just stood there, her chest heaving, blood dripping from her blade onto the still body of the guard at her feet. Zander took a single step in her direction, slowly, as if he were approaching a frightened animal. Then another.

Suddenly, Ace sucked in a loud, rattling breath and dropped her blade. It clattered on the ground.

"Zander," she said, the word half a sob, and reached out her hand.

Zander ran to her, the tether between them finally snapping into place, pulling them together like two magnets. He wrapped his arms around her, stooping so he could bury his face in her neck. Her hair obscured his vision, and her nails dug into his back as she sobbed freely.

He pulled back, bringing his hands to each side of her face, holding her still so he could get a better look at her. Dark circles sat under each eye, and fresh bruises marked her face and neck, previously obscured by the darkness. Zander made to examine the rest of her, looking for evidence of more abuse, but she slapped at his hands and grabbed the lapel of his jacket, pulling him toward her for a kiss.

His hands left her face and wrapped around her once again, gripping the back of her vest. They kissed like the meaning of life lay just beyond one another's lips, like they'd been starved for each other far longer than five days. Zander's tears mingled with her own, falling to the bloodstained path beneath their feet.

It was Ace who finally broke the kiss, looking up at him with a mix of exacerbation and relief, their arms still wrapped around each other.

"What are you doing?" she asked him.

Zander looked around at the dead bodies littering the ground, wondering what other explanation she needed.

"I'm... rescuing you," he said. He looked upstairs at the door she'd destroyed. "What are *you* doing?"

"I was escaping," Ace said, laughter in her voice. "At least, I thought I was. Something woke me, and then I heard Ig—" She faltered, the toll of the secrets she'd held between them suddenly come due. "I heard... Ignacio. I heard him talking about a fire, and then there were gunshots, so I took my chance. Oh Zander, I'm so sorry." New tears filled her eyes.

Zander shook his head, unwrapping his arms from around her and taking her hand in his. "Don't fret," he said, and softly traced his fingers along the edge of a bruise on her neck. His voice took on a dark tone. "Did he do this to you?"

"Actually," Ace said, turning to look at the man Zander had executed minutes before. She pointed at him. "He did, I think."

"Oh," Zander said, his shoulders dropping a bit. "Well, it's a good thing I killed him then."

Ace chuckled. "Ignacio doesn't like to get his hands dirty." She turned, taking in the scope of the carnage visible from where she stood. "Actually, a few of these guys got their hits in." She whipped her head back to look at Zander again, a look of appreciation on her face that bordered between professional and carnal. Zander's cheeks burned, and he smiled.

"They'll never touch you again," he said. "Now, let's get you out of here. Theo and Yarrow are waiting."

Ace nodded and retrieved her cutlass from the floor, her expression steeling. "Aye," she said. "Lead the way."

After collecting his daggers from the bodies of two of the men he'd killed—two of many men he'd killed this week, an existential crisis he would deal with later on—he made his way to the east wing. On the other side of the door was a foyer similar to the one he and Theo had entered, but instead of emptying into a long hallway, it led to a large dining room. Open archways led to more rooms, the darkness obscuring what lay beyond them. He looked at a closed door to the right and pointed, looking at Ace.

"Kitchen?" he asked. She nodded.

Zander rushed to the door, taking a candlestick from a nearby table on the way. He opened the door and held it, fishing in his pocket for his flint and steel. When he looked back at Ace, he noticed she was favoring her right leg.

"Is your leg hurt?" he whispered.

Ace waved her hand dismissively. "I'm okay. Landed wrong when I jumped from the balcony is all. It's my shoulder that will be throbbing later on."

Zander brushed his hand gently across her back as she walked through the door.

"Let's just get you out of here," he said. "Then I'll take care of you."

Ace turned to look at him from inside the dark kitchen, a soft smile on her face.

"You look like you've been through hell yourself, Chicken Leg. Let's say we'll take care of each other."

Zander nodded, smiling. Tears pricked the corners of his eyes as the joy and utter terror of the past hour began to settle in his bones. His hands threatened to start shaking again, and he gave them a mental scolding, willing his inevitable meltdown to hold off for a few more days.

He lit the candle. The small flame threw the cooking supplies into sharp relief, casting strange shadows on the walls. Replacing the flint and steel in his pocket, his eyes searched the space for a trapdoor in the floor. Spotting it, he placed the candlestick gently on the floor and gripped the edges of the door, prying it open. A wooden ladder led downward into a black abyss.

"This is how I left before," Ace said. "How did you know about this? I didn't even tell Theo and Yarrow."

"Ah, we ran into your Uncle Hugo." Zander paused to admire the look of shock that crossed Ace's face, then continued. "He's living in

Almogia now, with Ignacio's former household manager. He would like you to visit more often."

Ace laughed, throwing her head back slightly. It was a truly magnificent sound. Something inside Zander—something that had shriveled in fear and anger, believing he may never hear her laugh again—bloomed upon hearing it. He smiled at her, content to make her wait for the rest of the details, and lowered himself into the ground.

Finding solid ground beneath his feet, he reached up toward Ace, gesturing for her to pass him the candle. When she did, he took stock of his surroundings. The tunnel was about seven feet high and four feet wide. It appeared to be well-maintained, but he couldn't speak for the extension beyond the house.

"I'll go ahead and make sure it's safe," he told Ace. "Wait here."

He turned and walked down the tunnel, looking for any signs it was going to cave in on their heads. Hearing something behind him, he whipped around to see Ace climbing down the ladder, ignoring his instructions completely. He made his way back to her, holding out the candle so she could see where she was putting her feet. Of course she'd followed him, he thought. What made him think she would be content to stand around and wait when she'd been trapped in this place for days?

Zander took Ace's hand and led her forward, his left hand holding the candlestick out ahead of them. As they walked, he kept his gaze straight ahead, his eyes peeled for anything from a root jutting from the ground to an assassin lying in wait. He tried to banish the million things he wanted to say to the woman walking just behind him from his thoughts.

One week ago, he'd been tangled up with Ace in the bed of an inn, wishing he could stay there for the rest of his life. The next day they'd boarded The Valerian again, and thought being there on the sea with her, surrounded by pirates, was somehow even better. He'd felt, for the first time in his life, like he was right where he belonged.

Since then, he'd been beaten, captured, and abused. He'd killed, maimed, stolen, and fled for his life. He'd uncovered secret after secret, about the woman he loved and himself alike, and surprised himself in more ways than he could count. He was a different man now than he was a week ago. There was simply too much to say.

"The turn to get out should be just ahead," Ace said. "I never thought to ask Cristian why these tunnels were here."

"It's an old servant passage," Zander said. "It probably leads to areas only servants would go. Kitchens, laundry, et cetera. Cristian said it was extended beyond the house to the storehouses at some point, but he didn't say why."

His eyes never left the path as he spoke. They came to a fork, and he looked both ways. Seeing an area where the smooth, packed ground turned rougher, the ceiling lower, he turned right and headed that way. His hand still held Ace's, but he remained silent.

"I'm glad Tio Hugo is alright," Ace said after a few moments. "Did he really say I should visit?"

Zander looked back at Ace, worrying at the quiet tone she used.

"He told me to tell you he loves you. Then he demanded that I keep you safe, and that we all come visit soon. He called you 'Little Aracely,' and he has the same dimples you do." He reached out and gently poked at Ace's cheek, right where it folded into a dimple when she smiled.

The smile in question emerged, just as Ace's eyes filled with tears. She let out a sigh through pursed lips, squinting her eyes as if the combination of gestures would stem the flow of tears. It didn't.

Zander wrapped his arms around her and listened to her cry, rubbing circles gently on her back.

"I've got you," he whispered.

After a few last shuddering sobs, Ace pulled away, wiping her face on the backs of her sleeves. She shook her head like it would rid her of her thoughts.

"I'd always feared he was angry at me," Ace admitted. "My parents died, and then I ran away. I left him here to deal with it all by himself. I spent years running, afraid to return to Spain, afraid to face any of this. And then it caught up with me anyway, and it killed people that I love. All I had to do was say, 'No.' All those years ago, I could have prevented all of this if I'd just said, 'No. I won't have you.'"

Ace covered her face with her hands. Another sob racked her, and she spoke into her fingers, her voice muffled.

"He killed my parents."

Zander's heart stuttered. "That's what Hugo thought, too," he said softly. "How did you find out?"

Ace kept her hands on her face. "He all but spelled it out for me, on his ridiculous ship on the journey here. He was trying to intimidate me, so I would…" Her lower lip trembled, the words dying. "It's my fault, Zander. It's all my fault—my parents, the crew. And now here I am again, running like a rat in these goddamned tunnels."

Zander gently pried Ace's hands away so he could look into her eyes.

"Ace," he said softly. "It's not your fault."

"It is, Zander, you don't understand."

"Ace. A monster dropped into your life. You were very young. You did what you thought was right, and it didn't work, but not because you were wrong. It didn't work because he played by his own rules, rules someone as good and kind as you would never have considered to be in play. And yes, you ran, as many perfectly good and sane people would do after such a trauma." Zander's voice took on a harder tone, and he gripped Ace's shoulders firmly. "You didn't kill your parents, and you didn't kill your crew. You know who did."

Ace took a deep breath, her expression turning hard as she calmed. "Ignacio," she said.

Zander nodded. "Ignacio. Not you. Ignacio."

Ace looked back down the tunnel behind her, as if she meant to return and find him.

"After we meet up with Theo and Yarrow, if we find that none of us have killed him already, we'll make a plan to return and cut him to pieces," Zander promised.

Ace nodded, the steel of a pirate captain settling once more over her face. She gestured to the path ahead, and they continued hand in hand.

23

The smell of smoke signaled the approaching exit. When Ace and Zander emerged from the tunnel through an opening in the side of a knoll, the full moon did little to illuminate the thicket of trees awaiting them in the ashy night air. Zander snuffed the now-useless candle and replaced it with his dagger as he and Ace navigated through the branches, moving away from the source of the smoke. Behind them, one of the storehouses was alight.

Zander stopped to gather his bearings when they reached clear air. He pointed to a tree in the distance where horse-shaped shadows stood.

"There," he said. "That's where we're to meet Theo and Yarrow."

The two pirates continued walking, moving quickly.

"Stop right there!"

Ace and Zander whipped around to see a uniformed man emerging from the darkness, his pistol raised. The blood on his face shone in the moonlight despite the thick coat of soot on his skin, indicating he'd survived the second explosion at the storehouses.

"Don't take another step," the man said. "Lord Sanz will reward me handsomely for—"

The man fell over sideways, his declaration cut off by the impact of the large rock Yarrow held in their hand. They stood over him, squinting in the darkness and then hitting him again to ensure he was no longer conscious, before dropping the stone and rushing toward Ace and Zander.

When Yarrow reached Ace, they wrapped her in a fierce hug. A fierce, grinding cry escaped them, as if every moment of fear, anger, and frustration from the past five days left their body all at once. When they broke the hug, Yarrow took each of Ace's hands in theirs and gave her a look of ferocity.

"I told you not to come, you fool," Ace said, tears in her eyes.

"And you were a fool to think I'd listen," Yarrow responded. "God-damnit, I'm so glad to see you."

"And I, you," Ace said, pulling one of Yarrow's hands to her lips and kissing their knuckles.

"We must go," Yarrow said. They looked at Zander. "A few of the survivors from the second grenadier escaped and rode North. Theo pursued them on one of Sanz's horses. I'm going to go after him. We'll meet you two in Malaga as soon as we can. Ace, you know where."

"Yarrow, have you seen Sanz?" Zander asked.

Yarrow shook their head. "No, but I wouldn't stick around to look for him if I were you." Their eyes settled on Ace with a meaningful look. "Later," they said.

Ace nodded, and the three pirates ran to the horses tethered nearby and mounted them. Yarrow's gaze lingered on Ace and Zander before they took off in pursuit of their partner. Zander looked at Ace.

"We didn't come in on the main road," he said. "I assume you know the way to Malaga?"

"Aye," Ace said. "But I need to stop somewhere first. Do you still have my compass?"

Zander patted his pocket, indicating that he did. Ace smiled and spurred her horse into motion, and Zander followed her. The Sanz estate loomed in the background as they rode, the grand structure illuminated by fire on both sides that slowly spread inward, threatening to devour the remaining legacy of Ignacio Sanz.

They rode in the dark for a short time before they turned off the main road and followed a path east. After a few minutes, the sharp angles of a wrought-iron fence emerged in the darkness. Beyond it lay the ruins of a burnt building.

Ace approached the barrier slowly, then dismounted. Zander followed suit. He stood next to Ace as she looked up at a tall, arched iron gate. An ornate letter "V" decorated the top.

"This was your home," Zander said.

Ace nodded. "Aye, it was, once." She stepped forward and pushed on the gate. It swung open, creaking loudly.

"He never let me return here," she said as she stepped beyond the gate and onto her family's property.

Zander followed her wordlessly up the path to the ruins of her previous life. The roof and exterior walls were gone, either burned or removed after the fire. Most of the debris had been cleared away. Large stones around the base of the home remained, as did the foundation and much of the interior skeleton. There was a stillness in the air that reminded Zander of a graveyard.

Ace stopped at the threshold and turned to look at Zander.

"I need a few minutes alone," she said.

Zander nodded and took a step back. She walked on, disappearing into the crumbling structure.

Zander waited anxiously for Ace to return, twisting and twirling his daggers in his hands for a long time in silence. He scanned the landscape in the direction of Ignacio's estate, expecting to see men on horses dotting the horizon any moment.

After a while, a sound to his left drew his attention. The snap of a branch. He held his breath, listening. Another sound, like a footstep on gravel. Then another.

Zander crouched low and carefully made his way around the side of the house toward the sound. Turning a corner, he saw a man dart inside the ruins. A hood obscured his face. Zander's heart jumped from his chest into his throat. Ace was inside, exposed, vulnerable. He ran, leaping over the remains of a wall in pursuit of the stranger.

Ace's voice slowly became audible as he navigated the once-grand home in the dark. She was talking quietly, steadily, as if she were having a conversation with a loved one. Likely, she was. He steadied his breathing, not knowing where the man went, and not wanting to alert him to his presence. He focused on Ace's voice, following the sound to the center of the house.

He found her kneeling, a large stone wall at her back. Her head hung, her curls falling on either side of her face like a curtain.

"I promise," she was saying, but she stopped short. Her shoulders went rigid, hearing the crunch of footsteps behind her at the same time Zander did. She shot up, unsheathing her sword and whipping around just as a figure rushed at her, his own sword held aloft. As the blades clashed, the hood fell back from the man's face, revealing the snarling features of none other than Ignacio Sanz himself.

"You stupid fucking woman!" he screamed. His face was coated with soot, and dozens of shallow scratches marred his skin.

Ignacio pushed hard against Ace's blade with his own. Ace's foot caught on a stone, and she fell backward, landing on her elbows as she held her cutlass aloft.

Zander crossed the room quickly, quietly.

"I swear to God, Aracely, I will tie you to this pile of rubble and burn it again with you inside!"

Zander loosed one of his daggers just as Ignacio raised his sword above his head, his features twisted in fury.

"Tell me *now*!" he roared. "WHERE IS I—aaaghh!" He dropped the sword, looking in horror at his hand. The handle of Zander's knife stuck out of it, the tip jutting from Ignacio's palm.

Ace took the opportunity to kick at his knees, knocking him to the ground. Ignacio lunged forward, grabbing Ace by the hair with his uninjured hand and attempting to slam her head into the ground.

But Zander was already there, leveling a swift kick to the side of his head. He grabbed the back of Ignacio's shirt, pulling him away from Ace roughly. He reached forward and gripped the handle of his dagger, ripping it out of Ignacio's bloodied hand. Ignacio screamed, then went silent as Zander placed the blade against his throat. His other hand tangled in the hair atop his head, holding him still as he knelt, panting.

"Don't fucking move," Zander growled, shifting the blade for emphasis. "Unless she tells you to."

As he spoke, Ace rose from the ground like a wrathful spirit. Her cutlass dragged along the ground as she moved.

Zander kept his hand tangled in Ignacio's hair, holding his lover's husband's traitorous, murderous head in place as the villain cradled his bleeding hand. He removed his dagger from Ignacio's throat and stepped aside, holding his head aloft like a gift.

"My lady," he said.

Ignacio looked at Ace with the contempt of a man about to die.

"You should have just told me where it is," Ignacio bit out. His breath came in short bursts.

Ace walked slowly forward. "My family's legacy is not yours to claim," she said. "I have made a promise, here on this hallowed ground. A promise to take what is mine. My life. My inheritance. My *vengeance*."

Ace raised her cutlass, pointing it menacingly at Ignacio's stunned face.

"Go to hell, Ignacio," she said.

Zander let go. Ace reared back her arm, whipping her cutlass out in front of her and slicing Ignacio's throat with a loud cry. He fell to the ground, and the world was suddenly very still.

Ace stood there for a long while, staring at his lifeless body. Finally, she looked up at Zander and gave him a wry smile.

"My lady?" she said.

Zander chuckled. "It sounded quite dashing in my head."

Ace's smile widened. "It was dashing," she said.

She looked down again at the lifeless body at her feet and her smile vanished. They stood silently again as Ace's eyes swam with emotion. "When we were on the boat, he told me how he did it," she said finally. "How he killed my parents, I mean." She looked up at him, and Zander waited quietly for her to continue. "He gave them a gift the last time I saw them. A bottle of wine. It was poisoned. One of Sanz's men watched as they opened it, drank, and eventually fell asleep. Then, in the wake of the lightning storm, he set the loggia ablaze."

"I'm so sorry, Ace," Zander whispered.

Ace took a deep breath. Tears ran down her face. "Aye, me too. But at least now I know for sure." After a few moments of silence, she said, "May I have my compass?"

"Of course." Zander fished the wooden compass from his pocket and gave it to Ace.

She gestured for him to follow her, and they walked outside to the back of the house. A group of pillars that used to be arches and a small empty pond marked the area as the loggia, where Chandace and Nicolas died.

The light of the moon pooled over Ace's features as she looked out at the vineyards, the only part of the property that appeared to still be maintained. She turned the compass over in her hands and twisted the bottom. The base of the wood came off, revealing a small inner compartment containing a folded piece of parchment. She pulled it out, spreading it open in front of her to reveal a map.

Zander took a few steps forward to get a closer look at the parchment. The outline of a building—the building that lay burnt at their backs—took up one side. The other side was dotted with small landmarks Zander couldn't identify. A trail of dashes led to one of the landmarks—a large X—with the number 34 scrawled beside it.

"Is this..." Zander began.

"A treasure map," Ace finished. She placed her compass atop the map, pointed her body North, and walked. "This way," she said, carefully measuring her steps. "34 paces."

34 paces later, Ace stood at the edge of the vineyard a few yards away from a large Beech tree. Upon arriving, she folded her map, returned it to the compass, and sank to her knees. Zander joined her, using his knife to cut up the soil so she could dig it away with the handle of her cutlass. When the soil turned soft and moist, they used their hands to

shovel it away, eventually revealing a small wooden chest. They cleared away the dirt surrounding it, allowing Ace to wedge her fingers against the sides of the chest and lift it out with a grunt.

She squatted in front of the chest, a shy expression on her face.

"I... don't know how much you know about my family," she said finally. "Or about any of this, really." She gestured vaguely around her.

Zander settled onto the ground and folded his legs. "I've heard tale of the mythical Vidal pirate treasure, if that's what you mean," he said. "And I heard that while most of your parents' acquaintances were titillated with the idea, Ignacio was obsessed with it."

Ace nodded in confirmation, but she didn't meet Zander's eyes. Her fingers tapped rhythmically on the lid of the chest.

"Theo and Yarrow gave me the basics when it came to Ignacio and your engagement," Zander said. "I would love to know more, anything you'll tell me. When you're ready." He dipped his head down, attempting to meet her downcast eyes, and she raised her head to look him in the face.

"I suppose we have a lot to talk about," she said.

"No time like the present," Zander said, and smiled encouragingly.

Ace took another deep breath, settled more comfortably on the ground, and began.

"When Ignacio Sanz arrived in our lives, my family was at our height—at least as far as our land-faring days were concerned. My parents were comfortable and content. I managed some of their business affairs, and I was good at it. But I dreamed of going back to the sea. Every time Theo and Yarrow showed up on shore, a little piece of me thought about running away with them. But I loved my parents. I tried my best to envision my future here, not out there, like they wanted.

"When my father told me he'd received an offer of marriage, my first instinct was to run. I should have listened to that instinct. But my parents were *so* happy. It was a proper match, far beyond anything they'd dreamed for me. Their own marriage was born of a whirlwind romance, like something from a fairy tale. But their love was hard won. It required sacrifices. They wanted something else for me—something easier, I think. Because I loved my parents, I convinced myself they knew what was best. I convinced myself I could be happy as a Viscount's wife.

"One day, I planned to visit Ignacio's home for dinner. We had spent time together before, but it would be my first time visiting his home without my parents. It felt like a sort of test, an opportunity to imagine my life as a Viscountess before the wedding. I wore this terrible pink dress my mother picked out, and I remember my father teasing me, wondering whether the Viscount would recognize me when he arrived." She chuckled. "I left in his carriage... and I never saw them again. A servant rushed in during dessert to tell us my home had burned to the ground, and my parents had died."

Ace stopped speaking, her eyes closed and her lips pursed to stem a rush of tears. Zander waited in silence until she continued.

"After the fire, Ignacio kept me trapped in his house. He told me it was too dangerous to see my home—that the structure wasn't stable, that the land was too dry, that I must wait. He told me he would protect me, and that I must trust him to do so. I feigned trust, but in truth I had no choice. I was alone, vulnerable, and something deep in my bones told me I was not safe. But to let on that I knew would only put me in more danger.

"Ignacio came to my room every day to comfort me. He talked of our marriage and what it signified—the coming together of two families, two legacies. The joining of what was mine and what was his. He waited to ask me about my parents' famous treasure. He had mentioned it before, when he courted me, but he always phrased it as if it was a joke. I told him my parents had left me an inheritance, and he took it to mean the fabled treasure itself.

"One evening, in the midst of my grief, he came to my room. He told me he wanted to show me something, and then he took me to a locked room in the west wing. Inside lay the spoils of the Sanz fortune. Gold coins, tapestries, ancient relics from cultures I couldn't name. And in the center of the room, held aloft on a silver pedestal, was an emerald-encrusted dagger. He took the blade and held it out in front of me. 'This,' he said, 'is the legacy of my family. A blade passed down from generation to generation, valued for more than its jewels. It is part of me.'"

Ace took a deep, shuddering breath. Zander laid his hand atop hers.

"He told me that when we married, the blade would become mine as well. 'All that is mine will be yours,' he said to me. 'And just the same, all that is yours will be mine. The legacy of your family will be my legacy as well.' Then he pulled the emerald-studded sheath away from the knife and held the blade in front of my face. He said, 'I am all you have left, Aracely. You will see soon enough, there can be no secrets between us.' His message was clear: I would give him everything my parents left behind, or I would suffer until I did. I knew then I must run."

Zander squeezed Ace's hand. She twisted her fingers so they could wrap around his, and she squeezed back.

"When I left, I broke into that room, and I took the emerald blade. I stole his legacy, like he stole mine. I meant to return to his room and kill him with it, but Cristian found me and stopped me. He made me think of my Tio, who slept in one of the guest rooms, and what he would have to endure if I left with Ignacio's blood on my hands. So instead of killing him, I fled in the night, and I used the blade to buy back my parents' sloop. That boat was their real legacy... at least to me. But this,"—she tapped the lid of the chest with her fingertips—"*this* is the fabled Vidal pirate treasure. I wasn't able to return to it all those years ago."

Ace smiled fondly at the chest, memories dancing in her eyes. Then she looked at Zander and raised her eyebrows as if to say, *Ready?* Zander nodded, and she pried open the clasp, revealing the treasure inside.

Zander leaned forward, peering through the darkness at the contents in the chest. When he saw what was inside, he clutched his belly and laughed out loud. Ace joined him, her laughter ringing through the night and filling the valley. Zander wiped a stray tear from his eye and moved so he was sitting next to Ace, their thighs pressed together. He put his arm around her, and she laid her head on his shoulder so they could look at the contents of the chest together.

Inside the worn wooden box lay the treasures of a child, collected during her adventures at sea: a piece of coral, a sand dollar, a crab pincer, a doll made from corn husks, a seashell necklace, and a total of sixteen rocks of various sizes and colors.

And, tucked into the lid of the box as if it were a frame, was a detailed charcoal drawing of a little girl with curly hair and dimples, standing between her mother and father. Nicolas had the same broad smile as his daughter. Tendrils of his wavy hair fell across his face, his head tilted inward toward his little family. Ace's nose and strong brow were a spitting image of her mother's. Chandace wore a soft smile in the portrait, her hair pulled back from her face in dozens of small braids.

"What a beautiful family," Zander said, kissing the top of Ace's head as she gently traced her finger along the edge of the drawing.

"Aye," she said softly. "One of my mother's friends drew this, on a visit to Jamaica. I was eight, I think."

"And these are your treasures," Zander said. "Little pirate."

Ace laughed softly, her shoulders shaking under Zander's arms.

"Aye. When we came here, I buried my treasure. It was part a game, but mostly I did it out of spite. I thought surely my parents would come to their senses and take us back to the sea. They would see me burying the souvenirs of my childhood and be utterly distraught at the heartbreak they'd caused. I whispered a curse as I buried them, asking the magic of the sea to curse this land and drive us back into her arms."

Ace chuckled again, remembering her childhood angst. "It eventually became a family fable, a joke between the three of us. The Vidal family fortune, my grand inheritance, buried in a secret location known only to us. I made the map myself, and my father hid it inside the compass for safekeeping, to humor me. When I was trapped in Ignacio's home after my parents' death, one of my parents' servants snuck the compass to me, to comfort me. A memento."

Zander tightened his grip around Ace's shoulders and the two sat in silence for a while, listening to the ghosts of Ace's childhood. When Ace's breathing began to slow, Zander gently shook her. She straightened, yawning, and looked up at him.

"We should go," he said.

Ace nodded sleepily and stood. Zander closed the lid to her chest of treasures and lifted it, and the two walked back toward the ruins and the horses waiting beyond.

"There's one thing I still don't understand," Zander said as they walked.

Ace raised her eyebrows in question.

"Ignacio asked you where 'it' was. Was he looking for his dagger? Or your parents' treasure?"

Ace laughed. "The fool was looking for the treasure," she said. "All that talk about family legacies, and he never even asked me about the dagger. Honestly, I'm not sure if he noticed it was gone at all. He probably made up all that stuff about it being passed down from generation to generation."

Zander chuckled, shaking his head. "A villain and a fool."

They walked in silence a few minutes more. As they approached the horses, Ace reached out and touched Zander's arm, stopping him.

"Thank you," she said. "Thank you for coming to save me."

Zander smiled. "There isn't a force in the world that could have stopped me."

24

When Zander and Ace entered the port town of Malaga, the sun was just starting to peek over the horizon. Their bodies forgot their exhaustion as they rode, the sound of hooves on the ground a reminder of the carnage they left in their wake, pushing them forward.

Zander barely noticed their surroundings as they approached an inn Ace seemed to know. He was lost in his thoughts—thoughts of Theo and Yarrow and the men they chased north, of Hugo and Cristian and how worried they must be, of Ignacio's cold, lifeless eyes, forever staring at the wreckage of the home he'd destroyed—and beneath it all, intertwined like threads, was a persistent anxiety about the woman riding next to him.

In the last few hours, the secrets between them had become far fewer. But he couldn't shake his worries about what lay between them—or what didn't. As he pressed coins into the sleepy stable boy's hands, as Ace exchanged pleasantries with a large man named Henry who thought he'd never see her again, as he followed Ace up a set of tiled stairs toward their room, he ruminated on the depths of his love for the wild, mysterious, tenderhearted pirate captain who had barreled into his life one day out of the blue. It was a love that wrenched open the deepest parts of him, a love that made him feel vast and seen, a love that had no room for anything but bold-faced authenticity—a love that spanned lifetimes.

And he knew if he found out she didn't feel the same, it would shatter him beyond repair.

The sound of the door closing behind him snapped Zander back to the present moment. Before him was a spacious, comfortable room with a large bed. A fire was just beginning to roar to life in the hearth, and a plate of bread, meat, and cheese awaited them at a table near the corner. Zander turned to take in his surroundings, stopping at the sight of Ace standing still near the door, watching him.

Despite his anxiety, Zander couldn't help the smile that spread across his face seeing her standing there, whole and alive. She was giving him the same playful smile she often did when they retreated to her quarters at night, when the crew was good and drunk, and they knew they wouldn't be interrupted.

Zander removed his boots, then unbuttoned his coat and began emptying his heavy pockets. Ace stood and watched him. When he fished a handful of gold coins from his pocket and dropped them on the table, followed by another, her eyes widened.

"Where did you get those?" she asked.

Zander took off his coat, winking at her as he did. "I stole them," he said.

Ace's eyes narrowed mischievously, her grin widening. "Pirate," she said. She sauntered toward him.

"Oh, you have no idea," Zander said. "Not only did I steal those coins"—he removed his twin daggers from his boots and placed them on the table—"I commandeered an entire pirate ship, killed a quarter of the men on board, and ran it aground."

A mixture of emotions flitted across Ace's face. At first, humor, when she thought he was joking. Then, shock, tenderness, and admiration.

"Scoundrel," she said, her voice filled with lust and pride as she closed the distance between them.

"Aye," he agreed, his voice rough with emotion as Ace gripped the front of his shirt and pulled him toward her.

They kissed desperately, each of them starved for the other. Ace buried her hands in Zander's long, tangled hair, her nails pressing into his scalp as she kissed him. She lifted her leg, wrapping it around Zander's thigh and pressing her body against his. He responded by shifting his tight grip from her back to her thighs, lifting her up and walking forward so she was pressed against the wall.

"Ace," he managed to mutter between their kisses. He had her pinned against the wall with his hips, and his hands roamed freely, one cupping her breast while the other gently pressed against her neck.

Ace made a soft sound against his lips, and he nearly came undone. Instead, he stopped, pressing his forehead against hers so he could catch his breath.

"Ace," he said again.

"Zander," Ace said, her hand moving to his face as she tilted her chin forward, trying again to capture his lips.

"Wait," he said. He cupped his hands around her thighs again as he moved his body away, lowering her back to the ground. "Just wait a moment."

Zander took several steps back, running his hands roughly through his hair as he tried to focus on what he needed to say. Ace stood there, her expression one of wary concern.

"Zander? Are you okay?"

"Yes, I... well, no... I just..." Zander sighed and dropped his hands to his sides. "I love you, Ace. Do you know that?"

Ace nodded, a tentative smile forming on her face.

"I mean, I *really* love you," Zander clarified. "Run away and become a pirate kind of love. Lay down my life kind of love."

Zander's voice broke, and he took a moment to breathe deeply before continuing.

"Before you knocked me unconscious with the handle of that cut-lass"—he pointed accusingly at the cutlass in question, still hanging from her hip, and she grimaced—"you said you loved me, too. And before you say anything, hear me out. From the moment I laid eyes on you, I knew you were the only one for me. Something deep inside my soul reached through bone, muscle, and sinew, pushing through every layer of who I thought I was and bursting from my body just for a chance to touch you. That feeling hasn't gone away.

"The air I breathe feels stale when you're not sharing it. The last few days have been torture, knowing you're in trouble, knowing you could be hurt, or dead. Ace, I want to spend every moment with you for the rest of my life. I want to fall asleep with you each night and wake up with you each morning. I want to know everything, all of it, even the deep, shameful parts of you. Little by little or all at once like a flood, I'll take whatever you can give me, and I'll give you whatever you want in return."

Zander steeled himself for the next part, trying not to let the tears running down Ace's pretty face discourage him.

"But I would rather die than be another man who keeps you when you don't want to be kept. I want to know—I need to know. I need to know if you feel the same about me. I need to know if you see us as something that could last forever, or if I've just been convenient to have around."

Ace gasped softly, her face taking on a pained expression.

"Convenient?" she whispered, taking a step toward him. "Zander. You have been anything but convenient."

Zander's brows shot up, but Ace raised her hands in a silent plea for patience before she continued.

"Before I docked in Barbados the day I met you, I had committed myself to never, ever falling in love. It was a way to keep myself safe. I had Theo and Yarrow—my family—and the crew, and that was enough for me. But then you showed up, and god damnit if you didn't mess everything all up by chasing me down when I ran away." She laughed, a sputtering sound through her tears. "And you know, if you hadn't chased me, it would have only been a matter of time before I came back and found you again. You were stuck in my mind like a splinter."

Ace took another step toward him, so they were nearly touching. She took his hand and intertwined their fingers, holding their hands between them near their hearts, and looked boldly into his eyes.

"I bless the fated tides that brought me to your shore. If I could, I would kiss the very stars for guiding me to you, my love, my Zander. I'm sorry I haven't said it before. In every life I will find you. No matter how far I may travel, no matter the winds that push me this way or that, know this: I have always been on my way to you. And now that I've found you… and you've found me"—she smiled amusedly—"I am never letting you go again."

Ace kissed him tenderly. When she pulled away, she put her hand gently on his cheek.

"I do love you, Zander. And I'm so sorry for all the secrets that have lain between us. I'd kept them for so long… I didn't know how to let go."

Zander let out a long breath. With every word Ace said, he felt a heaviness leave his body, until all that was left was relief—relief that he'd found her, relief she was whole, relief they could begin their lives together anew even after all the heartache of the past week. He knew the pain of the last few days would follow them from this room. But they would heal, together.

Tears filled his eyes, and he wrapped his arms around Ace in a vice grip, holding her against him and finally letting himself feel the moment fully. He buried his nose in her hair and inhaled deeply, his tears running into her hair.

With every breath, he felt more whole.

Finally, he pulled back and smiled.

"Now, with that out of the way," he said, narrowing his eyes, "where were we?"

"Right here," Ace said, gripping his erection over his pants and gently squeezing.

A sound escaped Zander's mouth that was something between a moan and a surprised squeal not befitting a pirate of his caliber. As he leaned forward to capture her mouth with his, Ace leaned back teasingly so that all he could do was groan into her mouth as she continued to caress him. He tilted his head down to nip at her neck, then trailed kisses down her sternum and onto the top of her breasts as he undid the clasps on her vest.

Reaching the final clasp, Zander pulled her vest off and began working on her shirt, his mouth following his fingers downward until she was topless, and he gently kissed a bruise on her ribs.

Suddenly, a thought struck him, and he stopped.

"Wait."

"God, not again," Ace said. "What?"

"You're alright to do this, aren't you? I mean, you've been thoroughly traumatized these past few days. You were kidnapped, beaten. I don't want to rush you."

Ace's eyes softened, and she smiled down at him.

"I'm okay," she said. "I promise. Are you okay?"

"Yes."

Ace's hands tightened their grip in his hair. "Then undo the clasp on that belt, sailor."

"Yes, Captain."

Zander removed Ace's belt without taking his eyes from hers, standing as he tugged it away and tossed it to the floor, her ivory blade falling with a loud *thud*. She returned the favor, pulling off his belt so he could pull his shirt over his head. Ace's hands went to his chest, roaming downward toward his stomach, and the feeling was so achingly familiar Zander nearly lost himself in it.

He wrapped one arm around her waist, pulling her bare torso against his. His other hand cupped her face so he could kiss her, smiling against her mouth as he tried to shimmy out of his trousers without breaking contact. She laughed, pushing against him playfully so she could pull them down for him.

"You're so thoroughly covered in dirt and sweat, these never would have come down without a good tug, Zander," Ace said, laughing.

Zander tugged on Ace's pants, pushing her gently down to sit on the edge of the bed. He nipped at her ankle as he freed one of her legs.

"You're rather dirty yourself, Captain." He tossed the trousers aside.

Ace spread herself open for him, and he dropped to his knees.

"Come here, scoundrel," she said, and he obeyed.

Zander had intended to take his time, to kiss every inch of her miraculous body, to make her cry out in pleasure as many times as he could before he sated himself. But as soon as their lips met, Ace made a desperate sound and arched her hips toward his, and he buried himself inside her so quickly he wasn't entirely sure how they both ended up on the bed, her nails on his back, his hand braced on the headboard, moaning into her mouth as he took her bottom lip between his teeth and bit down gently. His other hand went to the pearl between her legs, and time lost all meaning as they rode a wave of ecstasy together.

Afterward, Zander rolled onto his side and pulled Ace against him, and they were both asleep within minutes.

***

They woke when the afternoon sun peered through the curtains, casting the room in an orange glow. Ace was still wrapped in his arms when Zander opened his eyes, her breasts pushed against his chest and her legs entwined with his. Zander kissed her face until she woke, giggling, and climbed on top of him, pinning his hands above his head and taking him once more.

When they finally left the bed, they found a note pushed under the door in Theo's distinct hand that simply said, *Here*.

"They'll be in their room," Ace said, sauntering toward the plate of untouched food on the table. "Likely beat as well. No rush."

She popped a small piece of cheese into her mouth. Chewing, she took the plate and the knife lying beside it and returned to the bed.

The two of them sat there, languidly eating, for a long while. Zander traced shapes on Ace's thighs absentmindedly as he ate, listening to the sounds of people and animals outside, the roar of the ocean a distant noise in the background.

"Can I ask you something?" Zander asked after a while.

"Mm," Ace said through a mouth full of bread, which Zander took as a yes.

"Why did you name your parents' sloop The Valerian?"

Ace smiled widely, and Zander chuckled at the way her cheeks turned up when they were filled with bread and cheese, like a chipmunk's.

"That's right," she said, "I can tell you now!" She sat up straighter, wiping her face and swallowing before she continued. "The day before my... well, my *wedding*"—she punctuated the word with a disgusted look—"I took a walk in the gardens by myself. I dug up one of the valerian plants and stuffed it under my skirt so I could take it back to my room. I screamed at everyone to leave me alone, that I needed a day of solitude before I became a Viscountess."

Ace chuckled at her past self's sense of humor.

"I broke a vase and used the sharper pieces to cut up the root, then I used the bowl of the vase and the toe of my boot to mash it, releasing what liquid was inside. I let the roots soak overnight in a glass of un-drunk wine a servant brought to my room before bed, then I strained the mixture through a bedsheet the following afternoon. I kept it in a glass bottle that once held perfume—smelly, awful stuff Ignacio tried to get me to wear."

She shuddered at the thought, and Zander leaned in to smell her natural musk appreciatively, making her smile.

"Anyway, the night of the wedding, I put it in Ignacio's wine. I dosed him bit by bit at first, but once he was drunk enough that everything tasted the same, I dumped the latter half of the bottle in his cup, and he didn't notice the difference. That night he brought me to the bridal chamber, closed the door behind us, and fell asleep while removing his pants." Ace laughed suddenly, as if she were seeing the image all over again. "And I was gone within the hour. So, I named the sloop The Valerian as a reminder of my incredible fortitude—and because she puts my enemies to sleep." Ace winked dramatically, and Zander chuckled at her theatrics.

"You are clever as you are brave, my love," Zander said, pulling her closer.

Ace giggled wickedly and wiggled so she was flush against Zander, their noses touching.

"Who are your enemies, Zander?" she whispered. "I will ensure you see them with their pants down before the end."

Zander laughed and kissed his fierce pirate's nose. "No need, my love. Any enemies I've ever had I made this week, and I've already killed most of them."

***

That evening, they met Theo and Yarrow downstairs for dinner. When Theo saw Ace, he jumped from his chair and ran to her. He hugged her silently for a moment, his eyes squeezed tightly closed. Then he drew back and examined her, his eyes lingering at her hair, likely looking for any more of those tiny needles.

"You okay?" he asked.

"I'm okay," Ace said, nodding. "Thank you, my family." She looked from Theo to Yarrow as she spoke, addressing both of them.

Yarrow put their hand over their heart in response, and Theo clapped Ace's shoulder affectionately.

"No need to thank us," Theo said. "You'd do the same."

"Aye," Ace agreed as she sank into a chair across from Yarrow. Zander sat next to her, and the man who'd received them earlier approached with two more drinks.

"I'll be honest," Theo said after they'd taken a drink. "I can't believe all of us are still alive. Did your man here tell you he nearly blew himself up before hanging off the side of a moving ship for an hour in the dark?"

Ace whipped her head toward Zander, a surprised smile on her face.

"He didn't. In fact, I know very little of this adventure you three had without me." She slammed her mug on the table authoritatively. "Spill."

Over the next several hours, they told Ace everything. The four companions took the threads of their lives over those past few days and braided them together again, laughing, gasping, crying together. They cried particularly over the loss of their fellow pirates, both to death and to capture. And in the end, they shared a bitter celebration over the story of Ignacio Sanz's long-awaited defeat.

After they'd cheered over the death of the fake husband/pirate and drained their cups, Zander asked Yarrow what happened after they parted ways near the storehouses.

"When I got to the stables and realized half of the pens were filled with sleeping men, I guessed the two of you would have your hands full as well. I snuck past the men, quietly unlocking the pens of the horses as I did, and took a single horse for myself. After I mounted, I screamed like a banshee to wake the men up, dared them to come catch me, and bolted out of there. Once they'd all mounted their own steeds and they came streaming out, I lit the grenadier and tossed it to the stables."

Zander let out a sharp breath, and Yarrow looked at him questioningly.

"I was afraid you'd killed the horses."

Theo laughed, but Yarrow looked affronted. "Of course not. The beasts did nothing wrong. I couldn't get them all out on my own without waking the men though, and then I would have been shot. So, I let them release the horses for me, and then I led them away from the estate and toward Almogia. There's a sharp turn about a kilometer from the Sanz estate that leads behind a hill. You remember it, right?" Yarrow looked to Theo, who shrugged. "Anyway, I lost them there, then I backtracked while they continued looking for me. It bought a little time."

"And then Theo found you?" Zander asked, looking back and forth between them.

"I ran for the storehouses after I left you," Theo explained, jutting his chin toward Zander. "I thought maybe Yarrow had gone there straight away. I was on my way back to the stables when I saw them riding up the main road."

"It was around that time men started spilling out of the Sanz estate like ants." Yarrow emphasized the final word as if they could crush the ants using their voice. "I heard Theo whistle and I went to him, and we intercepted the group of men sent to the storehouses with the second grenadier. We didn't know Ignacio was among the group. If we had, I would have presented his head to you when you emerged from that tunnel."

Yarrow looked pointedly at Ace. Ace wore a touched smile at the kind gesture.

"It was shortly after that I saw you both," Yarrow said, spreading their hands as if to indicate their presence together was the next and final piece of the story.

Zander sat back in his chair. He felt light, not just from the wine, but from unburdening himself of the previous week's experiences.

"I guess that's it then," he said. "That's the whole adventure."

He looked at Ace and smiled, then looked back at his friends, who were smiling at each other, and a piece of him knew that no matter how long the four of them lived, it would never be the end of their adventure. And he was right.

"What now, Captain?" Theo asked, wrapping his arm around Yarrow's shoulder.

"Well, it would seem we have another rescue to conduct," Ace said, placing her elbows on the table. "I heard word about the men who paid Sanz a bounty for our crewmates while I was there. They were fellow privateers."

Theo scowled, silently mouthing the words "fake pirates."

"Word has it, they brought our friends right here to Malaga." Ace tapped her pointer finger on the table in emphasis. "They plan to sail up the coast toward Barcelona, paying as many bounties for pirates as they can along the way. A mass execution is planned for next month in Madrid."

"Next month?" Zander said. "That sounds like plenty of time to me."

Theo snapped his fingers excitedly. "Yes!" he said. "Let's rescue more of our fucking friends. And some other guys, too, I guess."

"Right," Ace said. "Now, where did you say my boat is?"

Theo grimaced, as if he'd forgotten all about the damaged sloop they left stranded off the coast of Portugal. Yarrow looked at Zander, and he looked at Yarrow, each expecting the other to describe the location of the empty, fog-covered beach where they'd last seen The Valerian. Seeing each other at a loss, both of them burst into laughter. Theo soon joined suit, and eventually Ace laughed as well, shaking her head at them.

"You drunk fools couldn't pinpoint your own asses on a map," she said, waving her hand. "We'll figure it out tomorrow."

Ace placed her hand on top of Zander's, and their eyes met. As Theo and Yarrow continued to laugh, peppering each other with kisses, Ace and Zander simply stared at each other. The world narrowed, for each of them, to one blaringly bright and beautiful point.

Two souls—one hopelessly wandering, the other running for her life—yet they'd somehow met in the middle and become each other's solid ground in which to grow roots. Their lives until that point had been but a series of fractal paths leading ever inward, toward each other.

"Tomorrow," Zander echoed, squeezing Ace's hand in a promise.

"And the next day, and the day after that," Ace said.

Forever.

And indeed, they did—figure it out, that is.

Ace, Zander, Theo, and Yarrow retrieved their abandoned sloop and saved what remained of their pirate crew, plus a few more. It was their first pirate mission in the Mediterranean, a new frontier that opened to them immediately upon the death of Ignacio Sanz and the shadow he cast over Ace's life.

Ace visited her Uncle Hugo as soon as she'd saved her crew and finished repairs on The Valerian, leaving Theo and Yarrow in charge of the sloop and the resting crew. It would not be their last visit to Uncle Hugo and Cristian, who continued living in Almogia for the rest of their lives, happy and in love.

The Valerian crew continued to sail the Mediterranean after that, staying in the region over half the year and spending the remaining months in the Caribbean. They retained their strict moral code, taking only what they needed to remain free and alive, and prolonging their lives far beyond the most ambitious of pirates. And they remained wild and free, with none but the ocean and their love for each other as their master.

Some of the original crew stayed for the rest of their lives, including Bagu, who took up the role of Boatswain when Theo decided to dedicate himself more fervently to his writing. Saila stayed as well, mostly to be near Bagu, as did Sean, George, and Amir. Others found new paths to tread, like Santiago, who met a woman at one of their stops in Portugal and gave up his life at sea to stay with her. Douglas retired shortly after being rescued, and Echo left several years later.

Zander met more of Ace's family—cousins, aunts, uncles—in Spain and Jamaica. He even met her last living grandparent, Chandace's father. He eventually took Ace to England, where she met most of his brothers and sisters. Martha insisted they stay with her for a few days, and doted on her baby brother, whom she told her husband was a "sea merchant—just a particularly flamboyant one." By the time they visited, Zander had been a pirate for nearly a decade, and his parents, he found, had died. The loss simply became another pain shared by Zander and Ace, as they shared all things.

Zander and Ace had many more adventures together. They would go on to rescue each other many more times before the end. Theo and Yarrow remained by their sides as well, unfailingly devoted to one another and to their friends. Together, the four of them lived so fully, with such reckless love and abandon, Theo would eventually fill four handwritten books with tales of their adventures.

By the time this particular life had been wrung dry, both A and Z had found what their hearts longed for, what their souls required. For Ace, it was freedom—and the courage to keep it. Never again was she asked to sacrifice the life her heart desired for the sake of her propriety, nor that of a man's, and never again did she say "yes" when her heart knew she must say "no."

For Zander, the dreams he had as a little boy of a life filled with love and adventure came true, and they were far better than he could ever have imagined. The warmth and belonging he'd missed as a child, the community he longed for as an adult, and the adventure he was always too scared to ask for all fell in his lap that day in the jungle, ushered in with a kiss. And in the end, he became a rather remarkable pirate.

Perhaps, dear reader, you are still waiting for an adventure of your own. You have not yet been swept off your feet, taken to distant lands or to the bed of someone who makes your soul's metaphorical toes curl and the frayed edges of your heart braid together in a tapestry of belonging.

But there is time. Time for stories to be written, quests to be filled, and worlds to be saved. In this life or the next, there is time.

Perhaps you are like Ace, running for her life, sprinting toward her soul's match without knowing it. Perhaps you are like Zander, waiting aimlessly for life to start, unaware his life's purpose lay just around the corner. In either case, you are just where you are meant to be, cradled in the tendrils of the illusion we call time, answering the call of the universe to reach toward love, whether you know it or not.

Ace and Zander's love grew day by day, until one day death cut it short.

It was in the midst of a chase, 29 years after Zander jumped in the sea. Three members of the Royal Navy pursued Ace and Zander just outside of Porto, one of them having recognized them as notorious pirates. They were nearly to the sloop when one of the men cut Zander off, emerging from an alleyway and swinging his blade wildly.

Ace didn't spare a moment's thought before pushing Zander aside, taking the brunt of the blade herself. Theo and Yarrow arrived to fight off the officers, a moment too late.

She passed in Zander's arms, surrounded by her treasures, cradled by her love.

For the first time in 29 years, the world looked grey to Zander.

The role of captain passed to Yarrow, who remained the most capable sailor on board despite their advanced age. Zander served under them as a sailor, but he continued living in Ace's quarters. Not a thing was said about it, by any of the crew. It was their home, and it would remain his home until he followed her beyond the veil of this world.

He did, about a year later, during their annual journey to the Mediterranean. They had not yet reached Azores when a fever took hold of Zander. It burned furiously for two days, most of which he spent in his bed, dreaming of ships with octopus carvings on their bows.

On the second night, he woke suddenly from a dream he couldn't remember. His blanket was soaked through with sweat, and he shook violently. He instinctively reached his hand out and touched the other side of the bed, but found it empty.

Then he heard it. A voice, mingling with the still, small voice of the water with which he'd become so familiar. Her voice.

He walked to the deck of the ship in a haze, sweat soaking through his clothes, his fever raging. The water was still, and the moon hung high in the sky.

He followed her voice to the forecastle and peered out onto the water.

And there she was, like his own personal siren. She was standing on the water, her hand stretched out, inviting him.

Sighing contentedly, he smiled at the apparition.

"I'm with you," he said, and stepped off the edge into the arms of the ocean below.

And they lived happily ever after—again, and again, and again.

THE END

Thank you so much for reading *Fated Tides*, the second installment in the Metaphysical Love Stories series. This series of reincarnation romance novels can be read in any order, or as standalones. Visit www.sarahfaethsanders.com to stay in touch or learn about other books in this series. Or, you can follow me on Tiktok (@sarah_faeth_sanders) or Instagram (@sarah_faeth_sanders). I love hearing from readers!

It would mean so much to me if you took a few moments to leave a review on the platform of your choice. Honest reviews (good, bad, and in-between) are the lifeblood of an indie author. I am so grateful you've given your valuable time to my characters.

Want to hear the original songs from Fated Tides? Scan the QR code or visit https://soundcloud.com/sarah-sanders-102694884

First and foremost, thank you to my readers. I love you. To everyone who read and reviewed Soulmates, or reached out directly to tell me how much they loved the pirate flashback, this book wouldn't exist without you. Thank you to my editor Lwazi for loving my characters as much as I do, and to Lwazi and Amanda for sensitivity reading. Thank you to Rejenne and Marigold for making my book beautiful (again). To my amazing beta readers, Craig, Tas, Mello, Taryn, and Violet, thank you so much for your love and care.

Mom and dad, thank you for always supporting me. Kim, when I think of adventure, I still think of our adventure together after college. It, and your friendship, are defining experiences of my life. Kassie, thank you for bringing the pirate story from Soulmates to life with your lovely voice. You inspire me. Adam, thank you for everything. I love you.

Sarah Faeth Sanders has been a storyteller since she was a little girl, when she would sit her parents down and spin new tales on makeshift stages, always ending her narratives with the mysterious phrase "A Duck and a Rabbit" instead of "The End." Sarah received her BA in Sociology in 2012. After college, she backpacked through Southeast Asia with her best friend for seven months before returning home and meeting her partner, Adam, with whom she now has a beautiful son named Damian. In 2022, Sarah received her MS in Medical Cannabis Science and Therapeutics from the University of Maryland, Baltimore. She currently lives in the Pacific Northwest, where she draws inspiration from her natural surroundings to create new worlds. Sarah aspires to someday become an elusive hedge witch, increasingly one with the forest, communicating with the outer world solely through her increasingly whimsical and cryptic stories and a few friendly crows trained to deliver handwritten messages.

www.ingramcontent.com/pod-product-compliance
Lightning Source LLC
Chambersburg PA
CBHW021212310726
48971CB00006B/1533